Three Days

At

Millie Flowers'

LEAH EVERT-BURKS

This is a work of fiction. While, as in all fiction, the literary perceptions and insights are based on experience, all names, characters, places, and incidents are products of the author's imagination or are used fictitiously.

Book Layout ©2017 BookDesignTemplates.com

Three Days at Millie Flowers'/ Leah Evert-Burks. -- 1st ed.
ISBN 978-0-578-70299-5

For SuperPapa, "Silent" Edson Alexander Wilkins, professional baseball player, baseball coach, house boat and furniture builder, carpenter, cabinet maker, rock-hound, gold prospector, jewelry maker, stone faceter, storyteller, official wedding crier, politician, retired mayor, member of liars club, gambler, stunt car driver, used care dealer, movie star, commercial specialist, dog trainer, terrific dad, grandpa and great-grandpapa. A true renaissance man, who pursued each of his passions with a full heart and unceasing dedication. But most importantly to his family he was silly and engaging. It is from him that I learned to be a storyteller... and to hit a baseball.

"The sad part is that there is never much work for him. Yet a ballplayer has got to play ball like a singer has got to sing and an artist has got to draw pictures and a mountain climber has got to have a mountain to climb or else go crazy."

— Mark Harris
Bang the Drum Slowly

Contents

Abbott, Arizona

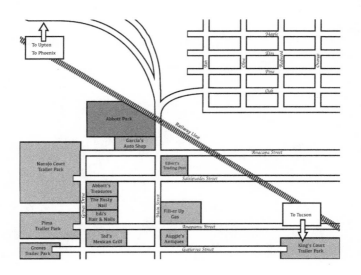

CHAPTER ONE

Running the

Bases

S afe at second. He had hesitated taking the base, but when he saw a delay in the wind-up he had gone. Grover Pendrell was not known for his aggressive base running, or even for making it around the bases. He was a pitcher who could hit, but beyond the RBI he didn't make it to second until and unless invited there by a force. With Rudy Flores a brawny hitter up to bat, his next move would be a base running advancement to third, if he was lucky. Art Ferrelli, the third base coach, began to move his hands up his sleeve to his ear and then back down again as if brushing off lint on a funeral suit. With sure intended strokes his thick fingers moved from two to three and then quickly moved behind his back as the hollow of the bat was heard hitting the ball and Grover was moving toward the next designated piece of square canvas cloth. Hopefully not to be thrown out.

Easily advanced to third with the big hit from Rudy he looked back at second base glad his steal had not been wasted. He bit down and closed his lips as his right arm had grazed the dirt. The mud layer dented with the slide of his arm making a narrow rut the remnants of which covered his inner cotton collar. He was much too disciplined to take a bite of this cake. Calling for time with a wave of his hand, he had taken a minute to adjust his cup and smile.

"You steal? Who'd of thunk it?" the slight built second baseman had grumbled with a right lisp at the "st." He made a quick motion to tag-check him though Grover was safely upright on the bag, then threw the ball back to the pitcher for the next round. As it hit the glove, he muttered "Pitchers," leaving the word to hang with the "s" slaughtered in sputter.

Grover hadn't allowed his mouth to curve up, but over the baseman's comment, he was certain he heard a cheer from someone in the dugout cheer. Looking that way casually as he released the umpire to resume play, he only saw the teams' worried, stone-expressed faces. Maybe they hadn't heard it. The club's Manager Birdie McCullen leaned on one knee lifting himself up the step in an arthritic pull to signal to Art, and soon those rapid jerks of movement would direct him on. No further fanfare for a steal well done.

Today as with almost every day, the Texas heat failed to hold onto the recent rainstorm that should have cooled things off - in concept. There was no need for the sun to blaze down or for the steamy moisture to build up to such a suffocating level. Inside the dugout there should have been some relief from the afternoon sun. But the tin walls closed in the heat, containing it and muffling the moisture like a shower stall. It was still hot and now the bodies of the fidgeting teammates contributed to the stifle. Rudy sat pulling at his socks as if they were too tight on his heel. The blue calf stripe of the Panthers separating into white cotton weavings with each tug. Cheap die job. Grover owned five pairs of team socks that sat in his drawer at home, all the same cheap AAA-league weave. Stained with all the bad weather games, cheap laundries and the heat. No matter how much bleach, they always held onto the mud from a day like today. Only Adele could get them acceptably white, but if she did it meant he was home and that pair would be placed in his top dresser drawer and not worn again. The next team, the next town, the next train, the next stripe.

Birdie stumbled into the dugout his belly imprinted with his belt buckle. His stubbled face was bi-colored and winged at the cheeks. The tips of the whiskers, still under the skin, dottings of black reached gray once they poked through the surface, making his face shadowed in pocked tonals. Grover knew him to shave twice a day and still the stubble surfaced by the seventh inning. He claimed he sweated whiskers and the team's record was the cause. Birdie was a talker. Maybe he had been a star in his day as he claimed, but most likely not. Regardless of his "record" he was now middle aged and pudgy, rotating from coaching jobs high school to AAA and dealing with transported players who weren't funded beyond a local sponsor, and pitchers who should not be stealing bases.

"Pendrell, jacket," he called loudly though he was only a stretch away from Grover's ear. Finding it necessary to point to the jacket beside him, at Grover's silent response, he turned his head quickly away and then turned it a notch back toward Grover, checking for his compliance. Birdie leaned on his knee viewing the next play, or hoping for the next conflict, but most likely he knew it would not come from the field. Grover's father, Ellis Pendrell had been much the same man, not wanting to ponder too long on lessons but wanting to be certain his son understood them and abided. He knew how this worked.

Grover had been about seven when he learned this for the first time. He had been playing in his father's workshop and had found a sheet of paper with some fine printing on it. The printing looked important and covered the entire length and width of the paper. Not being a good reader, Grover longed to find out what was on the paper, but somehow didn't consider the option of taking the entire sheet to someone who could read it to him. So as carefully as possible he began to tear small, delicate rips around the words, trying to capture just a sentence or two for later reading. But with each tear he clipped a letter here and there, making them, he feared, indiscernible to a reader, and had to start again with a new tear. Finally, Grover found himself with shavings of paper in his lap and no intact piece of paper large enough to read.

His father found him sitting just like that and at first had thought the shavings in his son's lap were wood from his own cabinet making. But young Grover began to cry and panic upon seeing his father and the combination of emotion circulated and blew when his father realized that the paper he had torn was a warranty for the new motor he had just purchased. For more than a half hour his father, a short but muscular man paced the shop in his tight strides, turning to tell his son how truly destructive this choice had been, but he never actually faced him, Grover got only peripheral clips of his expressions. It was almost like a nervous twitch of anger, reasoning, unreasonable, eloquent, and unintelligible. Through the tears Grover had tried to explain his purpose. But his father would not hear it, wanting to be absolutely sure his son knew what he'd done was wrong. He did not have time for the "why." Even as Grover was finally allowed to stand up, throw the chards of paper into the trash, leave the shop and run to the house for the round belly of his understanding mother, his father spit final words at him as if they were tobacco and Grover the ground; "Think, boy."

Grover grumbled, half pulling the glossy Panthers jacket sleeve on to his right arm up to a little over his elbow. It angered him that all the team colors went with black the heat soaking base color. Had anyone thought about the color choices when deciding what to call this team? Fort Worth Panthers, surely there was a better choice than black and blue. He could already feel the heat in his arm as he tried to move himself, or at least his arm into a cooler corner.

"Don't half-ass do it. Put it on or throw it out, your choice," Birdie crossed his arms together still balancing them on his knee but requiring that he lean farther in as if examining the mow of the field. Level, three quarter lines, half circular.

"Coach it's 100 degrees plus, not like it will freeze up on me," Grover snapped even while he complied. His voice sounded too youthful and novice to make this complaint hold any ground. He'd heard this too many times to continue to object, but he would never do as he was told without comment. Grover was not a talker but this was a familiar drill between him and the coach. He wanted it known he didn't think it necessary and felt too much attention was placed on the pitcher's arm. That aspect of his defiance would have to be maintained. It defined him by his managers as spirited. Young, foolish and spirited.

Third out, bottom of the eighth, 4 to 6, Blue. Grover hopped up the stairs to greet the next in the line-up. The direct sun met him and his right arm felt the weight.

Grover believed he had relatives here or not too far from Fort Worth, his home for now, but

never took the time to look them up. Maybe an
aunt, or maybe they were actually Adele's family.
He couldn't remember really. Nevertheless, each
home game he looked up at the stands thinking
he'd see some resemblance of himself. Fort
Worth, the shady-side of the dual city pairing,
known more for cattle than baseball, but still
loved the game. But instead of uncles and aunts a
few brimmed hats, brave baldheads, and baseball
caps met his stare, if any at all. The games were
attended by a few older men who didn't have
steady work to attend to, young bored wives
dreaming they were not in their already
sedimentary lives. Grover reasoned that if he had
relatives in north Texas they would surely
attend. Fingering a phone book one day in his
motel room he found two listings for Pendrells.
Jack Pendrell and E.E. Pendrell. Neither sounded
familiar, but each became his crowd when he
needed them during the at-home stretches. Jack,
a young and fit cousin who could never make the
minors, sat behind first base and called the
pitches to his four sisters who watched with
embarrassing admiration as their older cousin
pitched a no-hitter; and Elmer Edwin, Grover's

grandfather, who took off work for every home game from his cotton-milling business, stood the entire time, the full nine innings behind home so Grover would be sure to see him. His legs ached the whole next day but he would do anything for his grandson.

Today no one, not even imaginary, had showed to cheer him on and he had stolen second. No one but the regular strip of young boys behind the dugout who cheered for the players by name. That never failed to startle Grover though he had played here for a year. He had been one of these wide-eyed boys once in California, years back but receiving such admiration by name from strange eager faces still surprised him. That was not only for big leaguers, but as he struggled to be worthy he was just a prune-picker in the minors. Tomorrow he would be bussed out of Fort Worth to San Antonio for a three game series. No cheers tomorrow, or the next week. He would pitch the second game and play that full game, even if it meant ignoring the bruised feeling his throwing arm felt when he threw forty fastballs in five innings. But only one out five batters could hit that pitch and so he threw it.

It would be good to get out of Fort Worth, at least with its no more humid rain and stifling tin-contained dugouts. He reminded himself of this as the trip had been necessarily started too early, with Birdie calling "revelry" at 5:00 in the morning. At breakfast, Tracey his usual waitress at the coffee shop bid him "good luck" but had been too busy to chat long, and then they were herded off and onto the bus. He had always enjoyed Tracey's rapid chatter. She flirted with all the young ball players, and had some true love overseas. She would coldly turn away any true offers as if they were entirely unexpected, but she still flirted. Grover was safe, committed with wife and kid, actually a childhood sweetheart wife, very safe, so he got a lot of attention. It was only last Tuesday that Tracey had discovered Grover's length of marriage and had been so warmed by it that she sat and talked about expectations of married life every morning since. But this morning there was no time.

"It's nice to see a man in your line of work with such love for his wife," she said to him before the game with Shreveport. It was the way she said it that Grover realized this young soon to be wife who could handle the separation of the military because of the romance of it, may not handle the day-to-day more difficult conflicts of marriage. Grover never had handled the day-to-day well, and for that reason, many a time though he would never confide this to anyone, was grateful that his job kept him away from the everyday life at home.

Grover had told Tracey that his wife lived in a small bungalow home very near her parents who helped out while he traveled. He wasn't quite sure where Tracey got the rest of his story. She loved to see pictures of little Charlotte, now starting to pull herself up in attempts to walk, though Grover only had two he carried with him, and commented on having children of her own when her fiancée was back home from his tour and they had married. Lt. Larry Mannet it seemed was a Navy Seabee and was now somewhere in the Pacific building something. Tracey's explanations of his work always lacked detail other than approximate location. "He has two more years in the service, minimum, and then we'll settle down." The last years were to be in California close to where Grover lived. Another topic of conversation. Grover couldn't help but think of Tracey as one of those foolish pining high school girls who only loved the football players, though much better men existed. But Tracey was in her early twenties and because of her age, Grover felt genuine empathy for her. He doubted her married life would be what she imagined. He doubted Adele's was either and he knew his wasn't. Still, he watched her palm a shoulder and laugh with his team, wondering if she already knew she didn't want to be Mrs. Mannet and live that life.

Years later Grover had seen Tracey in a dress shop in Ventura while his daughter was trying on a dress for a junior prom, or some other formal dance of some sort, he couldn't remember the exact occasion. Charlotte had been particularly ill tempered that day and her mother had refused to go shopping with her, "Entirely." she has told her to her daughter's firm stance, "plenty of dresses." She told her she should be satisfied with the adding of an appliqué here to the shoulder and there to the waist of one of many dresses in her closet, but Charlotte had refused, citing some teenage tenet against wearing the same dress to a different dance.

Grover had agreed to chaperone the shopping, agreeing not to let her talk him into buying some ridiculous dress she will wear to this one dance and then hang in the closet. Now he sat in the corner of a young woman's dress shop waiting for his daughter to decide if the powder blue dress looked too cotton candy for the Spring Fling dance. He was looking idly at Charlotte swinging the hooped skirt like a bell and the facing mirror when Tracey came from the back carrying a stack of shoe boxes and ambled toward a woman who looked to be about her own age; she had to be in her mid-thirties or so by then. She laughed with the customer over some topic Grover could not hear and then got taken in by the conversation, forgetting that she was there to merely slip shoes over people's feet and make sure the toes didn't pinch. She sat down in the chair next to the woman and fell full throttle into a story. She had those same dreamy eyes and Grover tried to get a glimpse of her left hand to see if she in fact had become Mrs. Mannet. He also silently hoped that Lt. Mannet had not stayed in service too long to become part of the war. She was on the west coast now, which could indicate he was still in the service, or maybe she moved to California for the dream of it. A few minutes went by, just enough time for Charlotte to try on the yellow chiffon and ask the obvious question, whether she looked like a canary, when Tracey stood back up and carefully replaced the shoes in their boxes, apparently too small or too black or too something for the customer. Though she was standing straight her back was slumped and rounding at her shoulders, but as she passed, Grover saw on her hand was a simple gold band. Grover thought to approach her, and talk coincidences, but decided against it and only commented to his daughter that the blue made her look like her mother when they went to their first formal and she should choose that one. He did not want to go to the sad side of things today.

CHAPTER TWO

Another Pair of Socks

Rudy rumbled next him, something in Spanish, but Grover didn't know what he had said. For the last few games Rudy's focus seemed to be elsewhere. Where Grover wondered? In his game - with his family? Rudy was not like the rest of the team in that he not only spoke in a different language he seemed to have more to think about than the rest of the players. Things other than baseball. At every town he took the time to walk its streets, many times at night after a day game, or in the early morning on their days off. Grover always had an unrealistic fear that Rudy would be left behind and kept a seat for him on the bus just to remind himself to look for him in case he wasn't on it.

Grover had known boys like Rudy growing up in southern California. Grover even prided himself with the fact that he was born in Mexico. Born there during his parents' short attempt at making it rich with the precious minerals Mexico offered. Rudy had nodded to Grover's Spanish, helping him along with his own stories of origin. At first, that had made him stumble more. He could speak well enough to tell the tale, but having a native speaker made him self-conscious. When he heard Rudy rumble next to him in the bus to the next game, he knew the Spanish he attempted to speak was not the same as Rudy's Dominican verse. Was it dialect or circumstance? Grover's version of the language didn't have the hurried inflections of a man sending all his money home to his family in another country.

Grover did the same, with a wife and young daughter in Ventura, California, but his letters did not contain any urgency for replies back, only reporting of the games and towns and sometimes his hopes of being called up. Rudy hunched over his letters, penning frantic notes and carefully sealing the Airmail envelopes with more postage than required.

Today had been a day that ended with Birdie's shaving the second-layer stubble off his face after a slight victory and Rudy stuffing an airmail letter in his pocket ready to mail. This was the day that Grover met Tommy Cullen. He was walking with Rudy toward the post office and thinking he'd follow him through the streets, when Tommy had stopped him. He was a sports reporter for the Wichita Fall Sun and followed the Texas League closely while the league had a number of good seasons including bringing in the Dixie Series, the premier baseball series for the division. A fitting name he realized when Grover stood answering his questions without benefit of shade. Maybe he could switch to the Northeastern league and get out of the sun and the black uniforms for good. Damn cats.

He had pitched a good game but not an extraordinary one by any means, but decent. Tommy had asked about some curve ball hitters he had struck out, how Grover liked to pitch against lefties. Rudy waited patiently pulling the letter from his pocket and re-pressing the adhesive to make sure it was secure enough to make its long journey. His face turned listening to the words spoken between the two men and most likely getting three out of five; though they were better than Grover's Spanish odds. He laughed when Tommy asked if Grover intended to start a record on steals given his recent success. Grover smiled to his teammate who understood the humor of such a question.

Boss Elliott walked up to join them. He was always the unofficial spokesman, being a line-up catcher and self-appointed leader of the team. He frowned at Grover putting him on notice and then at the reporter for allowing this interview to proceed without him. As if he had been asked, he laid down his bag in the circle of men and rose to address the reporter's questions. Grover watched him knowing he would take the lead, his shoulders back, chest barreled ready to respond or take a pitch. But as he spoke, Tommy turned to Grover and asked about a wild pitch that clearly agitated an already agitated Boss. Grover politely responded as to why technically that had happened, and Boss road on his answer as to what he had done to make sure that didn't happen again. But again Tommy turned to Grover for further direct questioning. Rudy shifted his weight uncomfortably, not needing to know each word but knowing, this was not going the way Boss wanted. Boss adjusted his cap and crossed his arms over his barrel chest, listening to Grover's answers. He was a large man, a good target. Six five with wide hips that planted him solidly behind a base in his squat. Grover was only five seven, a small build though muscular, long-armed and long fingered. They looked like father and son, and the son was walking on shaky ground getting too much attention; the father was disapproving.

After the first few questions, Tommy then directed a question pointedly at Grover on his call to the Majors. Being more focused on Boss's building agitation, Grover thought he had heard wrong or maybe didn't hear the precursor of hopefulness these questions always began with. But Boss quickly unfolded his arms, asking Tommy for further information, his agitation fanning quickly and moving toward excitement.

"What?" he questioned. "What did you just say? Who are you talking about?"

Tommy looked at Grover and then to Rudy and at last to Boss. "Grover Pendrell's been called up to the Browns." The three players stared at each other but knew not one of them had an answer. "I got it on the AP back at the office some thirty minutes ago." He realized he should have led with this instead of springing it on them in a makeshift huddle on their way to the post office. But honestly he was surprised they didn't know. This was the biggest of news for small town baseball and yet they didn't know until it had hit the wire and Boss delivered it.

Rudy positioned himself on two legs evenly and lunged toward Grover with force. A cheer like had never been heard came from his hearty lungs. It was clearly the reaction of a friend. Boss stood firm and then looked back and forth for someone coming in with confirmation. Tommy understood the look.

"Check with Birdie, I'm headed to him next. Just lucky to run into you guys I guess."

Tommy didn't to regret that he had been the first to break the news to Grover, though not protocol, he was in fact somehow proud that a minor on his watch had made it. He slapped Grover's back with an open palm and began to shoot the questions rapidly - realizing Grover would probably tell him things he normally wouldn't given his apparent shock of news. Grover looked into Tommy's eyes and the eager possibilities lit out of him. But he also saw someone who at that moment had committed himself to him. Not because of who he was, but because he had hit the big time. He shared in Grover's pride, his shoulders straight and tall to match the new big league player's. Tommy Cullen would have a byline in the local newspaper and maybe on the wire and Grover Pendrell would have a career in the Majors.

The next hour Grover climbed on to barstools at the bar behind the last stall of the Stockyards and shyly thanked his team for their contributions to his call. He brushed his hair away from his face to get a clear view of every moment of this moment, because soon when he turned off the light in the motel room he shared with Bill Bantum the right fielder, the fear would mount and choke his confidence. But for now he was going to the Majors, something he had worked hard for, something he had dreamed of since sitting with that strip of boys on his block on the bench.

Adele couldn't believe he was calling her long distance. The cost of the call she "couldn't imagine" and when she did all she saw was a trail of dollars signs floating above her head. She wondered if her eyes glazed with the symbols, and she was looking for her reflection in the kitchen window when she finally understood Grover's words. Mr. Phillips was pulling into the shared narrow driveway in his pale yellow Chrysler, engine revving needlessly trying to impress, who she wasn't quite sure. Irritated, she turned her back to him so that he could in fact see only her torso capped at the waist and the back of her head. St. Louis. She didn't know anything about a place like St. Louis except she would move there with her husband and little Charlotte. Major League wives lived with their husbands. Charlotte waddled up to her mother, reaching for the phone as if she knew that would be the appropriate thing for a young daughter to do at this moment.

Charlotte's voice had been sweet and high-pitched. He had not understood many of her words and laughed at how often that seemed to happen to him even with adults.

He had understood Birdie's explanation of the call-up; he would throw batting practice for the Browns. Not a true ride to the big time but,"certainly at step tow'd em," Birdie had paternally commented. Grover was not disheartened, though he could tell Rudy and some of the other players were, and others snickered after finding out the conditions to his promotion. Adele hadn't differentiated in the line up or in hearing the news, though she knew there was a difference she had talked mainly about moving, what that meant and how they were to do it. She had lived in the same small California town her entire life. He had not been sure of any of the details and would have to call her back once he accepted the league position officially with the manager. But he was expecting nothing would change. He would don another team color and gladly roll the Panther socks up in his drawer the mud removed unnecessarily by Adele's hands.

Years after, when Grover allowed himself to remember the day he received the call, he couldn't help but think of another women, in addition to his dutiful Adele. He had meet Anita Bowen in St. Louis and she was a woman that made him feel juvenile, boyish and hopeful. She loved him only half-heartedly, he believed wholly. But it was not Anita that broke up his marriage to Adele. It was the warm and lustful thought of her that got in the way of every conversation from the time he met her.

CHAPTER THREE

Fly High

Millie's hair was to be envied. Thick, wavy, and light brown with enough blond to take the red dye properly. Her hairdresser at the El Rancho Vegas had told her not many girls can take that color, "Comes out too cheap, for most." It was somewhat brassy in the close spotlights, the ones that arched around the stage, but when the smoke was allowed to gather in the showroom and hang-on in sheets, her red hair turned a sultry deep tone;

the one her hairdresser admired. Millie loved the effect and so did her male friends.

Tonight she would put her hair up to hold a tiara of peacock feathers. "Thank God they are the feathers," she had commented when the designer showed her the sketches of new costumes for the upcoming show. Annie Wells and Joyce Candelaria had to carry heavy metal birdcages on their heads. Millie was grateful she was part of the flock in this show and not the hardware. It's nice to be a redhead, even if it's from a bottle. There were also advantages to dating the choreographer and designer, though there were the expected disadvantages. Things she didn't really consider at her age, but later could reflect on with a tired, more mature eye.

Pulling on her silver threaded nylons, Millie considered, as she had not in many months, other vocations. It had been a topic of discussion among the girls the evening before and had not been even remotely interesting at that time, but for some reason now it was, when she was with her own thoughts. It in fact dominated them. She had started noticing today the different lines of work that would require less effort than making herself up so thickly every night, putting on ridiculous heels and wearing heavy headdresses. She wasn't exactly complaining; she stopped herself, it was just that maybe something else would be easier, quieter. Like tonight she watched the costume assistant roll in the costumes, fluffing them a bit after their dry cleaning. Twenty to fifty costumes to manage every day and night, maybe that would not be the job she would choose. She had once not too long ago complained in a lengthy tirade when a zipper on the side of her aqua-sequined dolly dress stuck... the assistant had just shaken her head, yes, she would take care of it - like all the other "small" things she had to take care of. Russell, the costume designer, had been nearby, she realized and so there would be no objections from the girl. Millie had known she had an unfair advantage and took it. Poor girl, think of how many zippers stick in fifty sequined dresses and how many tirades she must nod to and politely abide.

She should be a cook. She had watched her friend Joyce cook a full meal for a dinner party of the cast during the holidays. It had been a fabulous spread and she seemed to do it with such ease. When Millie had asked her if she had considered doing this for a living, maybe cooking for one of those swanky cafes just off the strip, she had looked at Millie in horror. "And ruin a good hobby? Never."

Joyce clanked into the dressing room, taking her stall mirror allotment across from Millie's with the heavy deposit of her headpiece on a head-form.

"Gentle with that cage," Millie warned her "a's" elongated with her drawl. She had just seen Russell and he would have a fit if he saw disrespect of his creation. This was not something to say to Joyce, that Millie quickly realized, once she saw Annie enter holding a feathered headdress. She had been recast and it would be a difficult issue between them. Joyce had more years on the line and yet she hadn't been recast to more advantageous role in any show during those years.

Millie concentrated on her other leg and pulled the nylons up to the garter belt for some give. Spending more time than usual she was hoping it would appear that her attention had been unintentionally directed away from the cage sitting in front of Joyce as Annie approached her with the feathered tiara.

"Glad I practiced flyin'," she said with uncontained and obvious joy. Annie was from the mid-west. Millie and the others had called her "Farmer's Daughter," because she fit the jokes square on. Very well built with blond hair that could easily be secured off her shoulders in various styles if she desired. Her complexion when it did not have an inch of make-up, was milky and her eyes a doe-brown. This was her third year in Vegas, that made her a veteran to some and a novice to the others who were now off the dance lines and serving drinks in the lounge. She was a good enough friend to Millie, but she was not sure she would be further tolerated by the other dancers with such disregard of Joyce's feelings due to the casting. If she even realized it. This would not be made an issue by Joyce, who opposite of Annie was brown-haired and olive-complexed. She was not any less attractive in Millie's opinion, but she knew by Las Vegas standards if she wasn't blond or redheaded, disproportionately busted or towering long and thin, then she was average, at best. Of course "put her out in a crowd in Des Moines and she would be the talk of the corn haulers", Annie had once commented during a more compassionate time.

Joyce stoically finished applying the eye shadow to her arching brow when Jackie Knight stepped in to stir things up, as she always did.

"Still a caged woman, huh? Unlike your friend here." She bobbed her head in Annie's direction.

Annie appearing to not truly understand that she was the subject of Joyce's humiliation, misguidingly took her defense.

"The cage-heads are just as important as the birds."

Jackie moved closer for the kill. Annie was such an unknowingly easy target. "That why you fluttered in here, holding your head so high you'd get a nose bleed. Because what you did last night was so important?"

Jackie's words where not only harsh because of their content, they were hard because she was from Southside Chicago and she had that bitter severe edge to her words and her expressions.

Now it was Joyce, kind plain Joyce who came to Annie's defense. "She should be proud she made the bird line, don't make her feel bad about it." Millie watched with admiration as Joyce smiled at Annie and gave her a gentle swat with her right hand. "You fly high tonight, Annie." As she turned away from Jackie and Annie, Millie saw that the emotion was real. It had only been momentary jealousy that had affected Joyce Candelaria and it had passed. As the girls made final adjustments, Millie watched for any indication from Joyce that she held a true grudge against her more Vegas beautiful, more fortunate friends. Millie saw nothing, nothing but a young girl dancing in hot lights, in a red sequined dress with a heavy cage on her head with no chance to be a bird.

CHAPTER FOUR

Desert Flower

At 4:00 in the morning every place in the
world is quiet accept Vegas. Maybe
every place is not entirely quiet. Cities
like Houston wind down to a sleepy hum to allow
its occupants rest, to ready themselves for the
next 8:00-5:00 day. But in Las Vegas days didn't
end, you could walk downtown or the strip and if
the extravagant air conditioning of the opened
door of the casinos didn't shock you awake, then
the amount of people out on the sidewalks did.
Millie took her route about a half-mile to a

parking lot exactly three casino blocks away to
her car. From there it only took her five minutes
to drive to her apartment on Fremont and
Orange. She often wondered, as she walked, if it
made more sense to just walk to and from work
given the cost of gas, insurance and the hassle of
parking. She could get rid of her car, it wasn't
anything special to her, since she only used it to
get to and from work. If she went out on her days
off, it didn't amount too much, a quick trip to the
grocery store, to Henderson maybe. Her true
days off where she actually did something more
than errands, either Annie or Joyce drove. And
for work she could always ride with one of them
since they were now all in the same show and
lived not far from each other. Annie had laughed
at her when she brought up the idea of walking.

"Showgirls don't walk," she had laughed,
"That about the only thing that makes us
different from hookers." Millie had laughed too;
this was one of the many lessons the veteran
Annie taught her. Since coming to Vegas from
Houston, Texas, it had all been an education for
Millie. Auditioning in skimpy outfits only to be

put in a line and judged on how thick your eyelashes could be applied and whether your hair was the right color in the spotlights. She was not naïve, she had known when coming here that she would be judged all the time on her looks, and examined in her private life. Young Vegas was already getting that reputation. And she, as crazy as her family felt this life was, had wanted it all the more badly.

Millie Flowers had lived in Texas until she was twenty-three and two months. Her mother sold plumbing fixtures in the family owned hardware store. That was all she would sell. Her father as proprietor ran all departments and could answer your questions on roof shingles as well as grout, but Grace Flowers stayed in her confines of plumbing. Not that she wasn't good at it - she was and well recognized in that world, being wined and dined by the plumbing fixture manufacturers whenever they made their sales rounds. Only plumbing was what she was comfortable with, what she liked and so if someone wandered into her area behind the light fixtures asking about anything else but plumbing, she would very aptly and kindly lead

them toward Robert Flowers out of her domain
to where they needed to go.

Millie had worked in the store during and
after graduating high school, being the easiest
choice not sure what she wanted to do. A four-
year college had never been considered, not
because she wasn't capable, but because it wasn't
something girls she knew did in the late 1930s.
Most were married directly out of high school
and anyways didn't have to consider career
choices, or where to spend 8:00 to 5:00 each day.
They were at home and appeared happy. Millie
did not consider either. Though marriage was
out for now, she could never tolerate a boyfriend
for more than three months. After that period of
time his every mannerism, every twitch bothered
her. But what bothered her most was their
constant attention to her beauty and body. Millie
Flowers was beautiful, no doubt about it, and in
everybody's opinion and she didn't have to do
much to make herself that way. She was tall, 5.9',
this had been a problem at school dances, and she
was also shapely more so than her classmates.
Her hair was always willing to conform to the
latest styles and her eyebrows arched in perfect

crescents above thick curly lashes. Her bosoms, which were such an area of interest not only in Vegas, were large and symmetrical and made a breast-man sweat at the brow and quiver elsewhere. Sitting behind the cash register at Flower's Hardware made her a conversation piece for the local contractors and the Saturday fix-it men in town. Even her mother's crowd of plumbing fixture salesmen chose to speak to her about their latest products once she came to work there even though she attempted to steer them toward her mother.

It can't be said that this bothered Mille, it didn't. But when a man she was dating stopped dating her and began dating her looks it did. Her mother called it "hypocritical," knowing her daughter was proud of her beauty and the power it wielded. But Millie tried to explain that it wasn't that she minded the direction of their attention, she just felt that after the initial thrill her body could provide, they would then fall in love with her. But that hadn't happened, at least not yet, that she could tell. And when she turned twenty-three Mille thought it never would happen and made the decision to move to Las

Vegas where she had all the advantages her body offered.

"I've never heard you talk about moving."

"And Vegas?" Her father couldn't fathom.

Millie's older sister and younger brother all lived and planned to continue to live in Houston, why couldn't she? What was to come next, Millie hadn't wanted to hear, ever, "Why don't you make up with one of those boys you dropped and settle down?"

"Because I don't settle, Dad." Millie had retorted defiantly. And it was truly not until then that Mille realized that it was true. Settle, to her, meant staying there in Houston and working at the hardware store, the accounting firm or most recently the Bloom Boutiques. Her mother seemed to understand this more than her father, and tried to convince her to maybe move to another part of Houston, or even "Dallas", Grace had said to her own unhideable and husband's abhorrence. Seeing that "even" Dallas would still please her parents, thoughts of places beyond came to mind; places of mystery and advantages, so she chose Las Vegas. It was new and unchartered.

"You won't have family there." He said, adjusting his shirt, which had clung too tight at his belly.

"I know. That'll be hard." She said because it would, no doubt be the hardest thing. Millie had never been out of Texas. She hadn't had to make new friends in years.

"You can fly home whenev'r you like." Grace pulled her daughter close. They would not have the funds to do so, but she had said it anyway.

Gus Flowers cracked his knuckles loudly, rolled on to toes and then turning walked toward the den, closed the kitchen door quietly behind him. The hinges squeaked from lack of use.

The tenth of November next month would mark a year Millie had been here in Vegas. It hadn't been as hard as she had thought. She had made a few good friends, liked her work and for the most part the men she dated. Russell Berg was an artistic type and stereotypical in his moodiness and tendency to forget engagements they had made together. But Millie liked him because he could change a scene so quickly, magically and typically to her benefit; her advantage. He did this by taking her on trips with him and involving her in his designing exploits. Millie made a little extra money doing this since most often she served as a model for his costume creations, but it was fun and carefree. On the contrary, Evan Hamilton was elegant and wealthy, but their relationship had to be kept quiet, because he was married. "Of course," Annie had commented when Millie told her. "If I was married, I would never live in Vegas. All men here have affairs with showgirls, or even cocktail waitresses." Millie was about to defend him, but didn't, it was true Evan didn't deserve her attempts at a defense. "It's great sex." was all she would lend. "It always is," Annie advised in return and it was left at that.

Annie had had many affairs with married men. It was something she did without much thought to it. But lately, she seemed to regret some of the relationships she had with these men and feared they might in fact have been affected by her in some way. A deep, unsettling way. One night when Millie was over at Annie's apartment, she answered her door to a hesitant knock since Annie was busy trimming a roast she had splurged on at the Alpha Beta, and was met face to face with a teenage boy. He must have been about sixteen, and stood easily her height with a pimple-lined face and close set eyebrows. His thin arms shot out of his sleeves and were perches for clumps of adolescent hair. It was his arms that started the conversation - as he pulled at them in a tentative motion, settling on crossing them awkwardly across his chest.

"Is Annie Wells home?" Millie answered that she was and opened the apartment door wider so he could see her and her him. This must be a young friend or the son of a friend. Annie's apartment was like her's, what was called an efficiency cottage. You could see every room except the bathroom if you opened the front door wide enough. Annie looked up from the kitchen counter where prep was being done, straightening the towel that was slipping off her shoulder and wiping her hands as she did.

"Yes?" she called and then moved toward the open door. It was obvious by her question and the lift of her eyebrows that she had no idea who this young boy was.

Millie looked back. The boy cleared his throat and asked. "Are you Annie?"

"Yes?" Annie repeated but this time in answer to his question.

The boy straightened his back, and dropped his arms to his sides, but didn't move farther into the doorway, which he could have easily done since Millie had opened it wide to allow this conversation. She was not blocking, but offering full admittance.

"I want you," he choked, "to stay away from my father." This was said with some hesitation but clearly and in a forced deep tone. His throat constricted, possibly to lower his voice or just allow the strained words.

Annie pulled the towel off her shoulder and moved toward him as hesitantly as he had spoken to her. She had had to ask, "Who's your father?" Millie was struck by that fact that she honestly did not know.

"Nelson Miller," he said calmly, but suddenly sounded much more juvenile. "He's married and he's my dad, leave him alone." These final words had come quickly and with them the son of Nelson Miller's vision began to fog, "he's not yours to screw."

Millie had stood there still holding the open door and watching as the boy turned his back on the two women and crossed the lawn of the cottage complex toward a black sedan which was parked perfectly parallel to the curb. For a full two minutes she could not look at Annie. Who was this woman who slept with men with adolescent, feeling children. Who was this slut who had befriended her and shown her how to live in Las Vegas? How was SHE living in Las Vegas?

When Millie did turn she saw a pale Annie, shoulders in the process of slumping, as her face grew ugly with shame. Her milky complexion splotched and hived in the high points of her cheeks as the humility rushed in. Millie closed the door gently and with care as if that action was the most important at this moment; and then moved toward her friend, just as a high wail left her lips.

"His name is Michael." Millie didn't understand and lead Annie to her small table for two already set for the pot roast dinner, to sit. "Who's Michael?" Millie asked, she had thought the boy had said Nelson.

"The son." Annie bleeped a small sound and laid her head on the plate that was meant for the salad and cried.

Evan also had children. But Millie never asked their names nor allowed him to venture into any story about them. There was a girl and a boy and his wife stayed at home to raise them. Even with that scant information, Millie was able to draw a face, some characteristics, a favorite hobby, and the color of their rooms. On her days off when shopping was on her list of errands to run, she slowed in the sections of the grocery aisles with kid's food and wondered what cereal they liked best, if they had any allergies; and if they knew their father slept with a showgirl when he tired of his wife and the family dinners.

Once when Evan was dining with her in a restaurant on the strip, Millie had asked, wanting him to get angry with her and maybe, just maybe end the affair she could not seem to. "What did you tell your wife you were doing?"

Evan had been just about to take a bite of steak, almost raw so it was dripping in its animal blood from mouth to plate. He pulled the fork down away and held it there as the blood dripped the longer path to the dish. "Do you want to know?" he asked her directly somewhat accusatory. She had not even hesitated, "No." Now sitting at home taking her shoes off and placing them in her closet next to her tap shoes and shoes she wore only to weddings she wondered if he was sleeping soundly next to his wife not thinking about Millie Flowers, because he didn't need to.

CHAPTER FIVE

Girls of Height

She realized that she had been too tired this morning to draw the drapes in the front room. From her bed the sun-drenched her feet in intense heat, but only to the top portion of her first few toes. She pushed herself down to the bottom of the bed to take in more of the warmth. It was fall and still very warm for Las Vegas, but lately Millie craved the heat and because there was no humidity with it she loved it all the more. At about 3:30 she called Joyce, just to chat in hopes that her friend was not too upset about the recast of Annie. Joyce answered in a chipper voice, much too chipper for the time of day and amount of sleep Millie calculated Joyce would have received the night before. They were all actors on and off stage.

"How was your night?" Millie asked. Though the days and nights of all showgirls were reversed from the rest of the world, they spoke as if they weren't. The "need for normalcy" Joyce had quipped one day when Millie called her on it. Upon leaving last night Joyce had confided in her that her sister and husband were in town and wanted to be escorted through it with Joyce as their guide. The lights and glamour tour of Vegas all residents found themselves leading a few times a year when home came to call.

Joyce smiled into the receiver, only because her sister Louise was in view.

"Really fun, we went to The 91 Club, played some Black Jack and Roulette, Louise is a killer at the wheel. Millie imagined Joyce projecting that last comment toward her sister who probably "pashawed" her. Louise was a bird-boned woman who had married young and claimed to still be in love with her "one and only," though Joyce confided in Millie that Louise had a roving eye much to Joyce's dismay. Coming to Las Vegas was the couples one and only annual vacation from Los Angeles. This would seem really sad years later when Millie saw that most people who visited the emerging town of Las Vegas had such high expectations, as if this one trip would change their lives. It never did.

"We had breakfast buffet at Roy's and walked downtown," Joyce paused and quietly stated, "I'm exhausted." Louise must have left the room, good, Millie really wanted to talk this morning.

"Can you get in some sleep time before tonight? It's a full show." Fridays and Saturdays the girls put on a two-hour show with a short intermission. On the other nights of the week there were two shows of one hour and though it was the same total time, the break from early evening to ten o'clock at night seemed different enough to be preferred. The crowds were certainly different. No one with an artistic eye attended the weekend shows. They were in Vegas to party.

"I don't think so. Louise and Hank are coming to the show tonight. Russell got them complimentary tickets and at this point I don't know if I should thank him or kill him." Russell who never remembered anyone's name but Millie's had done the almost impossible to obtain complimentary tickets for Joyce.

"Russell got you tickets?" Millie demanded to know how and Joyce leapt into a story regarding some businessman who had purchased a whole block of tickets for tonight's show and had called to say he wouldn't need them. After finding out they were non-refundable the man had told the club manager, a fish-faced man with wide hips and a caved-in chest to keep the tickets and give them away. Coincidentally when Joyce was heading out with the sister and brother-in-law soon to be in tow, she had run into Russell who had been given six of the tickets and didn't know what to do with them and had gladly shoveled two off to Joyce. Joyce has acted casual about it with Russell and her sister but now on the phone with Millie she glowed. She was able to pull off the impression all showgirls try to make to their families in their home states that they have connections. That they were somehow important. The truth is they had connections, but they were

ones that they would never confess to their
family.

The heat of the sun was now fully on Millie's
body as she sat in the one chair in her efficiency
kitchen and now it did not feel soothing but
prickled her irritation. To Millie, Joyce was the
one girl who would end up happy and married;
she was the one who had a chance at that since
she was even-tempered and accommodating.
Millie did not like that her boyfriend, one of
them, was doing Joyce favors. Millie suddenly
found herself wanting to spend time with Joyce.
She told herself it was because Joyce was delicate
and under a lot of stress because of her sister's
presence, but truly she needed a friend. A friend,
other than Annie.

It was still hot when Millie headed out to the
club. She had dressed in cotton Capri pants with
a mid-drift tied at the waist. The print of her
shirt was checkered like a picnic tablecloth and
Millie wondered if it clashed with her red hair.
Hell she'd seen Lucy wear red many times and it
looked just fine. That somehow validated her
choice as she decided not to return to her
apartment and change. Millie's slip on heels

clicked on the pavement as she navigated around the cracks in the sidewalk pitted from what, she couldn't imagine. What could gauge concrete? There was never any harsh weather here only heat. Yet, each square of concrete had its own pattern of holes and crevasses.

Orange Avenue was crowded, full of people coming home from their office jobs. She could always tell the commuting neighbors from the tourists or casino workers, though they would inevitably mix in a mile or so up the avenue. The commuters were mainly men in dark family-sized sedans wearing white starched shirts, their navy coat jackets in the passenger seat next to them. She was certain that behind each driver's seat was a black attaché case containing important papers of some kind. When Millie reached The Flamingo, the mix of the traffic changed to tourists, gamblers and people in her own industry, no office workers or business executives. The traffic of the street flowed in spots and then clogged at Sahara where people entered the bulb lit passageways and dropped their pay on the craps tables.

Gambling had never appealed to Millie. It was difficult enough for her to pay her rent, car-related expenses and food. Why would she want to risk losing her wages? She never considered that she might be the one to hit it "big." She had considered the odds and the fantasy quickly faded, if there was ever one at all. It was the fantasy that fueled and plagued Las Vegas. Take Freddie Diego who was in her dance troop was one of those people that couldn't steer herself away from the gambling pull. Her gambling exploits had gotten so bad that she spent a good six or seven months last year rotating among friends' apartments because she couldn't afford her rent. She had been thrown out of a group boardinghouse, which had been her residence for at least two years. It was a great house with five bedrooms and as much independence or camaraderie as desired. Her roommates, who in better times had been friends, soon grew tired of hearing that Freddie would pay them back for their monthly footing of the rent next month, the month she would hit it "big." But months passed and her debts mounted, even beyond her rent, and soon bill collectors hounded her roommates for information on how to find Freddie, when they knocked on their door late at night that was it. The girls became fearful as the calls grew more aggressive and found that the only way to stop them was to say Freddie didn't live there any more and mean it.

Freddie was a glamorous showgirl in a much different way than the other girls. She was of the "exotic," being originally from Mexico and having immigrated to the United States in her teens. Her thick arching eyebrows, adobe skin and shaded features always commanded her a role in skits of the hot Latina woman in skits, or for this production, the wild and colorful parrot. Freddie wasn't insulted with this stereotyping, commenting to Millie that if Annie was forever the milkmaid, she was forever the Maria. Yet Millie noticed Freddie seemed to attract a different set of followers than the other girls. Las Vegas was far from being a melting pot at this time and so the men that were drawn to Freddie were men who favored the sultry dark women, and the Italians who often mistook Freddie for one of their own. Freddie didn't much care for the attention, but she did for the money it often came with. It was this weakness that led her to fall for Salvadore Degrasse, a young assistant manager at the El Cortez.

Salvadore had been very nice at first, to all the girls and that's what made all of them dislike him. Annie in particular made it a point to let him know what she thought of him and soon Millie had no fear of doing the same. Annie had educated Millie on the mob-connection in Vegas. Not what was written up in the pulp fiction novels, but the real connections to be feared therefore respected. To Millie it was unbelievable, fascinating and terrifying at the same time. It was all part of Vegas' history from its birth and was in the intricate operations of its heart. But Annie, and soon Millie, kept their distance from it as best they could. Freddie didn't, or she did and her illness for gambling made it impossible for her to do so.

One night after the show, when all the girls had removed their costume-gear and were back in their civilian clothes, Salvadore walked into the dressing room in search of Freddie. Annie immediately reprimanded him. "Hey, what are you doing coming in here?" The girls were all dressed but it was the nerve of intrusion that fired Annie up.

Salvadore ignored her tone, "Where is she, where's Freddie?" His voice was low and masculine, but his manner slightly feminine, with his thin build and his dapper manner of dress. He had obviously just come from the office and was still holding his attaché' in his wiry grip. Millie thought of the men in their sedans driving through her neighborhood and wondered if any of them were associated with Salvadore, or his kind. Freddie's locker was behind a corner that turned at the end of Millie's station. She was there; there was no need to look. When Salvadore had entered, Millie had heard a chirp coming from her. It had not been intentional but when Salvadore started past Millie to make the turn, Millie met him rising from her chair. Millie was at least three inches taller than him and it humored her the way Salvadore appeared so diminutive next to her. This discrepancy must either anger him or thrill him, since Freddie was only an inch or so shorter than Millie. Many men in Vegas seemed to prefer the girls of height.

They wanted to showgirl stature even without the lift of the stage.

"What do ya want?" Millie now asked. Salvadore scowled and lifted his chin to her, "I'm here to see Freddie not any of you sluts." Millie didn't know if it was the way he said it, the height difference or the sound of Freddie's sucked in breath, but she slowly brought her hand back and slapped him hard. For a second he stood in front of her not moving, then the other girls reacted to Millie's lead. From the corner of the dressing room twelve or more showgirls in all their height and glory moved in on him.

Salvadore touched his cheek lightly. It was red hot from the contact and below his eye was a small scratch from the ring Evan had given Millie last Christmas.

"What in the hell?" He seemed so truly pitiful, a short balding man with a carnation in his lapel and an attaché still latched in his right hand. She was almost sorry she had hit him, it was not a fair fight.

"Get out of here." Millie said.

"You're a crazy bitch," he said and turned to find the other dozen girls in close proximity.

"We all are," Millie retorted as they closed in. Salvadore stepped back, found a small opening between the girl guardians and the open dressing room door, he chided sheepishly, "I see that, well have that crazy Freddie see me, and soon." Millie shrugged like a defiant teenager and watched as the door closed hearing Salvadore's leather-soled feet run down the hall. When the latch sound caught the metal plate of the door, a nervous cheer broke out in the dressing room.

"Wow, you sure can hit," Annie said, pleased, as if Millie was now somehow an extension of her, someone to her credit. Her prodigy, having taught her well the rules of Vegas. They weren't rules she had ever hoped to learn, but had learned spectating in earlier circumstances and applying them here. Men like Salvadore were not only in Las Vegas, and the reality stung her. In Houston, they had been called Carl.

CHAPTER SIX

The Tale of Two Men

C arl was long and sleek with big ideas on all the business ventures he would start. David was "ethic" as Millie's mother would say, meaning he was Jewish, with a strong-medium build and deep-irised eyes. But they were no different really, and headed down the same road. The road of consequence to Millie.

They had both wanted Millie by their sides or on their arms, to show off. Millie had gone along on both rides. Carl Burke was someone Millie had known since high school. He had excelled in the social circles and established himself as the center of any given situation or strata. Millie had once desired to be within a center, and had been there in high school. Millie Flowers was such an anomaly, tall, sleek like him and captivating. She could also sing, dance and look lovely beside a successful man. It was the trophy part that caused her trouble not only outwardly but within herself. The beauty is what called her to Vegas and to her own person distaste at the attention caused her to be successful here. But in high school it had caused her more visible problems, many which stayed with her and even though hidden in thick skin continued to cause struggle in her adult years.

Carl appeared openly kind, if there were people around him, which required him to make such gestures. Should he want their respect. But in private he was cruel. His cruelty was tiered but the top layer was guided by his only true motivation, which was to succeed and to have other people acknowledge that he had succeeded. That is why he needed Millie in those years, to stand beside him, waltz into parties, throw her head back and laugh. At the time she dated Carl she worked as secretary for an accounting firm, a job she had landed out of high school before she joined her family's business. After months of training she found herself entering numbers on spreadsheets, whereby at the end of the day her fingers ached and the side of her palm and pinky were smudged with lead dust. Maybe that is why she opted for the glamour Carl offered. The jobs open to her were limited, and at that time avoiding the hardware store was a priority. Carl brought her out of that boring world and allowed her to forget she was an odd shaped creature, single in Houston, making tick marks on an oversized piece of paper all day.

Carl soon became established in his line of work, successful by his definition and the definition of some others who mattered. He was investing in car dealerships throughout the Houston area, which required capital contributions and the buying out partners as he went, when he could. He didn't control any one dealership in its entirety so he did not have to trouble himself with the actual day-to-day operations of management. Rather, he commanded from his high distant chair, squawking at the end of a phone line or conducting heated meetings at parties, which were meant to be pleasant affairs. It was at one of these meetings that Millie met David Bloom. David was one of the partners, but the only one who owned more single interest than Carl and on this particular evening walked away when he began his berating. His walking away was a decision; and more powerful than a scene. Carl watched him turn, back up from the crowd or whoever was in attendance and walk past him, always past him after a particular lashing to the group of partners. But he could only watch him walk and David would casually strip him of the intensity by leaving.

On one occasion, Carl attempted to counter the control and barked at David, "Where do you think you're going?" David turned slowly as if to match all the eyes that were not upon him. "Go? Well why would I stay?" His eyes locked Millie's, "when this beautiful woman wants so desperately to remove herself from this embarrassing predicament." He gently turned Millie away and led her toward a fold-up conference room table with baskets of bread and platters of triangular shaped cheese. He nudged her in the small of her back with his hand, coaxing her to move in front of him. He didn't need to coax, he was right, Millie wanted to remove herself, had needed to do so for a long time well before this cocktail party. David provided the opportunity, but she would have taken it from anyone, fearing she didn't have the strength or the aptitude to do it on her own.

For years Millie would remember Carl's stare, those wide blue-rimmed eyes looked at her with disbelief. By walking away with David Bloom, one of his partners and a total stranger to Millie, she had crushed him. Carl didn't approach them, though they stood only a few feet away and munched on the cheese and introduced themselves to each other in a polite social manner. Millie spoke gaily, forgetting she was merely a pawn in this duel of men. She was enjoying David and thanked him for retrieving her through attentive talk. He spoke softly and at times she had to strain to hear him. David was such a contrast to Carl, whose voice though not directed at them, barreled and roared on a "notice me" scale. David's dark curls were close-cut to his head and the sides of his brow were a noticeable shower of gray. Millie was twenty at the time and figured David Bloom to be in his mid thirties, but he corrected her on that first meeting explaining he was only twenty-five but worry had showed through. He was so at ease in this conversation, in the middle of this stance, Millie had dismissed the comment and told him so to which he laughed. It was his laugh that finally turned Carl's full attention to them. Moments later Carl accepted his coat from the hostess and left in defeat without a word.

After he left, the other partners slowly made their way to David, never mentioning the duel but obviously congratulating him with their favored attention. Millie saw Carl Burke only one more time in her life and that was some thirty years later. For the next two years she was the starlet of David Bloom. His success in the car dealerships was only a passing thing and his true profession was that of avoiding his destined field of retail management.

His father owned a chain of woman's boutiques; all located in an affluent area of Houston known as River Oaks. There were a total of five stores, each offering a different style of clothing, targeting a different taste. David confided in Millie that though the shops did well they didn't do as well as they could because of their proximity to each other; a fact David's father refused to acknowledge. When he started the business, Houston was segregated and Jewish-owned businesses stayed in the River Oaks area, and a few other pockets, one of the biggest being adjoining the Memorial neighborhood. There were no restrictions, per se, but his father feared the consequences if he branched out into other neighborhoods and believed the business would fail regardless, since non-Jewish patrons would not support the stores. It was not until David met Millie and explained this dilemma to her that he decided to once again broach the subject with his father.

Millie and David had been dating several months when David asked her to join him at a family dinner. He had been talking to Millie about managing one of the boutiques and Millie had listened with interest since she was still toiling through the bookkeeping job. Millie wasn't quite sure whether David's interest was honest since she literally hated her job at the accounting firm and wanted out. But when she thought about the proposition carefully she decided it was one that she would at least consider. Something to advance her toward something, though she didn't know what that something was. At least it wasn't hardware.

David had not opened his own family's door but had knocked like a visitor himself and had waited for his sibling to escort him in.

David's younger sister openly gawked at Millie this gentile, tall woman accompanying her brother. Evy, as David called his sister, was about seventeen by Millie's estimation and was introduced under his breath as a meddling little monster. She had David's dark hair but had ironed it into compliance to meet the latest style. It flipped at the ends and to restrain the top she secured a tight cloth scarf, which trailed down her back with even pointed ends and bounced as she walked. She was shorter than David, but not by much and stood stoutly on her squared, sturdy hips.

"Well hello," had been her challenging greeting as David ushered her into the living room of the house after a noticeably automatic lean to Evy's cheek. It appeared by their manner to be a more formal affair than Millie had anticipated, not just the event of dinner but also the family itself.

The living room was large and its wide windows faced the backyard, which housed mature shading oaks and stubby well-groomed crabgrass. A row of well-positioned stones at a corner of the yard appeared to be some kind of a rock garden alternative to grass. Upon arriving there they had passed a black and white diamond tile-floored room whose only occupant seemed to be a grand piano with some thickly oiled paintings on the two facing walls. The living room was not a contrast to the piano room but rather an extension. It was richly painted in a rouge red color and the paintings, also thickly oiled, were all rimmed in thick gold gilding of ornate overlays. It would have been gaudy except that the furnishings were also sparse and the room lacked a couch or sofa to sit on. Instead there were single chairs all beautifully upholstered in the same rich velvet material with trailings of gold throughout the plush. They were angled, offerings of perspective to the room, for different conversational groups.

Millie stood behind David, not liking the position but not knowing where to go exactly. When David had entered the room, he had stopped, not to ponder or rest but apparently to consider an approach; the right approach. Not yet sitting, Millie looked at the two opposite doorways expecting to be greeted, but they were empty.

Evy was still leading them and offered, "Please sit down and I'll tell Mother and Daddy you're here." She exited through the hallway that paralleled the glass cubed viewing to the outside and Millie watched her travel to another section to the house. In this configuration the occupants of the house could view persons in the living room from at least two directions. This made her even more nervous and she wondered if that nervousness was being observed. Millie sat down in the closest chair and David obediently took his seat next to her as if she had directed him to. Millie's own home was nothing like this. A simple wood and brick four-bedroom home with a front porch screened in so she could sleep out there in the summer heat when the four walls of a room of wall-contained humidity was too intolerable. But though a contrast in every way, she realized that this house also stifled the confidence of her date, who had grown up here, something 7722 Twin Hills Drive would never have attempted to do, much less succeed at.

David put both his hands on his knees, palms down with his fingers spread. "They should be here any minute," he looked over at Millie politely, and added, "My mother has a way of being late even when she's ready." A moment passed and David answered his own silent question, "I don't know if my father is home. I'm assuming he is." Millie wondered what indication had been provided for David to detect this possible absence.

"Did you grow up in this house?" Millie asked for conversation sake but also because she really wanted to know for sure.

"Yes, I never lived anywhere else until I went away to college." He looked down at both glassed corridors.

"And Evy? Is she still in high school or is she in college?" Millie wanted to confirm her first guess of Evy's age, but also make more conversation.

"She is in her first year of high school."

"Really?" Millie said, "She seems older, more groomed. If that's the right word." The choice humored David and loosened him up a bit. It somehow gave him the feeling that he could bring Millie in as a confidant.

"Evy is being groomed, she is following in my mother's footsteps. She spends her summers in Paris learning how to be an aristocrat with a Texas drawl." David said.

Before Millie could make a comment Mr. and Mrs. David Bloom Sr. entered from the opposite direction approaching the two sitting "guests" from behind.

"Evening," Mrs. Bloom offered as she fluttered toward Millie in a sweeping bell of belted polka dots. Millie and David jumped from their chairs, having been caught in some kind of rogue play of sarcasm. Millie took Mrs. Bloom's extended hand and then quickly Mr. Bloom's, who somehow moved as fast as his wife though he was a heavy and loud breathing man. His shake was an abrupt vertical move and then a quick release of the hand at the down stroke, causing Millie to lose her balance. She quickly righted herself. Millie's father had a strong shake also and had always told Millie to meet the strength of someone's shake with equal force. Millie had tried but it had been too quick and too forceful and when he had broken away his own hand had been left to slap his thigh.

"So nice that you're joining us for dinner," Mrs. Bloom extended her greeting and continued standing facing Millie. "Well thank you so much for allowing me to join you, I have been excited to meet David's family." Mrs. Bloom took this moment to look over at her son and lean into him to cup his cheek. Though she was a Paris-groomed aristocrat and her home made her own son an uncomfortable visitor, she loved her son and offered her affection to him.

"Mother, Daddy this is Millie Flowers" it was a delay but an introduction still needed. Mrs.

Bloom and Mr. Bloom nodded confirmations. "Flowers, what fitting name for such a beautiful specimen." David junior shrank a bit with the outward flirtatiousness of his father. But Millie lightened it with humor, "Thank you, yes well with such a surname I narrowly escaped the blessing of such first names as Daisy or Rose. I've always felt grateful for plain ole' Mildred."

Dinner was served in the dining room painted in a royal blue with similar gold leafed paintings lining the walls. A wait staff served them dinner and Millie began to crave a setting where the uncomfortable gaps in conversation could be broken by the hostess' necessary exit to the kitchen. Instead the five of them were left to be on their own-joined accord with no such reprieves, required to sit through the whole meal searching for conversation.

Millie daintily ate her salad and sorbet between courses while listening to Evy speak of her latest trip to Paris. She had only been back in the states for three weeks and was "having such a difficult time adjusting." Millie didn't find herself with a lot to add so merely nodded and politely asked a few questions. The few she could think of. She'd never been out of Houston. David sat to her right and spoke of business to his father in so much detail that Mrs. Bloom interrupted by saying so. "Please, no business at the dinner table."

Mrs. Bloom appeared younger than Millie had imagined and though stout and square like her daughter, had an appealing delicacy about her. The brown polka dotted dress of choice contrasted this a bit and to herself Millie questioned her choice of the brown color. Her hair was a chestnut brown and her lips a peachy orange. She had fashioned herself with pearls and matching earrings and thick pearl-banded bracelets. But her coloring was off and made her appear like a malformed mannequin. When she ventured bites of her meal, Mrs. Bloom's mouth curved in pleasantry but her body remained stiff, and formal.

"Have you visited our boutiques?" Mr. Bloom asked when it came time to retire to the study for some coffee and a touch of brandy. The irony of Mrs. Bloom's miscolored-style and the fact they owned boutiques was in Millie's mind. Millie was surprised by the question, since she had assumed

David had spoken to his father about the possibility of her managing one of the shops. But the way he had asked it was small talk not an introduction to a discussion of employment. Millie decided to step full into this subject line out of irritation of David's apparent omission. Her sympathy with him seemed to only go so far.

"Many times. I have been to all of them and have observed everything from buying of merchandise to customer service." If she wasn't going to be interviewed by him, she was going to interview herself in front of him. "The new lines of ladies handbags on display at the Memorial Drive shop were something I have seen selling like hotcakes at Foley's."

Mr. Bloom took his time sipping his liquor-laced coffee, as his wife for the first time during this visit acted like a hostess and refilled everyone's coffee cup with a fresh serving. Millie accepted a topping off only. She wasn't much of a coffee drinker but wanted to be polite.

"Really?" Mr. Bloom finally commented, "I hadn't heard that." Millie gave David a leading stare. He at first attempted to fain that he was occupied trying to settle the cup within the saucer. But after settled, he turned to face his father.

"Millie is quite talented when it comes to merchandising, she has a lot of ideas that are fresh and new." David reached for his coffee cup again out of nervousness since he had just set it down. This fueled Millie's desire to upset the balance, of this unfortunate intimidation David's family had over him.

"My talents actually extend beyond picking out purses, Mr. Bloom. I am very financially minded and have a background in accounting. I'm also a quick learner."

Mrs. Bloom went to reach for the coffee to once again pour but was discouraged realizing no one needed a refill so soon. Mr. Bloom sat forward in his chair. His large torso rolled into the saucer on his lap.

"Ms. Flowers, I would not equate secretarial work with a background in accounting." He wanted to set that record straight, then he launched further into, "But I am certainly ready to welcome any fresh ideas." He hit the word fresh with a bit of sarcasm.

Evy had not said a word through this entire ordeal in the study, Millie looked to her more out of curiosity than a request for support and noted that Evy was staring off out a dark window, her own untouched coffee cup in its saucer on the table untouched. Her eyes were glassy and at first Millie thought maybe she was close to tears but then realized that it was not tears but the fact that she had not blinked. Was this an onset of boredom or some successful means of escaping the life of a Texas aristocrat?

Millie thought about her response carefully though it only appeared to take seconds to deliver it after Mr. Bloom had concluded his trite diatribe.

"Mr. Bloom, with all due respect, I appreciate your views but do not necessarily agree with them. I believe your observations are clouded by the fact that you now operate your business at some distance. In saying so I mean to point out that it is the person making the entries into a company's books that knows the true strength of its numbers, not necessarily the person sitting in the boardroom." Millie took the time to examine David's reaction as she continued - it was null of expression everywhere on his face except his eyes that seemed to follow each word.

Millie continued, "I may only be a clerk in an accounting firm but I am in the numbers which makes me know the operation, just as I may only be a consumer in one of your boutiques but I know what sells and what doesn't." "And why," she added. Millie took a breath because she had not ever intended to say the rest until she saw that Evy's previously unfocused eyes were now on her.

"What you need to do is branch out, expand." Millie said. She let the sting and invasion of an outsider's statement to a continual family argument lay for a second until it quickly festered. "You need to get out of River Oaks. Your fashions are not only for the Jewish community and the community is not only in the confines of River Oaks, not any longer. Your boutiques are competing with each other and because of this they are all losing money."

Millie looked to Mr. Bloom for a response, when one didn't come he looked to David. "Am I right?" Millie probed offering him a chance to make a stance.

She had apparently inspired David a bit and he joined in her argument like a runner joining a race inspired by the pace. "Yes," he answered. Millie did eventually lend the floor and many times during the next few hours of discussion gave her frank opinion on how the business could be improved and why it was suffering, down to opinions on the paint of the storefronts. She stopped short of commenting on his mother's brown polka dot dress.

At the end of the evening Millie had secured an assistant manager position at a "to be opened" branch boutique just outside of River Oaks, "a risk area" but had already made the decision not to continue her relationship with David in any serious way. They dated for a few more years, but not exclusively any longer. She did stand by his side for many business affairs where he wanted to show a social presence. But in truth she pitied him and was sorry that he could not hold the confidence he held among business constituents with his own family. He had appeared suddenly unattractive and sad. But not the kind of sad she wished to invest herself in.

It wasn't David Bloom that Millie thought of when she confronted Salvadore that day it was Carl Burke. Millie had never told anyone of his subtle abuse and was resolved not to. When she saw Carl again they were both in their fifties. He had not aged in a dignified manner. His hair was thin and instead of cutting it short he swooped it over the crown of his head where it fluttered there like a dead feather. He had grown a substantial belly that hung over his belt and talked in elongated vowels. It was not a pleasant drawl. His car empire had appeared to have vanished, and he now worked on a lot he didn't own. He had been quick to recognize Millie, she not so quick. It was actually her sister that asked for his last name since his nametag only offered "Carl." "Burke" he had answered and used this as an opportunity to shake her hand again though he had just done so. "I thought so," said Alice in return. "This is my sister Millie. I believe you two dated years back?" she offered stepping to the side to bring them together. Millie wasn't sure at first, but then she saw a twitch of recognition. He remembered. "I'll be, Millie Flowers!" his grin opened up spaces of missing teeth. "Where have you been?" he moved toward her and cupped her arm. Millie's stomach started to take a tumble but recovered, she had not been with him for thirty years and she was grateful." "Vegas" she stated forcefully and walked off the lot with her sister following behind her with her whimpering about wanting to test-drive some car. "Not here." Alice didn't argue and didn't venture to ask why the short-clipped reaction. The past abuse had been subtle.

CHAPTER SEVEN

The Comfort of Cotton

A few months following this incident with Salvadore, Freddie finally ended up leaving the gambling life but had joined the different, more destructive ranks of alcoholics. Once an addict always an addict, another line - different verse. Millie did get a letter from her now and again, the last time she had proudly proclaimed sixty days sober. She should be praising Freddie, but really sixty days out of how many years? She didn't want to participate in any patronizing talk but Freddie had been such a beauty. When Freddie had crashed on Millie's sofa after the Salvadore slapping they had spent a few early mornings together talking when they should have been sleeping. Freddie kissed her cross necklace whenever she spoke of family, an apparent reflex, but didn't offer where they were. Millie never learned that part of her story.

It was Freddie who handed Millie the phone one morning. Millie had gone to get a gallon of milk at a local grocery. She dropped her purse and put her keys on the counter. Freddie had crossed herself before handing Millie the phone.

"Hello?" Millie offered tentatively.

"Mildred?" a throaty voice bleated.

"Pa?" Millie looked at Freddie whose mouth was quivering.

"She's gone pumpkin."

"Gone where?" Deep down Millie wanted to delay the fact that would soon emerge. It was a self-protective attempt.

She folded herself down to get blood to her head, listening to her father, and when she straightened Freddie was no longer in front of her.

"It happened quickly sugar, she didn't suffer" an honest comment. "That's what they tell me."

Millie found a chair and took the rest of it in. Her mother had died of a heart attack, early in the morning it was thought. In her sleep. She simply didn't wake up.

Grace Flowers had wanted to be a dancer but instead she was a plumbing specialist. Was that the way it should have gone? The way her life should have gone?

Freddie left that day, kissing Millie on the cheek while she was still on the phone. With her duffle bags and coat slung over her shoulder she closed the front door quietly. Millie was not of a mind to stop her, nor the mind to consider the timing of her leaving.

The trip to Houston for the funeral had to be hastily planned. Her father was in no shape to make arrangements so Millie and her sister, and little help from her brother, did the notifying and scheduling once Millie landed. The ceremony was subdued. The Flowers family was never very religious. Never had been. So it didn't need to be a religious affair. What warmed Millie's heart were the customers and industry folks who showed up to pay their respects to Grace Flowers. Plumbers, trades people and contractors in stiff suits mothballed for years, made sure to shake the hands of the family and some whispered a gentle message in her father's ear. Maybe not the life in the lights, or on the stage, but a life.

Going through her mother's things was a difficult task. Millie had known it would be hard but when it came time the process opened up a vision she had not expected. She started with the closet, positioned behind two large oak doors squarely in front of her parent's bed. Slide to the left was her mother's clothes to right her father's. She was glad to see that her mother's things took less space than her father's that would be easier when they were removed, not as much empty space for him to look at. Her mother had liked cotton, only cotton. When the synthetics made their splash in recent years with fade and stain-resistant claims, the onset of sturdy rayons and polyesters, Grace had shuddered - it was unnatural to wear plastic next to the skin no matter in what form or by what chemical miracle. When given a scarf from a friend's exotic travel in Europe comprised of thirty percent rayon she broke out in a rash so irritating she had to wear a towel seeped in Neosporin to the store. Millie had thought the aversion was all in her head and was merely substantiating her dislike.

Stroking collectively the sleeves of her blouses, as if gathering of arms, Millie felt soft age and comfort the cotton lent. Simple, no stripes, only solids and a few small prints of flowers on some dresses meant only to announce spring. There would be no spring this year.

She could not bear to go through her nightgowns or her "intimates." Instead she laid them in a gift box with a lid of Christmas angels she found in the hall closet and without telling her father or sister put them in the large trashcan waiting to be picked up. It would be too much to sort, not in volume but in emotion. The sleeves had been hard enough.

Millie folded the remaining clothes in piles neatly removing them from their hangers, but then returning them when she realized the empty hangers would be more harsh presence than the empty railing. Someone, she was not sure who, had dropped off some moving boxes, or maybe they had been in her parents' closet. She wasn't quite sure. But she had found them leaning in the front hallway expecting to be used. Sealing the boxes with duck tape because the house had no other tape, the fiber caught on her long fingernails. She looked down and for a minute had that feeling of panic that comes when you suddenly realize a situation has become permanent. She would never again have a conversation with her mother, never again see her wear the brown cotton sweater with the yellow piping, frayed a bit on the right collar. Her hand still secured to the tape Millie cried huge heaves into the partly sealed box. She would have to live the rest of her life without a mother.

She heard Freddie had taken another job with The Silver Slipper and had moved into another group house. The strange parting didn't make much sense to Millie but she reined in her judgment and let it be. Loss had done that for her, if it had done nothing else. How many people had walked through her mother's life? It had been such a show of respect at the service. Millie thought she knew all of her mother's friends and colleagues, but there were many faces she didn't recognize. Talking later to her siblings, they commented too that their mother must have been in some social clubs or maybe they didn't know all her customers because strangers sat in the church not just attending but grieving. People passed through a mother's life without their knowledge. It seemed strange and unfair. Should she have asked their affiliation if they had not offered it with the shaken hand of condolence?

CHAPTER EIGHT

Those Costumes

To relieve herself from the boredom of her work life, Millie auditioned for dance roles in small traveling productions throughout Houston that found stages and audiences wherever they could. She thought it would offer some distraction, an excuse to limit her scheduled work to days, time away from her kitchen table and a way to meet people beyond the "Charlie Girl crowd." Those had been her mother's words when she made the mistake of mentioning it to her in passing one morning. Millie's mother loathed the boutique's customers because they shopped to recreate themselves and in her "book" (not necessarily the Bible) that was sinful, or least reason to ridicule harshly. But what was even more sinful to Momma Flowers was that Millie should be working so hard and yet not meeting men. Men that would marry her.

"You sit at home every night, if you aren't locked up in that shop all day waiting on customers." Grace wiped her hands down her apron enough to put her stirring hand on her hips - making a point with her hips bowed forward like a rubber cowboy doll. "You haven't really seen anyone since David." She said his name with a long "a."

Millie had agreed to come to dinner because she had missed the last two pot roasts. Both times due to working late because of inventory season. She knew what the topics of the evening would be and immediately regretted her mention of the open audition call. She wanted to get off the subject. It had become her mother's cause de'momma, her sister Alice used to say after taking a French course at the community college.

"I haven't danced in years," Millie offered to the excuse-mix as she cut a chunk of the butter and lay the butter knife in the bar of cold curdled cream sliced halfway ready to make another square.

"I'm sure it's not like the dancin' you did in school or that you did as a little girl in ballet class." It will be more routines steps in a line." Grace had a thought, "Do they give you those costumes?"

"Momma, I don't even know what the story is about. What costumes are you talking about anyway?" Momma Flowers' indefinites always threw her.

"Well whatever the story, I can see you up there with those long legs can-canning." She turned and fluffed the mashed potatoes one more time before plopping them into the yellow Pyrex bowl for serving. With some reserve in her voice, and not really to Millie, "I'd do it if I was younger, much younger."

Millie looked at her mother from behind. Grace Flowers had always been an attractive woman, but was squat in shape, her thighs touching each other down to her knees under the belted skirt, unless she'd had her hands to her hips, legs straddled. The back of her arms wobbled as she lopped the last of the potatoes into the bowl. Large muscles, gone flaccid with age. She had never had Millie's body, could never line up to do the can-can; costume or not. Millie had always been told she got her height from her grandfather, her father's father and her bosoms from her mother. Now Millie looked sadly at her mother who longed to stand in line with other long-legged girls and kick to the right and after two beats kick to the left. But did Millie want to?

Grace placed the rest of the meal on the oak wood dining table and called the family to it. Millie would try out because she could. When the chance came for her to move to Las Vegas to work in she would do it because she could. Her mother smiling broadly and announcing to Cyrus the dry cleaner who had a shine for Momma Flowers that Mildred Lorene Flowers was going to dance in Vegas and "wear those costumes." That was all the direction she had, but the look in her Momma's eyes when she finished telling ol' Cyrus was enough. A shove toward an oncoming car could not have been stronger.

Walking out into the Vegas heat, Millie thought of those years between adult and adolescence in Texas and how they had brought her here. She had tired of the retail world, enjoying the success she gained but never happy to be a slave to the opinionated, shortsighted shopper. She had worked weekends and every holiday was a setup for another sale and every night she came home to soak her feet in a low plastic vat of warm Epsom salt. Mr. Bloom had had a thing about never sitting down on the job, even for the managers, so paperwork was done at home where she could sit comfortably at her kitchen table, tabulate daily receipts and fill out orders for needed stock. It wasn't that Millie didn't appreciate hard work, it was just that once she had accomplished what she could accomplish. Las Vegas had not been her first choice, had not been well planned, in fact it had not been expected at all.

CHAPTER NINE

Partnerless

Dances

Millie walked alone to her car. It was four o'clock in the morning and the day's commuters had not yet pulled themselves from their coupled-sleep, but the town was still alive with its usual gamble driven hordes. They were an easily discernable mix of those discovering Vegas for the first time, or third, and those still trying to make it "big." The drive to her apartment saddened Millie more than usual and she longed to again belong to the world that worked eight to five, that meet their family for Sunday dinners discussing the "why-not's"; who commuted to work with men in blue suits and crisp white dress shirts. Was she just tired this morning?

When she reached her street it was quiet, as always. Far enough away from the neon glare, not another car in motion, yet, only hers. She pulled into her designated spot under the carport, dimming the lights as she made the turn in. A porch light was on in the apartment next door and she was almost tempted to knock on the door and tell her neighbor about her slap to Salvadore. Maybe invigorated rather than tired.

Oscar would be pleased-maybe, though he had no idea who Salvadore was and why this slap held such meaning for her. Millie stopped herself in mid-self-discussion, Oscar was sleeping now until about six o'clock. She could not justify waking him when he had two solid hours of rest to go – such coveted sleep. At six, or six o' five he would rise to his alarm, pop some toast in the toaster and down a glass of orange juice before pulling his car out of the carport, not clicking the lights on until he had cleared Millie's window. He would gently avoid disturbing her in the midmorning hours as carefully as she restrained herself from disturbing him in the wee hours. They were good neighbors.

Oscar Moody worked in the assembly plant in Henderson, managing a staff of twenty gasket assemblers and barely had energy to talk to his neighbor. He was a nice man, close to Millie's age with no girlfriend that she knew of and very few acquaintances, as best she could tell. Millie had conjured up his life story in her head when she had first met him. She had a habit of doing that, one easily concealed since only she knew the stories. She came up with intricate backgrounds and associations, probably the particular subject of the life story one would never imagine. So it goes, Oscar Moody was single by choice, or actually by default since the love of his life had married the town pharmacist who had been his lab-mate in college organic chemistry class. He was from a large Irish-American family who had moved from Iowa to Reno, Nevada for the senior

Moody's asthma and health-related issues. He had left Reno shortly after Jannell, his true love, married Edward, because he had to pass the pharmacy on his way to work everyday and he just couldn't face it. When he arrived in Vegas he thought Jannell would follow him since she had always wanted to be a showgirl and would rely on his connections since he now, that he lived here. When she didn't follow, Oscar settled into his small one bedroom apartment on Orange Street and took the job at the gasket company to put money away for his eventual marriage to her when she left Edward. And there he stayed for the past year, waking up at 6:00 am, drinking orange juice without pulp and arriving on time every day to the factory, Monday through Friday, and sometimes 8:00 to 12:00 on Saturdays when the government required more than 10,000 gaskets in a month's time, which typically happened right before the end of a fiscal year.

Maybe 8 to 5 was not to be coveted. Maybe what she was doing at this time in her life was just fine, maybe. Performance life was amusing, and with the frequent changing of the stage roles she was able to transform herself every few months or so, believing this was the role for her for a short time until the bust of the bodice started itching and the sequins rubbed off when you sat down, leaving haphazard tailings.

Millie took a hot shower and rubbed her limbs down with rose-scented lotion before pulling her hair back away from her face. Her sheets were cool from the air conditioning unit in her bedroom and she actually shivered under the covers before shutting it off. In the next few hours she would toss in the dry heat and get up to turn it back on. But for now the coldness made her lonely and sad. She pulled the afghan her mother crocheted her for her sixteenth birthday up and over her shoulders. As she drifted to a forced sleep she thought of Salvadore and of David Bloom, and Carl Burke and sadly of Oscar pining for Jannell in the neighboring apartment, hoping for a knock on the door that would not be Millie.

When Millie had taken dancing lessons as a young girl in Houston her teachers had always veered her toward partnerless dances. It was the common consensus of these simple women that no boys would want to be paired with such a tall girl. So Millie tap-danced and did solitary ballet exercises while the smaller girls lindy-hopped and Charlestoned with their male classmates. Millie wished those teachers could see what she was doing now, maybe through Grace Flowers they at least knew. Sweet vengeance that she had succeeded but they had been right. Because of her long limbs she was one of the most graceful dancers in a line with the other solitary dancers, all misfits of size and body and muscle.

Millie woke in the morning she had turned too far from the air blasts and the thin sheet now stuck to her thighs turning with her as she peeled it off of her sweaty legs. The air conditioner unit shot the cool air directly to her brow and her damp hair, now more from sweat than from her pre-dawn shower, she lifted it up and let the coolness enter her pores. She was tired, but she was more hot than tired. She rolled over to allow the air to cool her neck, the force unable to lift the weight of her hair, which she pulled up into a ponytail up to the top of her head. The unit had been an extravagant expense for her but she figured that if she had to sleep in the heat of the day she was entitled to feel more comfortable. Now she didn't feel comfortable enough to climb back in the hot sheets so she moved closer to the unit and rose above it so that it blew the perspiration from her underarms. Millie twisted rotisserie style from her waist and rotated.

It was on the second twist that she saw Oscar. It was not his fault; he had not been intentionally watching her. She had known this immediately. Lifting up over the unit just enough to be seen from the small courtyard they shared. She must have looked as if she was posing, dancing for her audience against the air of the unit. An average size girl would not have been seen. Oscar looked immediately away from her but brought back his gaze back as if he couldn't help it or either wanted some confirmation.

Millie pulled her arms down and without obvious perusal examined herself. She was wearing a loose cotton top with spaghetti straps tied hastily in red bows off her shoulders. Her breasts were bra-less for sleep and she was sure the material shone sheer in the light of the glass reflected window. Millie bent down below the unit to watch as Oscar retreated back into his apartment, laundry wrapped bulky around his forearm. Would they talk of this? How would she approach it if at all? Would he? Would he now dream of his neighbor instead of his beloved Jannell? The thought actually pleased her, though she felt as if she may be betraying the mythical woman, even though she was as unreal as a desert breeze.

When later afternoon came and it was time for Millie to get ready for work, Oscar was not in his apartment. Millie had decided that she would stop by before going to the club, be blunt, and not hide from what had happened and make sure he was not himself embarrassed. She wasn't, really, but embarrassment to a man like Oscar would be difficult to relinquish. But it was about 4:00 he would not be home at this time of the workday. Millie brought back to their encounter earlier that morning. What time had it been and why was Oscar not at the plant? That could be further excuse for her window show and she stored it away for use in her eventual conversation with him. It was Wednesday, yes, she cleared that thought in her mind. He should not be home on Wednesdays.

When Millie drove into the carport that morning she took her usual care to dim her lights in making the sharp left turn and coasted into the parking space. Even though the lights where dim she could see a bulky figure leaning against Oscar's car, his calves crisscrossed ankle over ankle leaning back on the bumper. Millie turned off the ignition and looked in her rear view mirror. She could still see him. For a minute she thought maybe she shouldn't be so unguarded, maybe she should back out until she was sure it was in fact Oscar.

In the past few years a number of showgirls had been attacked. The attackers were either demented admirers or men who had some women hating disorder which caused them to loath the dancers and prey on them. Penny Laws had been one of the girls who had been attacked one night as she walked down to her car. They could never park near the casinos themselves because the available spaces were only for the paying tourist. Instead, they were forced to park in some back alley spot that welcomed the opportunities for attacks blocks away from the bright marquees. Penny had not faired well after the incident and though her physical wounds, which were many, healed, she lost that attribute showgirls have and need; the head held high confidence that allows them to touch their four-inch heels to the dance floor and know that all eyes are upon them. Penny had returned to her hometown of Sacramento, last Millie heard, and was working as a waitress. Wearing low-heeled gummed soles and working mornings.

Millie adjusted the mirror slightly as if that would allow her a full view of the man leaning on Oscar's car at 4:30 in the morning. The man pushed off the bumper or really more leaned with his back and rolled, coming up to his feet through the miracle of gravity. He had Oscar's form and what she thought it would look like in the dark. With Penny in her mind, Millie kept her hand on the ignition keys in case she needed to quickly start up the car and throw it into reverse to flee.

As soon as the man started down the narrow driver's side of the carport path, Millie could see it was in fact Oscar Moody. She allowed herself to examine his silhouette with a more inquisitive than investigative eye. The darkness allowed her to do so without a chance of detection. She pulled the keys out of the ignition and opened the door in front of him before he could attempt to squeeze by the door and the rusted support pole of the carport.

"I hope I didn't startle you," Oscar said. He lowered his head to her but still kept a distance.

"No." Millie answered and was surprised to hear the quiver in her voice. She had been scared. Oscar didn't know her voice well enough to detect it.

"It's just that I wanted to be sure to catch you and I thought if I waited inside I would be sure to fall asleep." Oscar still spoke at a whisper as if concerned he would wake the other rows of apartment neighbors with this early morning discussion.

Millie looped her purse around her forearm and closed the door of the Chevy, locking it. As soon as she had done so she wondered why since she never locked the car in the carport before. Maybe it was thoughts of Penny or was she still questioning why Oscar was here?

"Why are you up, Oscar?" she asked as he backed out of the narrow passage to let her pass.

"Well our schedules are so different." Oscar dropped his head and began walking her the short distance to her door. Millie walked but then waited. Oscar didn't continue.

"Well, yes, they have always been." Millie found herself getting irritated with this man, first he scares her and then he can't explain why he's there?

Millie turned on her toes on the second step of her porch, "What is it that you need to tell me, Oscar?" She realized the awkwardness in emphasizing his name too many times, but didn't care, she was tired.

Oscar looked up at her. Her porch light was on so Millie could see clearly his expression and at once regretted her sternness.

"I just wanted to tell you that, well I've switched shifts. I'll be home in the afternoons until about noon and then I go into work until about ten o'clock."

Millie shook her head and again waited for him to continue, but this time allowed the time to pass to where he could continue, comfortably.

"I just wanted to let you know so that you won't wonder why I'm around." Oscar turned to make his way to his apartment. His porch light held a yellow bulb and though you couldn't see his expression as sharply you could see the shadows of his features making him sorrowful.

Millie now understood. "Like yesterday?"

Oscar's head turned a bit away from her and in the light his nose shadowed his cheek. "I'm sorry about that, I was taking my laundry down. I knew you didn't see me, but I really needed to take my laundry down." The pitifulness of this explanation humored Millie. She laughed and this brought Oscar's face into full view again.

"I'm not laughing at you Oscar, I'm sorry. But you came out here at 4:30 in the morning to tell me that?" Millie adjusted her purse from one arm to the other and her hip to the opposite side. "I know you didn't mean to be there. And believe me I didn't mean to be there either." The irony of it hit her. "I was just hot", Millie now giggled, "hot and tired and you needed clean clothes." "And we're neighbors."

Oscar's voice was still soft and quiet. "I know I just wanted you to know so you don't think I planned it." Oscar looked directly at her. With this angle she could see him clearly and Millie noticed that he had a small scar above his right lip that made it curve up a little more than the other. He is not an unattractive man, and through the authoring of his life Millie had included a few episodes of his falling in love with her and dropping any idea of returning to Jannell.

"Maybe we could have lunch together sometime since we're both home during the same time now." She offered Oscar, who was heading into his apartment. "An early lunch that is."

Millie smiled and hoped her smile could be seen. She lifted her chin to the porch light just to be sure, though he was now a good distance away. " Yes, that would be nice, Millie."

Millie threw her purse on the couch. Maybe Jannell's heart will be broken after all.

CHAPTER TEN

Think Before You Cross the Street

M illie thought about Oscar more than she would have anticipated. She had met a lot of men; typically men who had seen her show or knew she was a showgirl. These were not men Millie wished to associate with but that was her world so that is who she met. But Oscar Moody-there was an interesting man, a baffling man, so different from the standard Vegas offerings. Since meeting in the carport Millie had let go of the fabricated story she had carefully developed for Oscar. She was suddenly ashamed of herself and at the thin mottling life she had made for him. She cleaned his slate waiting for him to develop and only examined what was actually happening between them to determine who he was.

Millie set a date with him for lunch at her apartment the following Friday. She always dreaded Friday performances because of the type of men who attended, so she had set lunch for that day hoping a lunch with Oscar would balance a bad evening.

Oscar appeared at her door at 10:00, which required Millie to lose some of her coveted sleep time, but allowed them two hours to eat casually and chat before he had to head to the plant. She would nap after. Millie prepared a green salad with mandarin oranges to sweeten the bitter lettuce, accompanied by toasted tomato and cheese sandwiches. Millie was not much of a cook and was relieved when Oscar had told her he eats light lunches so he doesn't feel sleepy on the job, "which could prove very dangerous." He advised. He sounded like a safety-training manual. This may be a longer lunch than she had hoped.

"How did it come about that you now have this schedule?" Millie asked as she folded a paper napkin onto her lap, making sure the side with the salad dressing drippings was face up so as not to stain her skirt.

Oscar had settled himself at the small red Formica kitchen table set. This had taken him no shorter than three minutes after he arrived for their date. Millie was about to ask him if he would prefer eating on the couch when he firmly sat down at the table. Now Millie saw, that the table, small for her, was tiny for him. Oscar was large yet slow moving and timid.

"Well, William Bolton, the swing-shift superintendent got fired, and well, I was asked to take over temporarily." Oscar took a mandarin slice by itself into his mouth. Was Oscar one of those men who had to have his food separated or who wouldn't eat foods of different consistencies together? This salad was a violation of both.

"Oh," Millie commented searching for a continuation of the conversation without being nosy. "Do you like this shift? I assume they'll return you to your regular shift once someone is hired?

Millie realized her questions may have contradicted each other and did not allow for comment between the two of them. She was relieved to note that Oscar was busy eating anyway and this time a leaf of lettuce with an orange slice on top together brought to his mouth.

"Well," Oscar started and Millie wondered if he started every sentence with that word. If he did she would soon tire of him quickly. "What a bitch." Millie said to herself and continued. "How judgmental can you be? It's just a language tick, like a man who clears his throat constantly." She immediately decided she would rather have a million "wells" than someone running snot up and down their esophagus.

"The shift is OK, I just haven't quite adjusted." Oscar took a polite moment to take the triangle of one of the corners of the napkin to dislodge some greens. Succeeding, his hand came down again to rest in his lap. Millie saw his bare forearm flex and relax. She noted his hands were bulky but immaculate. His forearms, they seemed disproportionate to his size, like a Popeye-arm. She noted too that his arm had the distinct tanned outline of a "permanent" shirt, much like her father who spent most of his days in the Texas sun when he was not in the store. He was a man of some outside labor that really didn't equate with what he was doing in Vegas. If she would have allowed herself she could have come up with a very intriguing story for his arm tan, but instead decided she wanted to know the truth.

Oscar had moved in next door after Millie had been in her apartment for about a year. She really didn't pay much attention to his arrival. They lived in a quad on opposite sides with two sets of neighbors above them. It seemed Oscar's apartment had had the most movement. In the year that Millie lived there before Oscar, it was home to an older women and a middle-aged Chinese couple.

"Have you always done this type of work?" Millie asked.

Oscar put both hands on the napkin on his lap, spreading his fingers. "No never before this one." Millie waited, the conversation was becoming much too difficult for her. Then a minute after a loud passing car made it to the next corner he continued, "I'm from Iowa, I repaired farm equipment before coming here. Also worked on a farm."

"Why'd you come here?" Millie asked abruptly but followed up, "I'm always curious as to why people come to Las Vegas." Millie popped a loose orange slice into her mouth. They were good by themselves.

"Well, my wife left and I was looking for a clean start." Millie quietly choked on the juice of the orange that was suddenly too much to swallow when this personal fact was so suddenly revealed. She would not have imagined this as part of Oscar's story. Or maybe she didn't expect it to be so close to what she had concocted for him.

"I'm sorry to hear that, it can be difficult to go through a break-up like that." Millie immediately felt she was too insincere in her consolation.

Sensing her lack of knowledge, Oscar finally naturally ventured, "You ever married?"

Millie thought about all the situations that could have turned into marriage and at this moment was glad none of them had. "No," she replied simply feeling foolish and possibly somewhat slighted that she did not have a failed marriage to discuss to match up the conversation.

They finished up lunch with some fruit cocktail with the cherry slices and Oscar had confided that he had not dated another women since his wife, that in the community he grew up in you stayed married and that he felt he had to leave because of the stigma of failure; that Vegas had not proved a wise move for him since he didn't have a social life and merely went to work and came home; that his true hope was to find someone to marry and move back to Iowa City and be accepted back into the community. He had not stated the last part, but it was strongly implied. Millie had only lent that she had almost married David Bloom and had wanted to marry a man named Evan who was already married, but was disturbed to find the character beneath his smoothness and had not been very serious since. She had not shared the character appraisal with Oscar but it had played in her head painfully.

Once Oscar had left, Millie felt as though their 4:30 meeting had been a pitiful occurrence and Oscar a pitiful man. He was handsome and more handsome to her as she examined him carefully throughout their meal, but he fell short, he was too weak, as David had been, too waiting for life to start, too dependant on circumstances to repair choices that didn't need repairing. Would he always be watching windows?

So when Oscar showed up one night at her show and she saw him there she pretended she didn't. That was until she saw him talking with Salvadore in one of the fire exit aisles of The Painted Desert Showroom. What would a washed up tractor mechanic have to do with a weasel? The contradictions in character were too great for her to let this go, even to avoid the pitiful Iowan.

Into the second set, Millie strained to see into the exit corridor. This was during the steps in which she and the other birds held hands and escorted each other around an imaginary circle, then glided into a figure eight. It was obvious to no one but Annie that her concentration was not on her dance steps. When they went stage right Millie was able to get an unobstructed look into the corridor where she saw Oscar standing alone, leaning against the wall, smoking, and looking up at Millie as she fluttered her sequined wings to the quick beat of the piano and drum duet.

Oscar hoped not to be seen by Millie but when he was, he couldn't help but be a bit glad. He had wanted to see her perform since moving into the apartment complex, but could never really afford it and was a bit embarrassed to ask her for comp tickets. Women like Millie were pursued and he didn't want to pursue her, he wanted to get to know her, but slowly, carefully. He had spoken in too much detail at their lunch and told her too much, more than he had planned. But he found himself wanting her to know right away that he was a settling man, one to be trusted, one who was not a playboy like the rest of the men in her nightly audience. Oscar almost let out a laugh at the thought. He was truly a farm boy from Iowa whose biggest aspiration had been to date a showgirl and show her decency.

The collar of his shirt began to itch. Just the brim of it where he had added some bleach by hand to make sure the sweat stains would not show through. He pulled at the neck of the shirt to separate the contact with his skin. Had he gotten it on his fingers too? He rubbed his thumb and index finger together to check for burn, but they felt fine. Better than he was feeling at this point. Millie had just rounded the stage in a trail of feathers and Oscar wondered if she had seen him from the stage. He had risen from his seat to have one cigarette at the exit curtain but had gotten to talking to the manager and did not make it back to his seat before intermission was over. He felt like such a fool standing there smoking his third cigarette, giving him a reason to be there, watching Millie Flowers, his neighbor, glide by in her feathers and diamond studded costume.

She was so beautiful. No one would know by meeting her in the quad of their apartment house that she was a showgirl. Not that she wasn't pretty enough or sophisticated enough, just that when she wasn't working, her face was freckled, friendly and open. Millie didn't cower or hide her height, instead she walked with her back straight and long legs looping in front of her. She looked more like some of the women athletes Oscar knew back home, but they didn't have the addition of her perfectly curved red tinted eyebrows, her carefully manicured fingernails and her bosom. When Oscar had seen her that day standing in front of her window trying to get relief from the heat, he had been made privy to her breasts. They were shapely and supple with hollows to the side where her armpits curved in. When she had risen to pull her hair up they joined the tug of her arms and Oscar had nearly stuttered though he was not engaged in any conversation. When she had spotted him standing there his work shirts retrieved from the clothesline in his hands, Oscar had carried on as if it was every day a woman like Millie Flowers bared her breasts to her neighbor. A sad man who was only in his late twenties or maybe early thirties, already divorced, working at a metal parts factory instead of repairing tractors.

Millie waltzed by with two other girls and they mimicked the swinging from trees. Oscar watched her hands grab and let go of the rope vines. She twirled off the rope and danced close to the edge of the stage. From Oscar's view the stage lights lit her skirt of sequins and their colors reflected back on to the audience. The room full of mostly men, looked like speckled dogs as they sat obediently staring, waiting the next command.

Millie was glad that the end of the set was in sight. She was winded and struggled to appear not to be. Night after night she was a bird. Flight was exhilarating but stillness was what she wished for these nights. When do birds sleep?

Returning to the dressing room she tugged at her pantyhose. They stuck to her thighs, then her calves and would not make it down to her feet even with the aggressive peeling.

"Damn it," Millie hissed and as if that suddenly justified it the stockings split open and ran in fifteen different directions. She was too hot and too sticky to be undressing. But she was too tired to allow time to cool down.

Why was Oscar Moody there tonight and why was he talking to that scum? An accustomed paranoia ran through Millie. Was Salvadore plotting to unleash some plan against her and was he soliciting the help of her neighbor? She could handle that Oscar was at the show. A lot of her acquaintances showed up at her performances and typically she considered the attendance a nice gesture. But not tonight – not with Salvadore.

Millie dove her index and middle finger into the cold cream and rubbed the cool smooth cream onto her eyelids caked with make-up. Reaching for the tissue, her hand fumbled for the box that was not in its usual place. Taking both hands she touched each bottle on her table. They were all her familiar perfumes, lotions, ointments and makeup, but where was the tissue? "Damn it!" this was becoming her battle cry and at that moment the fear hit again. Millie opened one eye though the cream burned intensely. It was quiet in the room. Annie and Freddie where in the shower she could hear the water. Janet was lying on the couch with a cloth over her forehead, from what Millie could make out through her cold cream tears.

"Janet," Millie called. Through the cream Millie saw some movement and heard her reluctance through a slow pulling of the cloth from her face.

"Yeah," she didn't appear to open her eyes.

"I need a tissue. Can you get me some?"

Janet pushed herself up. She was a big girl, not tall but big. She also had a tendency for the dramatic, which came in handy if you were a spoiled rich girl, but not when you needed something from her. Put upon by any interaction in life was her cross to bear.

"Really Millie, think about it before the cream." Janet shoved the box under her waiting hand.

Think before you cross the street. Millie wiped the plops of cream from the concave of her eyes, using the last tissue to make sure the thick eyeliner under her eyes had been erased. It was not until then that she noticed Oscar and could see that the dressing room was now empty.

"Millie?" he started. "...I hope I didn't startle you." Oscar looked dark and shaded at his position of barely entering the room, hesitant to move into the lights of the make-up mirrors.

"What are you doing here?" Millie asked checking herself slyly in the mirror to make sure she was not exposed, again. "And how long have you been lurking there?" Millie's anger had built as she considered the invasion he represented. She did not wait for his response.

"This dressing room is off limits, Oscar. You hold no privileges just because I'm your neighbor." Millie looked around again wondering where Janet had gone and why she was alone.

Oscar understood what she was looking for. "I waited until your friend left and I kept thinking if I said anything I would scare you."

Millie grabbed her robe and tied it tightly, too tightly around her.

She felt like an ad for Maxwell House, a housewife in the morning. No make-up, clean fresh face.

Oscar anxiously waved his right hand. He wondered if he looked as unsteady as he felt at this moment.

"I met your boss, Salvadore..."

The mention of this man's name turned Millie's anger to the all-familiar anxiety that exploded on to the other.

Oscar stared at the make-up-less face of a woman more furious than he had ever seen. He was making the situation worse but did not know how to tilt it back properly. He was in fact physically unsteady. "He said I should come back here," he bleated.

Millie barely heard the end of his sentence because of the sound of the roar in her ears. But when she did, the spinning anger slowed. She looked at Oscar Moody standing before her, barely before her in the shadows of a showgirl's dressing room wearing an over-starched shirt and a black wool suit though it was August. He appeared to be trembling.

Salvadore had told Oscar to go to the dressing room, knowing the reaction it would elicit. He put this innocent man on the tracks and sacrificed him to make a point.

Millie decided to befriend Oscar Moody at that very moment. She wanted to save him and maybe save herself. It was not that she was unfailingly kind and certainly not patient. It was that Oscar had been manipulated and she had been had.

When she considered Oscar Moody years later, after their quiet and plain marriage had failed, she allowed herself to return to this moment in the showgirl's dressing room, her eyes stinging with cold cream and the anger rolling down her brow in pre-wrinkle creases and know she had not married this man for love. It was because he lasted through her simmering rage. In five years he wouldn't, but he had offered her dedication and that's what she wanted. That's what she needed. Someone who saw her without her feathers.

When Oscar left Millie he left Vegas also. He had not succeeded in finding a woman to bring back to Iowa. Instead he had shamed himself even deeper with yet another ex-wife. Their parting had not been difficult other than the defeat it defined. He had told her he was taking a job again with John Deere in Ames, Iowa. It was a good company and a good job. When she did not respond with any indication that she was following, he told her simply "We gave it a try," and Mille nodded. They were married four years and ten months in total. During those four plus years Oscar continued working at the Henderson plant and Millie danced, but Oscar was moved off the midday shift and onto late night for most of those years. It should have helped things since they were on the same schedule, but the opposite had occurred. Their life became a passing in the hallways of the duplex they shared on Albert Street a few more miles off the strip than Orange Street. There were opportunities to talk, more opportunities but they avoided them. They were neighbors again. He was thirty-four, Millie thirty-two. They had no plans to have children. She wanted to continue dancing. It was what she did and it afforded no time for pregnancy and motherhood. He understood, she had found what suited her best. What suited him best was in Iowa. A low-light life with possibilities of a family.

When Millie finally left dancing five years after her split with Oscar it was for a reason no one would ever have anticipated, or could have. Many couples were joining and splitting post-war, no one gave it much thought. It was through the cruelty of cancer Millie lost her breasts. Not her life, for which she was always grateful, but her livelihood and more than a part of who she was.

The news came after a routine exam where a lump that should have been obvious was not, until pointed out with some frankness. Reflecting on it some thirty plus years later, she was lucky to survive. At a time when medicine had not made the advances it made her feel like a cat with lives to spare. She had had a radical double mastectomy because that is what they did then – nothing else. Cut it out was the approach. She was left severely scarred at thirty seven, "so young" with adequate falsies for her costumes but an end to a desire to be on stage. As shallow as it sounded when she answered the question in her head, she didn't want men looking at her on stage anymore. Everything felt false. She took the cocktail waitress route that was less taxing, lacked a stage and required less of her and the bald-headed row in people skills. She didn't have the spotlight on her and but had to hold conversations with the bald-headed row that had previously been in the shadows. It was near a Keno board while waitressing in a small dark bar that she met Grover Pendrell, almost twenty-five years after she left the stage.

CHAPTER ELEVEN

Waiting for a Train

The acrylic of her nails made a tonal succession of hollow clicks as she rapped them on her steering wheel. Millie drummed the severely squared tips in octaves large and low to small and high. The wheel itself was hot and because the train was still rolling by at its steady, slow pace she removed her palms for the moment but continued to click in impatience as the sound fell in line with the metal clicking of the train in front of her. She anticipated the end to the line of train cars and gripped the wheel once again making a loud clack when her dinner ringed age-spotted fingers hit the plastic. It was not the end but just the end of the boxcars now being trailed by the flat empty railway cars.

"Damn train." Millie commented to the air, and her passenger, without taking her eyes off the movement of the train cars in case the scene changed. Grover Pendrell merely looked up to view the flat cars quickly and returned to the task in his lap, the tying of a fishing fly. He'd rather sit in idle anyways. Didn't bother him one bit.

Millie a bright light, in this low-wattage desert waited in her 1970 Chevy Impala. A lone car impatiently idling for a train to pass on an already hot desert morning. She was dressed as if she were ready to walk into a scene of Alice's restaurant, the T.V. show version. Her brassy red hair pinned up in a modified beehive secured with the assistance of twenty or so bobby pins.

The u-shaped kind that is good at getting zits. One or two of the pins secured hair-sprayed curls that were pinned to her temples. She wore a rhinestone-punched blouse that ended in a triangle in front to the tip of her white Capri pants. Rosie, Millie's best friend in town had read an article about the limited number of women who should "dare to wear" Capri pants and shared the stats with Millie over tuna and pickle sandwiches. Millie had not fallen into the narrow parameters of acceptability, missing the age requirement by some forty odd years.

"Never wear white pants even if you have the figure for it and khaki capri's can prove to be just as disfiguring." Rosie had reported, folding her Cosmopolitan over in a hump anchored by her elbow to allow herself to continue to eat as she read.

"Black is the color of choice for the twenty to thirty crowd. And always adds a sliming effect to those of us who don't have those slender ankles."

"Those of us." Rosie repeated a bit hypocritically. She reached for the salt and added a layer to the slices of tomato that Millie had added to the plate. Nice and juicy from her garden.

"Says here that large print or small print, solid color, no matter, they don't belong on older than middle aged thighs."

Millie had risen to pour some more tea into Rosie's glass though it was still halfway full, she knew Rosie would inevitably gulp down the fluid once the salt kicked in. Rosie pressed down her brightly flowered skirt before retaking her seat to hear more confirmation that women over seventy and over should not be wearing orange.

"Really?" Millie commented though she never agreed with anything that magazine ever said. "How to Please Your Man" had infuriated Millie back in the early seventies and since then she rarely read an article from this rag unless Rosie was reading it to her. That article had claimed that a man wanted a women to be "quietly assertive" in the bedroom, but exploring for the purpose of what pleasures she could grant her partner. "Grant her partner!" Millie had been more than pissed off. She was not there to serve anyone in bed. Since reading that article "Grant" was the name she labeled men who thought they should be "served" and in fact became the common name for any man she met in the casino days. She and the waitresses would go through the list of Grants they had met the nights when reminiscing, before dipping to despair hoping one would develop into and deserve his god given name. Only Oscar deserved his Christian name upon careful reflection. Oscar had been a good guy.

Grover took the fishing line in his mouth and tried to cut it with an incisor.

"That's how you lost the first ones," Millie said sternly. Grover pulled the line out and bent down to search for the small scissors somewhere in his tackle box. He found the pair of mustache shears and snapped the line close to the knot he had tied. Good thing he couldn't grow whiskers any longer.

"Good thing there's more than one purpose for tools." Millie said.

"Why are we up so early?" Grover asked as the train looked to really be ending this time. It was asked as if he had just now thought to inquire though he had risen at five to accompany Millie.

Millie shot him a look letting him know at this moment she would rather him break his dentures than to launch into this diatribe about early errands. It was a common one and this train had been just too long for her to tolerate, and the heat too loathing.

"Lottery," she said under her breath as he dug into the layers of feather to choose a neon marabou to add to the current fly. It would go nicely with the yellow buck tails.

He remembered, "We have to wait until nine o'clock anyway and at ten' clock the numbers would still be the same." Grover was pushing it but he had had a good night's sleep and he felt frisky.

"I couldn't sit in that house any longer or Rosie would come bangin' on the door." Millie plunged forward as the last train car finally passed and the wooden piece of plywood lifted itself up with two distinct jumps. Grover held onto the door handle as the car cleared the tracks in a u-shape not waiting for the wood to completely rise before she was over them.

Rosie Rodriguez had been Millie's best friend since she moved to Abbott, Arizona, four years ago. And Grover believed, never were there two more opposites. Rosie was younger than Millie by a good fifteen years or more, rounded at every original angle and short, her neck rolled twice into the bend of her collarbone. She always wore Lycra stretchy pants with large t-shirts, hanging her breasts and midsection over waistbands unless she was feeling particularly gassy and then would opt for the moo-moo ensemble her husband had bought her during their fortieth wedding anniversary trip to Honolulu. Her dark hair matched her features and though age had settled in there were only narrow strips of gray rising up from the crown of her head and a few splattered on her eyebrows. Rosie wore no jewelry other than her modest wedding band and a gold crucifix she had received for confirmation when she was a young girl. She had been without the necklace for some fifteen years when her daughter wore it following high school, but her daughter and Rosie had become estranged due to Estelle's choice in husbands and one day after not speaking to her daughter in several years, the crucifix showed up in a simple envelope in the mail addressed to Rosie Rodriguez, 58 Pine,

Abbott, Arizona hand-stamped in Phoenix with no return address. Whenever Rosie was particularly upset she would reach for the cross and hold on to it until the moment passed - maybe due to the expiration of a coupon, or Manuel, her husband, missing dinner.

Millie loved this woman who tended to laugh too long making conversation hard at times, and who had welcomed the flamboyant towering aging showgirl into her desert town. Millie with her layers of chains around her neck like an eighties cop star and earrings which Rosie commented threatened to eventually pull through the long slitted-holes of her ears, did not dress in desert clothes. She still wore hot vinyl mules of orange and purple and insisted on wearing capris even when Cosmopolitan and her best friend told her not to.

Millie sat comfortably at the counter of Elbert's Trading Post drinking an overpriced miniature glass of orange juice and two fried eggs severely peppered. Grover sipped occasionally at the coffee in front of him, and read yesterday's sports section of the Arizona Republic. Elbert the proprietor of the store scraped the griddle and prepared the fixings for the day. He agreed to allow Millie and Grover into the Trading Post but refused to give them the winning numbers until 9:00 when he "officially" opened. "There are rules," though Millie could have disputed this and had almost grabbed today's paper from the bundled pile outside to check herself. She was always arguing but this morning also wanted breakfast so kept quiet.

Elbert Begay, a Navajo who usually wore his thick hair back in a ponytail of successive rubber bands when he was cooking, wore no net. Since he was not officially cooking only tolerating the Pendrells, his hair hung loose and met his back well below his shoulders. Millie badgered him about the questionable hygiene of chopping onions with loose hair, but as with the rules-comment decided not to protest since he was allowing her to sit here in the coolness of his small Trading Post while waiting for the clock to change and the numbers to be announced once he turned on the machine.

Elbert's younger sister Esther milled around the Trading Post making sure shelves were stocked and ready for the day. Since it was summer, the typical coating of dust hadn't settled on the small amount of merchandise stocked for the stranded tourists. These were always interesting encounters of mid-westerners who turned the wrong way off Route 66 thinking they will get to meet "real Indians" or an artist community tucked in the side of wandering mesas. Instead they found themselves in Abbott, which offered a main street with a few odd antique stores, two restaurant/bars, a gas station on opposite ends of the same block and four side streets, two of which fed directly into trailer parks where most all of the residents lived. This was it for downtown streets other than the few like Millie's that lived on Pine street which was across the railroad tracks and to the north of town and fed into another tributary feeding Phoenix.

Millie's part of Abbott was comprised of four streets that were divided by four streets and contained small post-World War II "postage stamp" homes, two bedroom one bath squared residences. They had at one time been much the same in exterior and paint color but by now had taken on their own embellished identities some forty years after they were built. Most hosted plastic or ceramic animals with a few stone wishing wells and brittled plastic flowers with glass soda bottles lining the walks. For landscape design in the desert one had to be resourceful.

Millie had spoken many times to Rosie about Esther Begay. She couldn't figure her out. That was not typically the case for Millie. Esther was about fifty, attractive, always wearing some of the jewelry she made to display in the one glass case below the register. But Esther had never married, had never even dated as far as Rosie knew. Rosie remembered her as a young adult, quiet, reserved never in any trouble, which was quite a contrast to her three brothers.

When Elbert opened the store in 1976 Esther joined him, settling into her role as cashier and keeper of the Post while Elbert cooked. Millie could count two maybe three full conversations she had with Esther in their years of being acquaintances. Once when Elbert sliced his hand and they had to close the grill for a week, and Millie expressed concern, and once when Millie had purchased a turquoise necklace to send to her sister in Houston.

Esther was territorial and had not liked it when Elbert was in her part of the Post and he openly complained to Millie as if her experience as a wife of an old man would allow her to understand this frustration. There was one other time Mille and Esther had spoken a few years back. It was on the year anniversary of John Hinckley had shot President Reagan. Esther had confided in Millie that she had known for quite some time that something bad would happen to this man since he had first been elected Governor of California. "He has never known who he was because of all the roles he played, Governor and President were just his next roles." Esther had claimed, "Someone will figure that out and want to be in one of his movies." Hinckley had a crush on the young movie star Jodie Foster, maybe for the same reason. Maybe he thought "the assassin" would be a great role for him.

Ten minutes before 9:00 Millie reached for the Style section of the paper, with Grover barely noticing since he was now talking to Jerry McLean about baseball players and in particular

Cal Ripken. When had Jerry snuck in? When she turned in her stool to allow herself some elbowroom to fold out the paper, she noticed a young man outside with his back leaning against the storefront. He appeared to be reading a paper himself but was facing directly into the sun. It was not like there was a lot of refuge he could take on this side of the street since it faced the east, but Millie couldn't help but wonder how he could make out newsprint with the sun beating down on his face. What was the paper he was reading? The type didn't look like the one in her hand. A traveler?

The man looked to be maybe mid-twenties with spiky reddish/brown hair, natural, unlike Millie's. He turned his head toward The Post examining the occupants, waiting for it to open. He must be desperate to get in - no one in their right mind would sit facing the sun trying to read a newspaper in this summer heat. Five minutes to nine. Elbert was on the tomatoes.

"I think you need to open up for that boy," Millie said, pointed to the back of the boy just in case Elbert needed a point of reference.

Without looking at his watch but looking at the boy, "It's not nine." The boy stood and wiped his brow with the newspaper. He'd surely have newsprint smeared on his brow. Guess he gave up on reading.

"Five minutes Elbert. Hell you let us in early and I bet that boy will sit down and order some of that fresh concentrated California orange juice you charge some two dollars for and maybe even pay for one of your omelets."

Elbert grumbled, "Not likely. Looks like a picky eater."

Grover found this humorous. "Sure don't want to place one of your omelets in front of a picky eater, that's for sure."

Elbert returned to his task, his back to Millie, and started chopping again. Millie examined the boy closer, who had now about-faced again and was clearly begging to get in.

"Hell Elbert Begay," Millie popped off her stool slammed the paper down next to her plate and marched mules slapping to the door. "What happened to Indian time?"

Millie clicked the lock of the door counter clockwise and opened it up wide as the three old men and Esther looked on. No one stopped her or said anything; no one had the guts to. Millie was a train herself when she was set in motion. Grover added some sugar to his coffee and stirred.

Millie greeted the young boy who now in her closer estimation was only about twenty-three or four. He was dripping in sweat and looked awfully skinny, she would later report to Rosie who was always concerned about underweight people.

"Come on in son," she said almost shoeing him with the clanking of her bangles of bracelets. "It's too damn hot for you to be out there leaning on glass." Patrick Emery moved into The Trading Post with the woman's greeting. He couldn't take the heat much longer and was regretting all the decisions of the morning.

"Thank you ma'am," he said politely. In truth he was so grateful he actually wanted to hug this odd looking grandma. The emotion was truly from desperation, also from extreme hunger and travel fatigue. Maybe also dehydration given the amount of sweat his pores emitted in the last 30 minutes.

Millie pointed to a seat next to her at the counter, sliding off her beaded purse, which hung from an equally elaborate beaded handle. She slung it onto her kneecap and it hung there swaying to the kick of her leg.

"I'm not ma'am I'm Millie Flowers, This here is Grover and Jerry," she pointed to the men with a casual nod of her head.

"Order up with old Elbert and he'll fix you up good. I can tell you're hungry." She motioned to the old Indian whose manner did not look that inviting, in fact a bit discouraging as he washed his cutting knives and placed them neatly in their magnetic hanging wall. Prep was now complete.

Patrick scanned the room, or rather its current occupants who he had not been able to see clearly through the sun-glared storefront window. Grover sat very close to Jerry because the two old men were both trying to read the same sports page of at the same time. Jerry kept standing up to try to get a better angle when Grover's big hands would block some of the type. Millie sat directly next to Patrick pushing the one page laminated egg stained menu into his view.

"Elbert makes a mean omelet and a load full of eggs is just what you need honey."

Patrick looked at the list of "innards" as Millie called them and ordered up a cheese, spinach and mushroom omelet. He tried to not sound too desperate for the meal but was sure he did, but the Indian not looking at all sympathetic went to work directly regardless.

"Very healthy combo," Millie commented and promptly took the menu from his hand to re-stow it in the metal forked rack next to the napkin holder.

"Haven't been eating very well lately. I figured that vegetables is what I need."

Before Elbert could get started breaking the yolks smoothly with the cupping of his palm, Millie rattled further commands at him. Seemed that all she needed was a confession of the boy's need and she was set into action.

"Make it a fluffy one Elbert, like you do for old Mackie, more eggs. This boy could use a few pounds unlike that truck of a woman." Millie leaned into him as if she and Patrick had been having this conversation for a good four hours or so and was now getting to the conclusion of the story. Patrick looked at the watch with the huge dial Millie had on her wrist along with the other bangles. He had only been sitting here for five minutes, but he was her friend.

"Mackie is the type of woman who would sit at this counter and order a light appetizer first," Millie catches herself, 'no, no, no' better to the truth, she would start with a cup of coffee, only please. Black no cream."

"And ten minutes later she'd be on pie after plowing through her middle course food," mumbled Grover in Patrick's direction giving Patrick a broad welcoming smile. He was his friend too.

"Grover Pendrell, you are not a storyteller. Millie winked a surprisingly seductive wink in the boy's direction. Introduction to conclusion type of man," she told him. Patrick wondered how this glittered old woman lived in what, on first read, appeared to be such a dull town. His mind wandered in search of the start of that story, when she grabbed his forearms leading him in and continued.

"Hell my whole life's been full of 'em." Millie climbed nimbly over the counter while still on

her stool and grabbed the orange-handled decaf
pot to top off her coffee. Most likely old Elbert
had gotten a full view of the bosom from her low
cut blouse.

"So..." her southern voice lilted as she settled
back into her seat and looked at him, palm open,
to fill in the blank.

"Patrick." he answered obediently.

"Well Patrick." Just why haven't you been
eating healthy? A young body like you, if I had
that body years back I would have treated myself
better."

Grover's eyes peeked over the paper as if he
was ready to lend a comment but thought better
of it and retreated back to his sports stats with
Jerry close at his side, and then over his head
trying to get a view of the numbers.

"I've been traveling for quite awhile, and well
I just haven't had many square meals." Square
came out hard a brusque sounding more like
"air" with an S in front of it.

"Now what does that expression mean, square
meals?" Millie looked to the other men for help
with this one. "I've always had three meals, three,

doesn't make a square. Yet every day when you're young you're told to have a square meal."

"I think it relates more to the food groups." Patrick flattened the napkin smoothly in his lap as he watches Elbert slide the omelet on to a chipped plate.

Millie pulled back and smiled, "You're a bright boy Patrick. I think you're exactly right." She moved in closer to him positioning salt and pepper shakers to the right of his fork.

Grover rolled his eyes. Patrick is in the web.

It was not until 10:32 that Patrick finished his meal in its entirety. As hungry as he was, there was a lot of talking between bites and yes, pie. By that time he had confessed to Millie that he had not kept good company in his travels, had not chosen these travel companions well and had just that morning chosen to abandon them. It had not been a very "bright" move because he chose to leave them in Abbott and the prospects of making this a positive chapter in his tale were not too promising, currently.

"Well son, if you had jumped ship last night in Phoenix, you would have been worse off."

"How so?" Patrick asked folding his well-used napkin neatly and tucking it under his plate.

"Well the main road here in Abbott is clean, straight, directed." Millie points ahead of her as if mimicking an ascent. You can clear your head in a town like Abbott. Phoenix clogs your reasoning, but Abbott, Abbott's lines are lean honey." Millie pursed her lips, pleased with the accomplishment of her description. She stood up and straightened the line of her pants.

Patrick could not figure out how Millie Flowers would end up in Abbott, Arizona, and now she had presented the perfect lead in.

Millie was surprisingly hesitant at first with her answer. Patrick feared he had asked the wrong question or gotten too personal, but Millie gathered her thoughts, turned a bit on her stool facing out the storefront, and looked down the clean, straight road that ran through Abbott.

"Grover over here married me, and well, as a married woman, Las Vegas just didn't have the same appeal anymore." Grover puts the paper down with a motion that looks as if like it was for good, and smiles at his wife.

"Now that's a story." Grover leans and turns toward the conversation.

"Yep." Jerry chimes in for the first time, but takes the folded paper, reopens it and begins his solitary read.

"How long have you been married?" Patrick asks caught up in the sentiment. His pleasure is not unnoticed.

"About five years." Grover responds, "April 25, 1979."

Patrick can't help but be taken aback. By the looks of them Millie is in her seventies, Grover easily eighties. The obvious rhythm they have together is one that must have been developed through a lifetime of companionship, not just a mere five years.

"When I met Millie she was still running with the wrong crowd. Probably the grandparents of those friends you left." Grover finished before Millie could protest, "Maybe great grandparents but she was ready for me, all I had to do was walk into that club and she fell for me." Leaning in over Millie, "Hell all over me." His grin was conspiratorial.

"Hell he threw a fast ball at me and that's really all it took." Millie also smiled at Patrick as if giving him some unstated advice he could use at some later date. "I wasn't running with any crowd, I was waitressing and tending bar by then. The second shift for showgirls."

Patrick could see Millie Flowers in full glitter costume and heavily head pieced garb, floating across a stage eyeing the pot-bellied men as if they were Clark Gable. Even with her advanced age, he could picture her beauty and her glide.

Millie outlined it for him. She was young when she came to Vegas, in her mid-twenties and old when she left. She loved the dancing and the costuming and all the wildness about it, but it tired even a young beautiful girl. And the one thing you never heard about was the politics. Everyone heard of the large-scale roots of the operations and "the mob", but the club owners, managers, other showgirls, it was a constant struggle to stay on that stage and to stay on the right stage killed you. Patrick listened with the rapture of a pulp fiction reader. It was Millie who grew tired of the talk of her showgirl life and Patrick was soon partnering with Grover when

Millie exited left to the ladies room, "to freshen up before her long two blocks home", Grover gripped his coffee cup with long bony fingers as Millie's absence drew a silence into the room. He was not a talker. Patrick noticed now with an unobstructed view his torso was short but he had long legs, obviously a bit bowlegged and noticeable even when sitting. In front of his stool and acting as a footrest was a tackle box.

Patrick couldn't imagine that the fishing was too good here, but Grover corrected him.

"Fishing's good anywhere you make it good." He smiled. All those meaningful sayings displayed on shellacked pieces of wood hanging in the tourists' shops. That would be one of them for sure. He looked around at the walls of the Trading Post. They were relatively bare except for some posters for rodeos of the past.

Patrick took an immediate liking to Grover Pendrell, who notwithstanding Millie's comment had the face and voice of a storyteller when he wanted to be. What were his stories? Millie had presented an opening so clearly but Grover, Grover kept his shirt buttoned up to the collar.

CHAPTER TWELVE

A Shade Tree in Abbott, Arizona

Millie stuffed the losing lottery ticket into her purple snake-skinned wallet. Not even three.

"Want another?" Esther asked, splitting a roll of quarters on the counter as if expecting the need to make change some time in the day.

Millie hesitated, the next drawing wasn't until Saturday, maybe she should wait, may be she shouldn't buy at all.

"Hell yes, but two quick picks." Millie reopened her purse.

"Two!" Grover yelped bow-legged at her side.

"Esther, you got to learn to cut her off. That's my coffee money and every day there's the threat that I'll have to switch to Sanka."

"I'm not a therapist." Esther said as she handed Millie the tickets.

"You sayin' I need a therapist?" Millie looked at Esther and demanded an answer before accepting the tickets. There was a friendly, yet stern pitch to her voice.

"I ain't sayin' nothing." Millie tore the tickets from her hand and Esther resumed her seat at the register and didn't take her eyes off her peacock make-uped customer.

"You bet you ain't." Millie growled.

Grover looked to Patrick, letting him know this was standard procedure and quite frankly tiring. But nothing to be alarmed by.

Millie patted Patrick on the back and wished him well as she headed out the door of the Post.

"Honey, you are welcome anytime." She smiled. Thinking that sounded a bit hollow, "Grover and I live over on Pine, number 25, gray house, rock front, cuter than the rest of 'em."

Patrick thanked her with a wave. He followed them outside thinking he had over-stayed his welcome here and would be asked to leave The Post without them. Millie opened her driver's side door and turned. "You're a sweet boy and you were right to get off of that train." As the doors closed, Grover safely seated, Patrick heard Millie make a few unintelligible comments as she fit herself under the steering wheel. Interesting pair but most enjoyable conversation he'd had in awhile; in a long while.

Alone now, Patrick blushed, thinking he had told her of the night before, than realizing he hadn't told her the details, his natural pallor returned. He exited The Post but stayed standing in front of it until Millie had safely pulled out and cleared a large blue Chevy truck, whose bed stuck out into the street. Grover's head was down attending to something in his tackle box but Millie was in full wave as they headed down Main Street.

Main was a clean and straight-angled street, and hot. It was around noon and if Patrick had not known for sure before, by the glare of Elbert through the window that he and the old couple had over stayed their welcome at Elbert's Trading Post, he would have headed back in for the coolness. Instead he headed northwest toward a small park with a single tree. Millie had thought the next train would be by about 2:00 and if that was so, he needed some shade.

The street had few inhabitants, an older man pumping some gas standing next to the tank with the aid of a walker. A woman about Millie's age leaving what looked to be a barber shop/nail salon. Was the whole town was inhabited by senior citizens like so many of the communities in Florida? This was the Sunbelt so maybe old people migrated down to the desert from colder climates, as well as to the gulf-lining states.

When he reached a spot of grass he was grateful to see that the single tree spindly towered over a splinter-ridden picnic table and was providing some limited shade. He settled himself in and opened the sports section of the paper Grover and Jerry had finished reading and given him to replace his sweat soggy Wall Street Journal which he unsuccessfully used as a towel. He was surprised to see that handwriting on the pages.

With block lettering Grover had made careful notations in the margins of the baseball stats. They appeared to be acronym numbers, RBIs ERAs, homeruns with names attached to them as if an extension column to the grid. Patrick used his hand to shade his eyes to read the names; he was able to read, "Gehrig, Ruth, Alexander." He looked at the numbers again and noticed this time there were also dates attributed to the stats, 1928, 1930. Grover had highlighted Cal Ripken Jr's stats in one of the printed columns with an asterisk. What did that mean? Was The Iron Man going to beat some historic record? Patrick wished he could ask Grover. He loved his Soxes but couldn't help but admire what Baltimore was putting together. And also why would he scribble some numbers with the great ballplayer's names? There was a story there, he was sure.

Patrick was still pondering the questions when he looked up to the sound of a metallic ticking. He almost looked immediately away because it was only the sound of a stroller, when he realized that it was someone under the age of sixty that was pushing it down the clean stretch of road. It was a woman close to his age, maybe twenty, twenty-two. She had dark hair pulled up on her head to expose her neck and remove the heat and the weight. Her eyes were brown with thick eyebrows that arched, and making her eyes appear huge and smiling naturally. She wasn't smiling though. The baby she was pushing was young, probably under a year. A blanket was pulled over the top of the stroller to protect him from the infringing sunshine that the canopy could not cover. The baby was sound asleep and Patrick wondered how. Anyone, even a baby, could sleep in this heat?

The girl caught Patrick's eye briefly, examining him as if wondering not particularly who he was, - as he had her- but why he was there. Patrick liked the attention even though she had not spoken. As she got within speaking distance, her eyes moved to the bench itself and the blank space next to him; she then looked at the tree as if to judge the movement of the shade. It was there now, but the sun would continue its move west with its blazing rays. It would take at least thirty minutes to shade that end of the bench.

She had come to sit here in the shade. She was not pleased Patrick was there in her favorite spot, and even more he realized, she was openly irritated. It was probably the heat since she didn't appear to be angry by nature.

"Please, sit down." Patrick gestured and moved to the other end of the bench, which was only partially shaded but better than nothing.

The girl looked around and down the street as if being watched or looking for an alternative. And when there wasn't either, she wheeled the stroller to a halt, parking it next to the bench in the shadiest part and took the offered seat.

"Nice spot this bench." Patrick looked straight ahead, not wanting to make the girl feel anymore uncomfortable than she obviously already was.

The girl nodded her head and attended to adjusting the overhanging blanket so that it was sure not to block a breeze, if there were a chance of one.

"Is this the only park in town?" Patrick suspected the answer, but desperately wanted some conversation.

"Yes," the girl said, this time looking at him long enough to offer an answer.

"I'm Patrick Emery."

The girl turned more toward him and he expected a name in return. "Are you from Boston?"

Patrick laughed. He clearly had an accent, but it was not what he had expected her to say.

"Yes. Well outside of Boston, Quincy."

"Ah." The girl pulled her hair tighter onto the top of her head and took a baby wipe from the baby bag to wipe her own neck. Patrick could see it was gritty with sweat and embedded dirt lines. Something he had not noticed when she approached or when she had sat down. It felt intimate.

"You know Cliff, Cliff Clavin?" she asked still pulling her hair off her neck and wiping again.

"From Cheers?" Patrick asked.

"Yeah, the T.V. Show."

"Yeah." Patrick wasn't sure where this was going but it was a conversation.

"Well you sound like him." She wadded up the wipe and threw it toward the trash barrel in front of them, making it easily. "You don't look like him, for sure, but you sure sound like him."

"Great." Not really.

"I'm not sayin' something bad, Patrick. It's just we don't hear many Eastern dialects in the desert."

"Ah well." Patrick was surprised she had used his name so soon. Not that she shouldn't, it just sounded so personal, too soon.

A few minutes passed and Patrick noticed that the street was becoming more deserted. No customers at the gas station or the barber shop, though it did look like Elbert had a good crowd inside The Trading Post. At least half a dozen. Six was a good crowd he determined.

"Is this a retirement community, like those Sun City places?"

"Well it's sure Sun City here, but no not officially, just a lot of old people." The girl took out a bottle of water from the stroller and drank from it. One could live a week off the supplies in a baby stroller.

The girl continued. "This is their nap time, too hot for older people to be out on the street. But it's the time I like to be out here, just me and Nathan."

Patrick feigned some interest. "How old is Nathan?"

"Nine months, August 30," the girl answered.

Before Patrick could to ask another question, the girl interjected. "I'm Jennifer," to Patrick's surprise she extended her hand to him.

He shook it timidly, "Nice to meet you Jennifer and thank you for letting me share this bench, for awhile." Jennifer looked at him for further information.

"I'm waiting for the two o'clock train."

"We don't have a train station, you'll need to go to Upton, about thirty-five miles west." Considering, "Don't think we get many passenger trains through here, so I guess there's no need for a stop."

Train hopping had sounded intriguing to the girls he met on previous stop-overs but now he wished he hadn't confessed his mode of transportation, because now he was either going to have to lie or tell this beautiful girl that he has been breaking the law and planned to continue to do so. He decided on a compromise.

"Oh, OK" He said, as if thanking her for the information.

Jennifer looked at Patrick's belongings.

"Do you plan to walk, that's too far to walk and I hate to tell you but no one will pick up hitchhikers here. These old folks watch too many cop shows, and the news."

She laughed. "What are you going to do?"

Patrick panicked because he didn't have an answer, "Well I had promised to visit some friends. So I'll probably just spend a few days here and then have them take me to the station."

"Who?" By the one word question, he had taken the wrong escape route. This was a very small town after all.

"Millie Flowers and Grover." He said trying to sound casual, Bob and Carol, you know.

"Millie!" Jennifer gasped.

Patrick began to sweat. If Jennifer is her granddaughter he will just die, or worse have to tell her he was lying or was he? Millie had extended an offer for him to come stay with her and Grover, but had she been sincere? She'd given him their address. Maybe he could still save himself.

"Well actually I just met them, but it might be nice to stay for a few days." He said it. Good or bad he was now closer to honesty than before.

"Maybe a few hours, but days? If you're used to Boston, you're not going to be wanting to stay here in Abbott."

"So do you know Millie and Grover?"

"Well of course, I do live here ya know." Jennifer laughed again and the range of the sounds that composed her laugh woke Nathan, who began to moan and move around in his stroller. The heat finally penetrating his unconsciousness levered out by his mother's laughter.

"Millie Flowers is the only thing that makes this town halfway interesting." Thinking she should be a bit more tactful Jennifer added, "She is a really nice lady and if she invited you, you should accept."

Nathan began to cry; small puffs of guttural noise really, a contrast to his mother's joyful laughter.

When Jennifer picked him up Patrick was surprised how big he actually was. She set him on her pressed-together knees facing him toward her, bouncing his legs. Jennifer's legs together barely provided enough space to hold the chubby extensions. She was not skinny, but small, a young small woman with a huge crying baby. With the motion, soon Nathan calmed down, aided by a pacifier that Jennifer pulled from the life-support stroller bag-of-tricks.

"Millie got me my first job here." Jennifer said. "I take care of some old people, not a nurse really, just help them out with some of the basic things." Jennifer cooed at her son who smiled through the pacifier and drooling saliva down his chin.

"That's gotta be hard work." Patrick couldn't imagine what the 'basic things for old people' entailed, but he knew he wouldn't have the humility, or the patience to handle it.

"Not really, it's nice to spend time with people, plus I bring Nathan with me." She looked across the road, in a stare as if the people she assists are all standing there in a line supporting her statement. "They're so lonely. Especially the ones that are widowed, the long marriages and then their spouse is gone." Jennifer switched the angle of Nathan's legs. His little chubby knees were wet with sweat. "Actually Millie is the age of many of my clients, but she's stronger than me, has more energy, 'specially since having Nathan here." She gave him a loving consideration.

A whistle blew announcing the approach of the train slowing at the town crossing. Patrick considered walking off and ending the conversation so he could hop the train and get out of Abbott like he said. But Jennifer continued to talk and he couldn't think of a breakaway line, and is really not sure he wanted to.

The train soon left Abbott, having slowed at the one crossing only, but not actually stopping in town just as Jennifer had said. Patrick found himself walking down Main Street toward the tracks, though not to catch the train but to try to find Pine Street and the home of Millie Flowers and Grover Pendrell. Jennifer left the bench twenty minutes before when the sun started moving to the West and the bench was almost fully exposed. Now Patrick was stuck. In Abbott,

Arizona of all places. He could kick himself - but only if he could do it in the shade.

CHAPTER THIRTEEN

Heavy Lessons

He had already yelled at the T.V. for some error the Red Soxes had made that, "One a minor league rookie would make, not a million dollar money wing." He had followed Millie into the bedroom where he had announced that she had "too many bottles of nail polish and why did she need more than one moisturizer?" Grover had not taken a nap today and Millie was not tolerating his grumpiness well.

She banished him out to the yard to tend to tomatoes or "head down the road." So there Grover worked, re-staking tomato plants whose branches hung heavily with the fruit. The yard was no bigger than a small dance floor in a Baptist hall, but housed some twenty plants, all healthy, all happy to provide this old man some forced diversion for a bad mood. The afternoon sun was now baking the front of the house and Grover was well shaded by the overhanging roof. He promised to stay there so that Millie did not have her reoccurring fears of heat prostration realized.

Rosie's husband, Manuel had been struck down with heat stroke when Rosie sent him out to fix the screen door. She had not taken care to note that the sun was blazing directly on her husband's back and neck, until she saw him collapse on to the concrete porch-block that served as their front steps. She was forever re-living the event to the point where Millie told her if she didn't stop crossing herself every time she sent her husband out to do chores she was going to cross her "up side the head." But Millie worried. The desert was brutal especially to its elderly inhabitants who toiled with boredom even in the heat.

As Grover tinkered with the tomatoes, Millie cut out her Sunday coupons. It was a quiet ritual for her. She had a system in whereby coupons were organized by food groups and reverse chronological order so that a coupon wouldn't expire or go unused. Such an event would be unforgiveable. Millie claimed this is how she was able to save all those years living in Vegas when pay was "scraping by." She tried to live moderately, rented a studio apartment, shopped for clothes only at end-of-the-season sales and allowed herself to go food shopping only if she had at least five coupons close to expiring. Grover "poo-pooed" this method saying when he wanted something, he wanted it and would buy it coupon or not; blazon. This mentality came from his days on the road while pitching. He bought what he needed when he needed it and sent the rest to his wife and daughter. He hadn't needed much, and they needed more. When they settled in St. Louis for a bit, when Grover had been called up by the Browns, he had changed his habits and spent too much of the little money that he made because he had foolishly thought his baseball career would continue and progress until he was ready for a comfortable retirement, but it hadn't.

In his second year of throwing batting practice, he had not advanced to pitching a game and was punctuated with aches and muscle pain he had never experienced, in his many years of playing the game. He toned it down, as he appreciated the coach's reflection that batting practice meant, "they needed to hit", but he still threw hard. Grover was so determined to pitch in a game that he declined any suggestion that he rest and let one of the other guys warm up the team. Instead he threw night after night, his elbow on fire by the time the first game pitch was thrown. As he did with everyone else, he dismissed concerns, his own and the well meaning; he was going to make it into a game. His wife, Adele, fretted whenever he returned home with ice-wrapped around the perimeter of his right arm and begged him to sit it out; just a few times. "Don't be so willing to pitch, coach will understand." But he didn't get paid when he sat out, not like the game today, and no one praised him for his curves when he didn't throw them.

So the inevitable and the predicted happened in 1932, he threw out his arm and couldn't control his pitches any longer. At the same time the Depression extended itself out to every family in the U.S. in some way, every way painful. Many of the AAA ball clubs closed because no one had an extra buck to waste on a baseball game. Even the "The Show" suffered. The only leagues that survived were the company teams. Baseball was the entertainment in a world without television and without money to spend in ballparks, games against a bakery and a local oil company allowed Grover to play a bit longer, but not for living wages.

Grover said he learned heavy lessons after he lost his arm and what he learned was that he had made a number of bad choices. He had not gotten an education, he had married too young and he had counted on a career few could ever count on. Still Grover never regretted the game, it was his love, and he held his experience close in his character and in high esteem. Millie squirmed with some of the stories, not because she necessarily knew the truth of the struggles but because she suspected Grover was romanticizing the time as he did with any difficult circumstance. In truth this was true of us all; revisionism is the safe harbor of philosophers and storytellers.

Early on in their courtship when Millie asked him about his first marriage, he reported on only the good times. When he bought their first home in a small quaint section of St. Louis, when his only daughter Charlotte graduated from high school and he helped her pick out her prom dress, when he taught her how to throw a baseball and she threw straight and hard, when his wife sat with the other baseball wives in the stadium and cheered even though he never played a regulation game. To hear Grover tell it, you couldn't imagine that he and Adele had divorced in 1950; and would be at a loss as to why they divorced when you found out that they had. It was a good thing, Millie never respected a man who made a practice of denigrating his ex-wife or talked badly of her to their kids, but Grover, Grover was the extreme opposite. He not only spoken well of

Adele he spoke of her with such current fondness that it should have made Millie uncomfortable.

Millie had seen many pictures of Adele and her red hair, apparently close to the hue of Millie's own. There was a regal beauty to her and prominent dimples opening up welcoming features. When Millie prodded Charlotte on what Adele's life was following the divorce it was revealed that she had wandered into the Hollywood scene moving closer to Los Angeles. Never in films but reportedly favored by many film stars. Who Charlotte didn't say, but nothing serious was always the endnote. She reflected on this time with understanding in her mother's life as a need to spread her wings. She had been a young bride and mother. Later Adele lived a quiet life working at a small grocery market and retired back where they began in Ventura, California. Marrying again, but divorcing only after a few years. Even forced, there was not much of a story there. Grover and Adele's wedding picture was one of those old photographs that seemed to allow you into their souls, where they revealed they were in love, and maybe would always be in the very least reflecting fondly on each other. Adele passed away when she was in her fifties a good pair of decades before Grover made his bets on Keno board in Vegas.

Grover had other difficult losses. Reluctantly revisited with a protective detachment. When Grover spoke of the loss of his youngest brother Jack during World War II he did so with such expression that Millie thought his recount of the event should have been on Radio Free America; so gleaming with pride and bravery. It was this loss that woke him in the middle of the night screaming, his face burning with the hysteria, feeling his brother's fall from the Pacific skies. He spoke of the loss in censored terms; adjectives that praised and ended there. And when someone brought it up in conversation, maybe mentioning a loved one they had lost in the war, he was never prepared to tell the story. Instead, he looked blankly at the inquiring person and was openly astounded that they would ask him something that caused him so much personal pain. There was no reconciliation for Grover. He stopped attending veterans celebrations for this reason and instead mourned alone in his fitful sleep and draped Jack's ribboned medals over his picture on the mantel each Veterans Day.

CHAPTER FOURTEEN

Day One at Millie Flowers'

Millie was in the middle of the detergent coupons when there was a knock at the door. The door was not more than cheap press-wood with a tinny metal screen door, so actually she heard the combination of the two knocks hollow wood and metal, the sound couldn't help but resound through the small house. Millie looked at her watch, 2:15; people would just be waking up from their naps. Standing stiffly determining that it was most likely Rosie fretting about a call she wanted to make to her older daughter Marisol who she had at last located in Tucson. She wasn't sure she was in the mood. Certain she wasn't she stood for a moment and gathered herself.

But it wasn't Rosie. It was Patrick standing there, his backpack slung heavily over his right shoulder, duffle bag in the other, looking anxious and uncomfortable and not necessarily from the heat as before. Millie couldn't have been more pleased.

"Get in here," Millie exclaimed like he was a misdirected kid home late from an unauthorized outing. She opened the door widely to accommodate him and his gear together.

"I decided not to ride the train." he said.

"Well I'm glad to hear it, come on in and sit." Millie directed him into the small living room, past the card table that was cluttered with coupons.

"Giving up the train all together? Or just today?" Millie questioned as she took off the boy's backpack with both hands as if she were removing a winter coat. She disappeared with it and the duffle without waiting for his response. They were heavy but she didn't seem to need any help.

The room was darkly paneled and furnished with a crushed green velvet sofa and two matching Lazy Boy recliners. Between the chairs was a choppy circular table with heavy metal hinges and pulls. Patrick could tell which chair was whose by the contents of the table. On Millie's side was a dog-eared current romance novel, a coaster and pink-rimmed reading glasses on a chain, also a nail file and a bottle of bright red nail polish. Grover's side had a stack of neatly folded sports pages, must be at least a week's worth, a coaster with mallard ducks, two ink pens and a roll of Tums.

Millie returned, "I put you in Charlotte's room."

"Charlotte?"

"Grover's grown daughter." She laughed, "Of course grown, what else would an old man have, right? She stays here sometimes in the winter with the kids, lives out in Long Beach, California, and can't imagine why they'd want to come here when they live in California. Well we keep a room for her and the family anyways."

Patrick felt uncomfortable with the assumptions he had made in visiting.

"I hope I'm not imposing, it's just..."

"Please don't go down that road honey, I won't hear of it. If I offer, I mean it and when I offered, I knew it would be at least over night. No more trains run through Abbott until morning, on the run you got off of." Millie sat down in the Lazy Boy to face him. Patrick moved to the middle of the sofa not sure exactly where to go but the middle seemed right.

"Why'd you decide to stay honey?"

Patrick hadn't thought all of this through; he had only gotten to the part where he got to the front door and knocked.

"Well, it's just I'm not sure where I'm going. The plan was to see California, then head back, but I don't know if I want to make the trip alone."

"It could still be an adventure for you, even alone, hell may be much more if alone." Millie pulled out the leg rest and her orange mules shot up toward Patrick. She was ready for a good long chat.

It was after Grover came into the house, gulped down some of the sun tea, and joined Millie and Patrick, who in contrast were quietly sipping, that Patrick causally mentioned Jennifer.

A hesitant smile came to Millie's face. "She is a beauty isn't she?" Her head moved forward and focused closer to Patrick though her mules were still firm on the footrest.

Patrick wanted to quickly dissuade the point that that was why he stayed; exactly why he had brought her up was to make conversation, but didn't have a chance.

Millie leaned back in her chair and put her arms on her lap. "Jennifer's lived here about a year, or so. She was pregnant with that baby when she came here, no place to go really. But she set herself up pretty good. She's a sweet girl, listens to the old folks with all our aches and pains and that's something special in a person." Millie seemed to look past Patrick to the point that he turned to see is someone was coming up the rock-rimmed walk. But there was no one there. Millie refocused looking at him again.

"Lived for awhile with the baby's father, a real son of a bitch. Left some months ago and I can say thank the Lord I haven't seen him back." Millie paused and adjusted the rings on her fingers. Though they then didn't need adjusting. "It's a shame when a young girl hasn't been given the means to avoid men like that." Her eyes worked her glossy orange lips into a smile, "She'd be blessed to be fancied by someone like you." Grover took a sip of tea and let out a grunt.

Patrick wanted to say so many things. Namely that he was not interested in her, he had no intention or desire to get to know her better, and he was leaving town tomorrow. But as each thought came, Millie's look combated it, so he just smiled back at her abidingly. Abbott, Arizona why here?

"Promise me one thing Patrick." Millie popped her footrest down in one strong push and set both her feet onto the worn green-shagged carpet. "Promise me you will see past her circumstances."

"I promise." he told her and meant it. It was not much of a commitment for a day or so.

Charlotte's room was a virtual photo gallery of her, and her husband and their three children through all the stages of their lives. As Patrick lay facing the wall he traced each grandchild's life from being held in a hospital bed by their mother to what he believed must be their most current stage in life. Grover had listed them out for him when they spoke at dinner. Edwin who was the oldest was in college, California; one of the UCs. He must be the dark bushy-haired kid accepting a diploma in a black and purple trimmed robe. Then there was Heidi who was still in high school and "a bit of a handful", Grover had said under his breath but smiled through it. She was also easy to pinpoint since she wore thick mascara and a hemp-beaded choker in her school picture. And then there was Liza with her short-cropped hair and small features; Patrick determined she would always be pretty but never beautiful." But she was Grover's obvious favorite, a baseball player, Grover exclaimed proudly, asked to play kid pitch with the boys when she was only ten. There she was lining the walls in all her baseball uniforms holding the bats proudly with the gloves draped on her knee. It did look to be a natural pose and somewhat beautiful.

Grover had promised Patrick he would share his baseball album with him the next day. At first, Patrick had thought he was talking about more pictures of Liza. How many more pictures can there be? But after speaking of his pride of Liza, Grover confessed, " I was in the Major Leagues, a pitcher."

"I'd love to see the pictures of when you pitched." Patrick had almost begged to see the album then, but the age-infused exhaustion in the elderly man's eyes quelled his impulse and understanding the energy excitement will tap, scolded a silence and Patrick relented politely. "Maybe let's go through them tomorrow. I look forward to it." He would wait anxiously for the next day to arrive and memories to fall out of this old baseball player who had scribbled the names of the greats on a newspaper sports section. He was in his eighties? Who had he known? What had he seen?

In Charlotte's room, Patrick turned away from the framed photos to face the window. Millie had opened it wide to allow the desert breeze into the room, though the air conditioner above it was on full power. Patrick felt guilty about the wasted expense and got up about 2:00 am to close the window. No breeze had hit anyways, and it was doubtful one would. The quiet of the desert was remarkable and for a good ten minutes before closing the window, Patrick looked out on to the desert night. It was a clear night but for a few stars the sky was a pitch black. With the outline of an adjacent roofline, there was also the outline of saguaro cacti that dotted the hillside moving toward Phoenix. Patrick wondered briefly where Blake and Doug where, if they had continued the journey, or were hesitating continuing given the disruption caused or that of self-reflection.

He had heard their calls to him as he jumped off the train. Instead of heading back to them, he moved toward a shed that appeared to house some old auto parts. He stayed there until the train picked up more speed. He waited there for some twenty minutes making sure the two boys hadn't jumped off themselves and were looking for him, maybe checking out the town. Abbott, he believed it was called.

He made his way around the shed toward the direction of town when the train was a good two miles away. He had already forgotten the rules of train hopping and was walking too casually. Victor Garcia was finishing a transaction with one of the Bottom brothers when Patrick passed the front of the small shop he had been hiding behind so carefully.

"Hey where'd you come from?" he hollered.

Not knowing where he was pointing, he pointed beyond the shed toward a small mesa. Victor appeared to consider, nodded and returned to his conversation with a bearded man who waiting wanted to know about an oil pan. When Patrick had cleared the shop, rounding the falling down chain-linked fence, he looked to see where he had pointed but could only see a few speckles of houses, small square cottages with painted bordering rocks what appeared to be their primary landscaping feature. He had wondered why his pointing had sufficed. Why hadn't this man who could have busted him, merely dismissed him after the initial gruff interest in his voice? Patrick wouldn't find out the answer to that question until he had spent a few days at Millie Flowers'. People had little need to be suspicious of her in Abbott. If they ended up here they were meant to.

Had Doug and Blake thought him injured? Maybe fallen? Still drunk and unstable? They had seen him de-train that couldn't be a thought/fear; could it? The guilt of that had almost made Patrick reveal himself to them seconds after jumping, almost made him jump back onboard until he had heard Doug grumble, "He was a drag anyway." Blake had pleaded for a moment and then no more discussion. That he heard. He felt like a ten year old, wounded and mad. Damn them; let them believe he was dead, gone; tonight he had a bed at Millie Flowers'.

CHAPTER FIFTEEN

Sacred

Memories

P atrick had fallen back into a deep sleep finally in the early hours of morning. Millie later explained that though it wasn't "natural" to get up so early in the morning, it was the coolest part of the day and so desert people learned how to do their chores in the morning before the blaze of the sun curtailed most activity. By the time Patrick was awake at 9:30, Grover had fixed a rusty hinge on the tool shed's west facing door, mowed the small speck of lawn that guided the rock-lined sidewalk up to the front door, and taken the car to be gassed up for Millie's scheduled ride to the supermarket the next day. There seemed to be a schedule closely followed.

Millie spent the morning hours at the barber/beauty shop for a set and curl then, stopped by The Trading Post to redeem her big winning lottery ticket, she actually had three out of seven on a scratcher and was entitled to five dollars which was quickly turned into another ticket investment. Having accomplished her tasks of the day, she was happily chirping behind a frying pan cooking Patrick some "protein, which is what he needed." Eggs again, but Millie style.

"I have never seen a college boy so skinny," she commented more toward the grease splatter guard than to Patrick, "Doesn't your Momma live in Boston?" She questioned without sounding accusatory in any sense, just kindly curious.

"Yes, ma'am."

"Well you need to waddle on over there two, three nights a week and let her fix you something. No one ever stayed healthy on dorm food."

"Well I live in a group house, off campus. I cook. Really Millie I eat fine, I'm just from a skinny family. We're all pretty boney." As final statement because she may later think he was a rude glutton, "I eat a lot."

Millie reached over the plastic roses that centered the kitchen table and touched Patrick's cheek gently. It was an affectionate gesture Patrick didn't expect. "Skinny genes or not you need to fill out those cheek bones." She turned back to the bacon and expertly speared them into a grease drainer.

"Not fair being a skinny boy. I was one of those tall lanky girls, yes, people always asking me if I played sports. I didn't. Wasn't a thing in Texas. Girls playing I mean." She turned to answer as if Patrick was asking, "I just danced. But funny thing was I hit twenty eight and boom," Millie motioned to her hip spatula still in hand, Patrick winced for fear of flying bacon grease, "the hips start to widen and the pounds start piling. I swear I was on a diet for some thirty years and then boom," this time Patrick didn't duck, " I don't have to diet anymore same weight, same shape since I was fifty. Of course the fake boobs help, they never sag." Millie plopped the bacon adorned with eggs and toast in front of Patrick and took a seat. Patrick froze with the words "fake boobs."

"Sorry sweetie. It's been a fact of my life for so long I forget it's not an appropriate comment. I had breast cancer-early. Have lived with the falsies longer than the real ones. Way longer."

Patrick nodded, sure that's not appropriate. He hasn't known this woman one day. Millie continues, "Please don't feel sorry for me. I survived and it was a long time ago. Lucky I found a man who didn't care about the lumps of flesh, they would have been in full sag when we met anyways. Hell but I still miss them sometimes." Millie looks at Patrick's plate which is untouched.

"Eat Patrick don't let my verbal wanderings distract you or you never will. Eat."

Patrick smiled shyly, thanked her, and picked up a piece of bacon. He was amazed just how good all this "protein" was. "Were you married when you were younger?" he asked between bites kind of hoping to get off the subject of breasts or missing ones.

"Yes once to a man from Iowa. Short marriage, don't quite know why I said yes, but Oscar was a good man. Divorced in my early thirties. Loved the sex though. Dated a lot then met Grover."

Patrick smiled, the way she said things so casually were such revelations, easily shared. He wasn't like that. Not even close.

Millie moved in with confidence and sat down opposite, "Bet sex is somethin' for you isn't it? I remember my twenties, the boys were rabbits."

Patrick couldn't help but remember that he is talking with a woman who was his grandmother's age, but he also felt like he could talk to her about anything, even over bacon in a tiny cottage in the middle of a desert.

"Yes." He answered simply, but wanting to say more. How to weave in the revelations?

"Who's special to you Patrick? Do you have a girlfriend back in college?" Millie had replaced the empty space in his confession before he could object or fill it, which he would have done with something out of politeness. She also filled his plate back up with a second helping of protein as if to signal that the conversation was in fact to continue.

"No. I dated a few girls last quarter. Both law students. But first year was really difficult and well we just found ourselves arguing with each other, over, well nothing."

Millie grabbed a dishtowel from behind her, "Well that doesn't bode well for your profession." Millie looked at him seriously, "Nothing should come in the way of love, nothing," she said definitively.

Millie had fixed Patrick an iced coffee to wash down his meal with a caffeine-kick when Grover finally pulled out the photo album of his baseball years. There was breakfast taste to the coffee that Millie identified for him as chicory.

The album was remarkable with its obvious care in the making and artistry it held. The outer cover was wood with the carved letters in the center G. A. P., with the grains of wood prominent and shellacked with a deeply layered gloss. It was held together with thick leather laces.

"My mother made it." Grover stated proudly reflecting an admiration that he probably held since receiving it so many years ago. Grover took the album and laid it flat on the card table, which had been cleaned of the coupons from the day before. Carefully he turned the pages, showing taped-in yellowed articles and rosters and a few photos of his various minor league teams. The pages were hard and brittle with age but still held the evidence of his memories documented carefully in photos and newspaper articles. With each article, Grover allowed time for Patrick to read the article in full, and then told the appropriate back-story when he passed over the last period. This man had timing and control like the pitcher he once was.

"I was playing for the Frogs. Been there about three months, maybe two, liked it pretty good. Not too shabby a travel schedule, Adele and Charlotte could come up every once in awhile and actually see a game, spend some time together. Though Charlotte was just a baby then." Grover smiled at his mention of his daughter's name.

Patrick wondered if it was always that way with parents. Grover's daughter was now in her fifties and her father still smiled at the memories of her as a baby. He wondered if his mother was doing the same in Quincy, telling one of her co-workers that her son was on a cross-country adventure with his friends. For certain his father would not have that smile, his unwelcome opinion was certain to be that he was taking "crazy paths" and was "a good for nothing."

Patrick had not spoken to his father in years. He had tried but he couldn't tolerate even the idea of him without feeling his pulse race and seeing scenes he no longer cared to remember. Had there been good memories? A Christmas dinner? An Easter egg hunt? He no longer recalled. The line of photos of Patrick's years of growth lined his mother's house, not his father's.

Grover's voice broke in. "I was pitching oh about the fifth inning, the top. We were ahead by five runs, wasn't any way that team..." Grover took a minute to look at the printed article which was headlined "Pendrell Ejected," "Fresno, raisin-fed losers, was no way they could catch up. So I was figurin' this out, the third base coach starts giving me a bad time." Grover looks at Patrick full on so that he can apparently understand the gravity of the situation.

"I'm winding up for my signature curveball and he's yelling, 'you're a bum Pendrell, where's your arm, got no guts throw something worth swingin' at.'" Grover clears his throat, still angry about the exchange though by the clipping the game was in 1926. You hear this kind of talk, maybe by opposing fans, but a coach?"

"So I look over at the umpire, I know he hears it. He motions me to continue play and I do. That's what I'm there for. I get the next two guys out, one swinging, one a lousy pop up fly ball right into the glove of my right fielder Elliott, so I think its over." Grover laughs a sarcastic laugh. "I get back on the mound to wind-up next inning and there he is a big-bellied southerner cussing at me." I can't even let a ball go without hearing a four-letter word fallin' from his mouth. I look at the umpire again and this time he looks away. 'To hell with this' I say to myself." Grover puffs himself up and a flush comes over his face, his cheeks in particular take on a splotchy red with stubble, "I put my glove down, gentlemanly on to the mound, and walk over to that son of a bitch coach and belt him one. Hell he didn't even stop talking as I was heading over. A wiser man would have. I threw my left into his cheek, not going to hurt my right for this guy, and he was still talking. My boys pulled me off or I would have made sure he was silent for a good long time."

Patrick considers this man of eight decades, imagining what the rest of the pages will tell.

Grover continued well into the noon hour, spending carefully allocated time on each of the pages of the album. Mixing the print of a story or photograph with memories of the actual people and the circumstances all played out. Deep crevices of black ink, some handwritten or in newsprint, held the names and the dates and Grover gave the color. The language was as Patrick had never seen before. This was the entertainment and the sports writers were painting stories. A byline caught Patrick's eye, "Silent Pendrell tag-team no-hitter." Patrick didn't know where to begin. "Silent?," he read on. Grover's manager at the time was asked why he was nicknamed "Silent." Well Bud Gevers replied, "Pendrell is a talkative guy. You ask him

a question and he either answers 'yes' or 'no'."
Grover saw where his finger was pointing and
chuckled. "Yep." Silent had become a storyteller.
Patrick read-on, but liked Grover's telling, even
more than the adjective-rich writing of the sports
writers.

"I pitched the first six innings. No hits.
Peaches Ibsen finished the last three no hits." He
smiled, "only one I ever threw. Didn't mind
sharing it with ole' Peaches he was a good guy.
From Georgia. We all had nicknames, I didn't
have any problem living up to mine. I was a
serious guy." Grover turned the page.

"The circumstances," Grover was careful to
point out, "were not like they are today. Baseball
was not a profession you went into to be rich and
famous. Nah, it was the opposite. I barely made
enough money to support my wife and daughter.
They lived back in Ventura where we grew up, in
a tiny one bedroom cottage on a small plot of
land that had four of the same identical houses on
it." Grover reflected, "I know she regretted
marrying me when I was being traded back and
forth to minor league teams around the country

and was embarrassed by the lack of things we had. Adele never said so, never directly anyway."

Millie waltzed into the room, sliding two turkey sandwiches on to the narrow open space of the table above the album.

"I think that humiliation she carried around too quietly is what did us in," Grover reflected looking at nothing particular in the album.

"Maybe it was that showy asshole who lived next door." Millie concluded with such direct detest that it made Patrick turn to look at her. He couldn't help but be impressed; if she was in fact talking about a man who broke up her husband's first marriage.

Grover wasn't impressed nor did he appear to be insulted. Not in the least, but said definitively, "Yeah I'm sure he had something to do with, being home for her, driving his fancy Chevrolet." Grover took the plate with the sandwich and pushed himself away from the table. Sandwich in both of his large hands.

After two large bites of the sandwich, Grover quietly plead, "Don't think badly of Adele," as if Patrick had some reason to judge this woman of seventy-odd years prior. "She was young and I was away. I was away a lot, even when I was home."

"So you got divorced? That wasn't too common back then. Right?"

"We did, and it wasn't," wiping his mouth with a cocktail napkin that read "The Flamingo" in pink letters, "Well we did eventually, but not then, oh no I knew about the affair, she told me, but we didn't divorce until well after Charlotte had graduated high school some years later."

"Didn't you think she'd have other affairs? Didn't you lose your trust in her? I mean with the traveling, didn't you wonder?" Patrick thought he may be entering too personal of territory, but he really wanted to know.

"I know she didn't mess around again. I'm sure she wanted to, but she was a sweet thing and would never go through that again." Grover pulled a tomato out from between the bread and set it aside on his plate. Taking a minute from his tales, he pulled out a small shaker of salt from his pocket salted the bare tomato heavily, popping it into his mouth.

"Don't tell Millie," he whispered to Patrick after he had chewed up the small salty bite, leaning into him to give him that secret instruction. Millie was just around the corner but in earshot.

Patrick had wanted to ask and was growing more anxious when he heard the playing year-references. Had he met some of baseballs greats? Played with them? Grover answered him rather matter-of factually, "yes."

During the time he played for the Browns it was common to "borrow" players among the local big league teams; these were not "trades" Grover made very clear. So for a few home game series he was sent over to the St. Louis Cardinals.

"The Browns were in the gutter most of that decade, but the Cardinals...they were the heavy-hitters."

Grover chuckled. "You know how I told you my coach told me to throw something the batters could hit for practice?"

Patrick nodded.

"Well I threw my best at the Cardinals and they hit everything like I was throwing a softball." Grover showed no embarrassment shaking his head at the memory. He noticed the look on Patrick's face – anticipation, and continued. "Well it was a home game that the Yankees came through Sportsman Park. The way that park was set up the visitor teams had to walk through our dugout to get to theirs'. I wasn't pitching the game obviously but had pitched warm-up. The guys let me stay on the bench as everyone was in and out warming up in the field." To himself more than Patrick, "You have times where you think - I will always remember this and other times you think I should have realized it was a moment and paid more attention. I still thought at that time I was going to make the roster, still cocky, so I was cool when Ruth entered the dugout."

Patrick inched himself toward Grover. He didn't want to miss a word.

"Babe looked down the line. The other guys nodded. I looked straight ahead but was sitting only one in from where he stood. He came over and hit me on the shoulder and asked, 'You pitching to me today kid?'"

"He called you kid?" Patrick could hardly stand it.

"He called everyone kid, but of course I was."

"What did you say?" Patrick felt himself like a kid asking for information too quickly.

"I barely spoke, but forced out a 'no' unartfully. He just laughed and raise his head to me on his way out."

Patrick couldn't imagine. Had he ever met someone he admired so much? He was putting a list together in his head of those he would want to meet when another name continued the story-Gehrig.

Patrick took a quick slice of air.

"If I was Silent, Lou was mute but in a kingly way. He also stood for a minute in the dugout when he came through, after Ruth, but only nodded to the team. Some of the Cardinals went to talk to him but he merely smiled, nodded to whatever they said and walked on."

Patrick thought of the famous speech. He had such a heroes' presence. He wondered if Lou had any idea what a legacy he would have?

After the sandwiches, Grover was obviously feeling tired, ready for a rest. Millie tried to nudge him into taking his nap, but before he would he had to tell Patrick about Anita, Anita Anne Bowers.

"Oh, Grover this could go on up to dinnertime." Millie scoffed tenderly, but Grover assured her. "It won't, I just want to tell this last one." Patrick watched the old man turn the next page revealing a black and white portrait of a dark-haired girl with pins curls and a lace collar. Her clothes looked subdued and restrictive but it was easy to see that her manner was not.

He stroked the page gently, "She was quite a looker. Taking a moment to speak to the kitchen, "Like Millie."

"She had such beautiful long legs and such a grace about her. I met her in St. Louis after being called up to the majors."

Millie moved back into the room and took a seat in her blue Lazy Boy quietly. Patrick could tell she was listening to a story she had heard a hundred times, for the first time.

"Anita was at a social gathering we were required to go to as part of the team. I didn't mind. All the other guys fell for the blonds in attendance, always the blonds. Big bosoms, small-waisted. You know the kind you see in those photos of the twenties and thirties. Buxom. The kind whose picture hung in a GI's locker?"

Patrick had no idea, but nodded to keep the story going.

"I on the other hand was smitten by Anita Anne Bowen. She paid me a lot of attention that night, maybe being that the boys paid her little and we got to talking, spent a lot of time talking." Grover looked from Patrick to the picture. "She was from Omaha originally, moved to Missouri to be near an aunt of hers. She was a teacher and a darn good one."

"So you had an affair with this woman, Anita?" Patrick asked casually taking a sip of his tea. When he lowered his glass. He had been an impatient or just an insensitive listener, thinking there was a need to interject when there wasn't. He had not allowed the story to progress, as Grover had wanted, as the story should have. Millie stayed silent as Grover's paused, picking up a Reader's Digest next to her and thumbing through it.

"No I did not!" Grover. Millie seemed to jump a bit even though she knew it was coming. It seemed she might have expected the response but surely not the depth of the indignant tone.

"I'm sorry Grover, go on." Patrick urged.

"Go to hell." Grover closed the album harshly. "You boys just don't understand what loving someone is like. No I never had sex with Anita Bowen," his indignant voice rose as he himself rose from his chair, "I never even held her hand." He was holding his album and facing Patrick. "I talked with her all night and more over the next few months until I brought over Adele and Charlotte. But I loved her, as much as I loved Adele and as much as I love Millie." Grover pushed his chair with his leg to make room and taking the album with him retreated to his bedroom down the narrow hallway.

Patrick's heart was beating rapidly as if he had run up a flight of stairs. It was a physical reaction to the strain of shame. Millie had also closed her magazine and was now looking out the window.

"I'm so sorry Millie." He sounded like a small child trying to get out of due punishment.

Millie took a moment and rose from her chair. After a moment of stammered silent concentration that crossed from her brow to her jaw, she sat back down in Grover's chair. Patrick hadn't noticed before that her eye shadow had a descending trait, the closer to her eyes the bluer.

"I know, Patrick." She paused for an exhaled breath, muffling it a bit not to sound too dramatic. "You have to first remember that old men get grumpy, but most importantly that their memories are sacred." Millie touched Patrick's jawbone in her palm gently, not minding the rough stubble of his face. Patrick was clenching and hadn't realized it. "Do you have a grandfather? One that's alive that you've known in adulthood?"

Patrick hesitated. He did have a grandfather but his grandfather lived in a nursing home in upstate New York and he honestly hadn't seen him in more than two years. "Yes," he answered not having the courage to admit yet another shortcoming.

Millie smiled slightly. "When you get home, visit him, talk to him and let him tell you his stories, his memories." Millie lowered one of her hands on to Patrick's hand cupping it with an arch of her knotty knuckles. "What did he do for a living, your grandfather?"

"He worked in a furniture factory." Patrick saw him standing in his leather apron, and thick gloves to protect his hands from the coarse wood sheddings. He stood in line with other men of equal age and equal stoop. Guiding large pieces of lumber through saws and measuring with precision where the next turn should be. In his childhood home his mother displayed her father's candlesticks on the mantel, turned with care and painted in delicate metallic paints on his days off from the factory. Next to the perfect four-inch wide set of candlesticks was a wobbly two-inch wide three-inch tall stick Patrick had made with his grandfather when he was ten years old. Was it still there? Had failed to notice it anymore. The strong sitting with the small.

"Ask him about the feel of wood, what was his favorite to work with? About what he did at the end of his shift, about a girl he once loved." Millie's hand retreated, "but don't put it in your world, it doesn't belong there."

"He liked Beech. I think." Patrick offered. "His house was full of it. Big chunky furniture."

"Nice finish you can get off of white beech," Millie said. "I had the largest dinning room table made of white beech when I lived in Vegas. Used to host 10 or more for dinner. Gave it to Patsy." Millie slides her hands on the armrest as if feeling wood again.

"His girl?"

"No idea."

Millie rose quietly her lanky shapely frame retreating down the hall toward Grover. Patrick watched her move away from him, letting the regret of a question asked move off his chest, but it was replaced with much more heavy emotion and much bigger regret.

He heard the door of Grover's bedroom door close with a hollow pressboard clunk as Millie settled her husband down for a restless, angry afternoon nap, much the way you would a two-year-old child. Grumpy but that was not all.

CHAPTER SIXTEEN

Anita Anne Bowen

She almost didn't notice him at all, and why would she? Anita was not a regular at baseball games so would not have equated his build and manner of physical presence with that of a baseball player, or even registered his profession if he had walked toward her in a full home-stand uniform. But she did notice him finally not because he was introduced to her, but because he was a gentle speaker. She had met Grover at a reception held by the local Elks Club. Being a teacher at the local high school she tried to shoe-horn herself into these community gatherings because it was a chance to meet many of her students' parents; many of which rarely came to school gatherings but may be Elks, or veterans or members of some other cloister institution. She was not the only teacher that did this, and on this night Sheila Costi came with her with her husband leading the way to this event as an Elk himself. It had apparently been rumored that some of the Browns were going to be in attendance and Roger didn't want to miss that. Even if they had the worst record in baseball. The particular area where her high school was located and this Elks Club was an Irish immigrant blue-collar neighborhood. Its residents worked in brick factories and other industrial facilities. The working class was loud and festive and Anita enjoyed the mix these gatherings provided so she went.

Anita had come to St. Louis from Omaha at the urging of her Aunt Martha. An outwardly rigid woman who only having sons, doted on her niece from the very beginning, and indulged her when she was around. So in her aunt's fifties with the death of her husband, Anita's Uncle Neal, Martha looked to her niece's presence to bring some continued meaning or just company. Her two sons lived farther east one in New Jersey and the other in Philadelphia. One married with a young quiet life the other, Martha thought would never settle down. Anita had always loved her Aunt Martha and enjoyed her company so when she graduated from teaching college she made the move to St. Louis. She got her first job at McNamara High School in the Kerry Patch neighborhood and she settled into her life in the new city with a real profession, and one she was proud of.

That night at the Elks was like any other at the mixers, some food, drink and a small amateur band. She made her way around the large room, skirting men who had been drinking too much and instead striking up conversations with couples who were in the age-range to be a student's parent. A few she recognized as those few who attended school fairs, and she gave a quick "hello" of recognition but took more time to speak to the others. Sheila worked the room in a similar manner but most often spent these evenings with more familiar friends since as a teacher of more than ten years she didn't have the drive of a youthful teacher like Anita.

About an hour into the evening Anita saw Sheila motioning to her. It was a poor attempt as subtlety since Sheila was a rather loud woman with gestures to match. Anita took the time to wrap-up her conversation with the Donnellys, Lily's stick-thin parents with equal rushes of jet-black hair, and made her way to Sheila's motioning arms.

Sheila smiled triumphantly when Anita joined. If there was an order to the configuration Sheila stood at the top of the semi-circled conversation, Roger to her direct right then next to him an attractive man in his mid-twenties, followed by two other men a bit older? The four men seemed to be in a technical conversation of sorts using multiple acronyms in their sentences. Anita hated acronyms they were so alienating. She first heard Sheila breaking in with questions.

"So what is your ERA?" she inquired of the younger of the three men.

"Well ma'am I haven't actually hit yet in a game so no stats on me," he answered softly not out of any embarrassment to be stat-less but rather because that appeared to be the way he spoke. The other two were not such soft speakers.

"Pendrell here is our batting practice pitcher," exclaimed the more broader-shouldered of the remaining two. His words barreled like his chest. With that he slapped Pendrell on the back, "We hope to see him on the roster soon." He looked up and nodded a welcoming greeting to Anita, "ma'am."

"Hello." Anita greeted the three men, and reached out her hand to each of them, as Roger introduced her "This here is Anita Bowen one of our high school teachers." She shook the last hand ahead of the introductions, "Anita this is Grover Pendrell, Tommy Fitzsimons, and Kip Knotts of the St. Louis Browns." The last part of the introduction was in baritone.

"Nice to meet you all." Anita offered.

"Anita's from Nebraska," Sheila added to the offering. The men nodded. The blond man apparently Kip Knotts commented, "We will pass through that way in about a week or so." He smiled, "nice country."

"Yes it is, a surprisingly forested place in otherwise vast acres of farm land." The group smiled; she must be a teacher.

Grover quietly asked, "What do you teach?"

"English," Anita responded. "Literature mainly but I also have to teach grammar to the horrors of teenagers."

Grover smiled and not just in a polite way but a smile that indicated pleasure.

The other three men started talking about baseball again, there was a home game the next night, and then they wandered toward some attractive women that apparently did know they were baseball players. Sheila excused herself to go speak to a couple she knew.

"Do you like reading?" Anita asked, wondering if that was the reason for the smile.

"I do," Grover answered a little bit louder since the music had also gotten louder, people were starting to dance so they moved off to the side.

"It's about the only thing that keeps me sane."

"Who do you read?" Anita always liked to say "who" rather than "what." Books were written by people.

"I like it all." he sounded like a kid with the enthusiasm only kids had when it came to something they truly loved. We lose that later, Anita recognized. She hoped to hold on to her loves maybe a little longer.

"Just about everything, Fitzgerald, Forrester, I like some EE Cummings too. But I also really like good westerns, Zane Grey can make me miss meals."

Anita smiled broadly, "I hate to hear what James Joyce makes you miss." She teased.

Grover grinned. "Yes, he's definitely on the menu." Thinking a moment, "Good if you teach him around these parts. Good for the kids to know an Irish writer." As if testing her humor, her knowledge, or how well they were to get on, "If you're wondering, Cummings just makes me miss punctuation."

Anita's laughter had filled the hall, even with the brass instrument din of the music, she could be heard over it. A few of the dancers turned to look.

Anita and Grover's friendship grew from there and they never tired of talk or the subject of books. But they did tire of the lack of future they had together. Grover was married with a young daughter in California. And he was in love with her, and he was a good man. Anita loved him too and it broke her heart she could not have him. After a year of playing with the Browns, and not pitching, or batting in an actual game, Grover was called back down to the minors. It was just as well, she would remember and then scold herself for such selfishness. She did need him out of her town to forget him and to move on with her life. In the naivety of thinking she thought she could forget him. She did move on with her life, married a few years later and also had a daughter. She also eventually knew it was all right that she continued to love Grover Pendrell, and she did all these decades later.

CHAPTER SEVENTEEN

Riding the Rails

This summer had been all about sex, maybe that's why he was so used to its mention and making it applicable with every reference, making it cheap where it shouldn't be. Patrick had lived freely, away from care and worry. Away from his family, away from the pressures of performing well in school. This had been his summer to not care, and for most of it he hadn't. Yet now he found himself in this small paneled room in a house with a kitchen facing tomatoes, a tidy living room to the east now drawn thickly with drapes, wondering what he could do to make up for a fleeting, foolish comment to an old man he didn't even know.

This was his failure. It had been the numbing mindlessness of sex that had finally pulled him off the train and dropped him in this small town in the Arizona desert. It had been the fury of the mindlessness that had caused him to move away from a person who he thought was a good friend.

Doug and Patrick had met registering for the first semester of Contracts 203. Both had heard that though this section of Contracts was difficult, it was best to take it first year, first semester if you could. They discovered standing in line that this comment had been given to both of them but by different people, it therefore must be solid advice. Doug and Patrick soon discovered that this was "the" class that weeded-out the high G.P.A., yet ill equipped students entering law school. The fact that it was advising professors who had suggested they take the class that made them both feel that they fell within that screen and thought it best to know whether they sifted out to the bottom and should find another profession. Make it an early determination.

They hadn't discussed this revelation with each other that day, in that line, but both had been driven to prove they could make it through, that both could go beyond merely making it through. Doug and Patrick spent so many hours together studying that when a room became available in the shabby group house that Patrick lived in on Hennings Avenue, Doug logically moved in and their study hours were more easily extended.

The next semester brought Torts and Constitutional law, but through these daunting subjects, both felt the satisfaction of entering these courses with high grades having emerged from Professor Sorkin's 203 Contracts. Both held the dangerous arrogance that comes from success in one tough course in law school. It had been all this work without much play that convinced Patrick to join Doug and Blake, another roommate in the group house in the risky summer adventure. Riding rails was somewhat illegal, they knew, and absolutely crazy. But those were the exact reasons Patrick decided to do it. He had been too abiding for too long.

Patrick had lied to his mother when they took off for his journey. He had never regretted the telling of that lie until now. Instead of the truth he had told her that they were driving cross-country, but doing it slowly to see the middle states and to see where they ended up when they had to turn back. They were shooting for California. Patrick's mother, Beverly, had never been out of Massachusetts so the vision both scared and thrilled her. But this was her third child telling her this, and the only one who had pursued college much less graduate school. So when Patrick told her of their plans, lying only about the means of transportation, really, she did not deny him his chance with any shown hesitancy. It was a chance she had never had, marrying young and having three children. She asked only that he act responsibly and not make her regret her decision to support him. Her decision. His father made no decisions anymore except to lose a string of jobs and drink on Wednesdays when the bartender who would tolerate him was working.

One month on the rails had lengthened to two because the three didn't want to face what they had been required to face at school. The rails removed them. None of them spoke of law school and Patrick began to wonder if any of them would actually return. But why wouldn't they? Patrick and Doug were at the top of their class. Blake was not too far behind, though he did not seem to have the same motivations as the other two to excel. It was highly probable that Patrick would lose his ranking to Angelo a handsome Italian American who came from a line of lawyers and was already assured a place in a New York law firm when he graduated. But did he really care?

The longer into the trip the more irresponsible the boys became. It was as if the farther west they got the more removed they were from the structure of their responsibilities. They were trying to run. Blake began to drink excessively and it was not the liquor Patrick had seen him sip at his family's weekend dinners. Now he made sure he had a six-pack of beer when they were on the train, instead of having a drink when they settled in a town for a daily meal and an occasional rest at a motel. Doug, drank too, but did not do this to extreme. He took on a much more disturbing obsession. He picked up girls, any girl, and tallied his sexual experiences for the other two upon each rail jump. At first it had been entertaining, a juvenile conquering that Patrick took part in also from time to time. Meeting someone unknown to you in any sense other than what they drank that night and ending up sleeping with them was part of the adventure. Patrick even spent an extra two days in Kansas City with a twenty-year-old girl named Leesa who he not only had great sex with but also enjoyed during the times out of bed. But mostly it was about getting laid and enjoying getting laid for the pleasure and the power of it.

It was in El Paso that Doug had begun the practice of truly soul-absent sex and the accumulation and conquers overflowed into New Mexico and then Arizona. The three were staying at a Motel 6 for a few days enjoying the proximity to the Mexican border, Blake drinking Tecate for breakfast and rounding the day with shots of Tequila without lime or salt, "unadulterated." One morning Patrick slept in late and joined the two later in a bar called "Juanita's" adjacent to the University of Texas campus and met the local attendees who were enrolled in summer courses to fill some missing course requirements from the previous semesters.

The narrow bar had a collegial décor, housing ten four person booths below large televisions that were suspended in each of the corners of the room with cable wire. Doug and Blake grabbed a larger booth, which allowed them two viewings of sport events, the Texas Rangers on one screen and soccer on another. Patrick was more hungry than anything else and ordered what was called a "Texas Toast Burger" with a thick bread slice-shaped toasted bun Before his meal arrived, the bar started to fill up with people mainly his age, with a few older barflies hanging on at the counter on a rotation from other neighborhood bars. Both screens becoming boring, Doug noticed two co-eds at the middle booth, snacking on peanuts and throwing the shells to the floor, which was the custom at Juanita's. Patrick saw the exchange of glances, but concentrated on his burger, which was covered with the accompanying chili fries bringing cautionary comments from Blake though he helped himself to the bounty of the gaseous treat. Patrick had reached down to the last few bites when the girls stopped by to talk about their courses, where they were from and asked the typical scores of questions related to college life. They were young, undergraduates in their second year, twenty. The two girls, Geneiva and Ellen finished each other's questions and vowed that the guys would have a great time at a party at a friend's house. "Come on by, really." They offered.

Geneiva was a particularly attractive girl with long brown hair that framed her round face. She had waited only moments into the introductions and college jabber to squeeze into the side of the booth with Blake and Patrick, her shoulders and thighs touching Patrick's. She talked of growing up in Houston and trying to get into the University of Texas at Austin, but not being able to quite meet entrance requirements and taking the alternative of El Paso, that didn't have the same prestige. Patrick realized that each state must have the same cast system of universities and cities-even the ones within the same system. From her background, it sounded like Geneiva evenly matched Patrick, coming from a large middle class catholic family. They small-talked about music, reporting on recent concert attendances. Patrick threw in a few comments when it came to the likings and dislike of college life. He had had the opportunity to go away for undergraduate, attending the University of Colorado mostly on scholarships and considered that his most enjoyable time of life. Law school had proved much different with his living close to home and working to make enough money for his starchy-fueled meals. He did not respond to adjusting to being back in his hometown. Geneiva had some desire to return to Houston he had not had the same draw to Boston. Still he had ended up there.

Geneiva led into the possibilities of conversational exchange with Patrick more naturally than with Blake. Blake picked this up, and without feeling insulted and increased his alcohol intake. Across the table Ellen and Doug were already engaged in some intimacies in what appeared even at this level to be, a squeezing of thigh, a nuzzle to the ear under the guise of telling a whispery joke. Doug and Patrick exchanged glances, as an almost estimate as to how long this bedding would take. Still the limping conversation between Blake, Geneiva and Patrick continued. Patrick was asked what type of law he wanted to go into, if he wanted to work at a law firm, if so where? The questions were tiresome and started to be unwelcoming. Soon Blake took control and ordered shots all around. Ellen giggled and Geneiva moved toward her over the table to confide some direction to her. Geneiva was the first to take a drink and rolled her eyes back as the liquor burned down her throat. Ellen followed wasting most of it through her incapacity to stop laughing. Patrick and Blake cheered each other and downed theirs together while Doug positioned a line of salt on the table licked it with his tongue and then gulped down the tequila.

From there the three men danced with the two girls. Doug had claimed Ellen but Geneiva was still up for grabs. She wove herself between the two men as if someone where calling a square dance. Soon it was obvious her choice was to be Patrick and it occurred to him that he could care less. As they spun together on the dance floor and later that night in her roommate's car, he wondered if she cared as little as he did. If she cared to know this guy from Quincy, Mass, more than a fuck. Had he even mentioned the name of his hometown or was it always Boston-generalized? Had she even recalled it, or cared to recall any of the information he had shared with her during the sex-courting.

That night, after he had dropped Geneiva off at her dorm, he lay listening to Blake snore drunken pockets of air next to him, hoping tonight would not be one of the nights he threw up at the side of the bed. In the next bed his best friend Doug screwed Ellen, as if no one else were in the room. Patrick asked the same questions he had asked himself. But this time he heard himself saying it out loud. It surprised him at first, and it was not until he heard Doug yell back, that he was fully alerted.

"What the fuck is wrong with you?" Patrick had said it out loud.

This was not right. This disregard for the way things should be. "The way things should be." He heard himself say. It didn't make sense, but as he was yelling what was coming out of his head

Doug turned on the light on the adjoining nightstand. The hollow of the coned shade teetering on a cheap base pointed into Ellen's face and bare body. She looked young and miserable. Was it his yelling, the light, or the fact that she was having sex with a man she didn't know in a room with two other men laying in the adjacent bed? Her eyes locked on Patrick, drooping slightly in the corners. He had not noticed this before.

"You're fucking her while Blake and I lay a foot from you." Patrick barreled rising out of the bed.

Doug also pulled himself up from the bed, the blanket falling onto Ellen's face covering her. "Yeah and what the fuck is it to you?" Doug was angry, but his erection was still blood gorged.

Patrick found himself laughing, not out of anger but the mere shock of this whole scene and Doug's attempt to defend it through asking a question.

Patrick sat back down on the bed hoping the cramps of the hysteria would leave. Doug was still naked berating him, building his case that Patrick was not the innocent here. Patrick turned away from the shrouded Ellen as he pulled on his jeans and slipped into his flip-flops. Blake who still hadn't raised his head from his pillow, except to push the other light away from his face. "Shit" he commented at the hot metal burning his hand and passed out, vomit starting to fall from his mouth. Patrick twisted Blake's head toward the floor and Blake heaved safely onto his piled clothes and shoes.

Rounding the bed and grabbing the room keys and car keys out of the glass-tiered ashtray, Doug's voice reached an irritating tone of squelch. Apparently Patrick's disregard of anything he had to say brought Doug to the brink, but Patrick was already there. Pulling the blanket from naked Ellen's head, he pulled her up cupping her clothes in his arm and with the other punched Doug in the mouth just as the work "fuck" was launched in his direction, again.

Ellen sat quietly next to him as Patrick drove her in the direction of the university. She leaned slightly on the car door and Patrick feared she may throw up on herself.

"I don't know," she said to Patrick as he eyed the street signs searching for the street to the dorm he had dropped Geneiva off.

She didn't know where she lived. Great.

"I don't know why I let him fuck me." She swallowed some air, "in a room with you in it." Patrick slowed the car, he didn't know where he was but didn't think it was a good time to bring that up. "I don't know," she said again.

Patrick stopped the car at a curb and turned the car off.

"I just wanted to have some fun." Patrick nodded though she could not see him because she was not looking at him. Ellen's hair curtained her face in long sweat-locked clumps. She must have been nineteen, Patrick figured. He felt paternal and terrible that he had been there.

"I'm sorry," he told her and felt the desire to hold her, but resisted.

"Why are you sorry?"

"Because," is all that he could come up with.

Ellen shook her head not needing the rest of the sentence anyways. Patrick noticed that her hand shook as she pulled her hair behind her ears. An acrylic nail hung to the side of her natural nail as if on a hinge.

"Can you walk me to my door?" She asked. Patrick hoped that maybe he had miraculously found her street in all this confusion. Or maybe the car had found its own way, because he still didn't know where he was exactly.

"I want it to look like the end of a good date." Ellen opened her purse and with shaking hands brushed her hair and pulled the visor down to meet the mirror, applying lipstick to her lips and removed the mascara smudges from the apples of her cheeks. Her tremors lessened.

Patrick pulled up in front of the Hope Dorms, which was only a few blocks away, and thought of the irony of the name. She had just wanted to have fun. That is all Patrick had wanted when he agreed to take this journey as if fun had no rules. But it did. And the rules had been broken tonight.

He gave Ellen back her keys so she could open her door and stood on the stoop of the dorm entrance. No one was around, the lobby light was still glowing but inside the couches that furnished the community area were empty except for mismatched pillows.

"Good night." Patrick said in a low voice.

"Good night." Ellen replied and entered the dorm house.

It was at least a three-mile walk back to the motel and though he didn't have a watch Patrick knew it was about five in the morning. He walked through the neighboring housing complex for the students who had moved from campus housing to the next step which was comprised of lean-to housing with bikes in the front yard and dented trashcans filled with beer bottles and circled with what else didn't fit. No one stirred. As he made his way toward the center of town, a man opening the shades of his stuccoed home and woman and child still in pajamas walking a bow-legged dog passed him. On his walk Patrick repressed an acknowledgement that he could have convinced Ellen to have sex with him just then but instead had done the right thing, the thing he had not been doing for quite awhile. A moment of lack of self-loathing, then realization, he hadn't done the right thing after all. Ellen had slept with Doug and he hadn't intervened. He had slept with Geneiva and hadn't cared.

Patrick hopped on the train hours later with Blake and Doug in tow. They spent the next few days barely communicating with the other than to agree to keep riding the westward train. They crossed the Arizona state line early morning and within an hour Patrick jumped off in Abbott with his backpack, duffle bag and the decision not to return.

CHAPTER EIGHTEEN

A Good Kid

Patrick walked into the room saw Millie but concentrated on the absence of Grover. She stood in the kitchen in a short silk robe with a line of puffy feathers around the sleeves and clinging leggings. Apparently nap attire. Millie was a woman who exposed herself in every way but in no way did it seem obscene.

With soapy hands she answered him, pointing. "He's attending to his tomatoes, again," she pointed to an unseen location in the backyard. "I make him wait 'til now so he doesn't die of heat prostration." Millie set up onto her toes to find him through the kitchen window. "There he is with his hands in the manure," very matter-of-factly.

"Snack?" Millie asked, "some fruit? I can whip up a nice fruit salad." Patrick was starved but didn't want to miss an opportunity to talk with Grover, out of Millie's supervision or scorn.

"I'll call to you when it's ready," Millie knew Patrick's intent, and let it go.

Stepping out into the yard, it was surprisingly cool. The roof overhung a good two feet from the house and the damp coolness of the potting soil made an impression of rising moisture. Grover was spreading it generously using his spatula hands to pad it down even and firmly.

"Afternoon," he called gently wiping some dirt on to his face.

"Howdy" Grover padding down the soil looking toward a wicker basket of bounty. "Millie likes my butter boys, claims she needs them for the big dinner tonight." Grover shifted his weight on a pad under his knees. Patrick recognized the shape.

"That home plate?" He asked.

"Yep." Grover rose and in doing so brushed off the raised pentagonal cotton plate with his hand like an umpire's brush.

"Wasn't paid beans, but got some memorabilia I can put under my knees." Grover picked up the plate and tossed it into the open shed. He raised and stretched his back. "Probably could sell some of this junk at a flea market."

Nodding, "Listen Grover," Patrick started, "I'm sorry about what I said, about Anita."

Grover straightened a bit taller still and faced Patrick. He was surprised how tall he still stood, he had thought it was just his long arms but standing face to face, Patrick realized Grover didn't hump over though his age would have afforded him to.

"You don't need to apologize to an old man Patrick, they don't remember one insult to the next." Grover bended down to pick up the basket of tomatoes he has just harvested from the garden but Patrick reached them.

"I'll get that." Patrick watched again the rise of Grover's body after relinquishing the basket. He does remember.

"Well I am sorry."

Grover patted him on the shoulder or used him to rise up to full stand, or both. His age was showing though he worked at it not to. His big open palm took up his whole shoulder blade.

"You're a good kid Patrick," Grover lead into the house, but Patrick didn't follow at first. The words stung him. He thought of Ellen and Hope Hall at UT El Paso.

"But I'm not, Grover." Grover stopped on the top step. He stood adjacent to Millie who is in the kitchen window finishing her chore of washing the dishes in her pink feather boaed robe. If not for the glass and framing they would be standing next to each other.

"I've done some things." Patrick wanted to tell this old man more, wanted to recover from his self-hatred. Was this the first step, confession? But Grover was not his priest.

"Did you murder someone?" Grover asked bluntly.

"No." Patrick replied. The basket was getting heavier so he squeezed his grip and allowed it down a bit, still holding on.

"Then you're a good kid. You don't have to be a saint, just understand a few things that are wrong and walk away from them," Grover noticed the basket. "and don't pop those tomatoes or Millie will have our heads."

Patrick followed Grover into the house, surprisingly relieved that he was "a good kid", not that Grover knew anything about him and used a ridiculous measure to come to that conclusion. He was a good kid to Grover and that is what mattered to him at this moment.

CHAPTER NINETEEN

Space A19

The trailer was no more than three rooms, or maybe four if you counted the bathroom separately which wasn't done. Jennifer's room was in the back of the trailer and Nathan had a little room off the hallway that had no closet so his clothes were piled carefully on the shelves meant for linens, with the towels. She had put them in flowered cardboard boxes she got at Longs, but they collapsed into each other when she stacked them so she gave up and moved his clothes into the hallway. They didn't take up much room anyway.

Jennifer walked through the small trailer looking for the blue rubber ball Nathan had again thrown from his highchair. She got down on her knees to find it, leveling her eyes to the floor, in hopes that finding the ball would stop him from crying if only for a minute. Quiet minutes were precious but not expected during his witching hour.

When she finally found it under a tossed aside jacket and pair of old worn sneakers, Nathan had moved on to other things, sitting contently in the highchair fingering his peach mush and blowing bubbles of translucent pale orange spit. Jennifer sighed, she had to stop the maniac tendencies she'd developed in dealing with an infant. She took the foil off her dinner and began to eat quickly, trying to get food in before the crying. Tired, she's just tired. The dish was still in the cardboard tray Rusty delivered it in earlier. Months ago she would have taken the time to properly eat the food. At least place it on a plate. But Jennifer had found that it was easier not to dirty another one and the box top made it easier to clear the table. She opened the mashed potato container to let it cool some more before she shared it with Nathan, and ticked off in her head what Nathan had eaten today. Applesauce for breakfast and a banana, well half, he mashed the rest on his head, carrots for lunch with that nasty beef stew stuff and now peaches and potatoes. Jennifer plopped some string beans on his tray thinking he needed something green and hoping it would be enough.

Ever since she moved to Abbott Jennifer had been on food stamps. She's got to be the youngest in Rusty's rounds of Meals-on-Wheels and some of the other recipients felt she should be delivering, not accepting, though they would never say so. Hell, Rusty is well into his seventies. At those many moments when such thoughts make her become too self-conscious, she had considered moving, things must be better in a bigger town. At least people may not know so easily that at twenty you're taking charity. But the fear of taking her baby out of Abbott's kind embrace to a city like Phoenix terrified her. She had lived in bigger towns and the size may make it easier to hide but certainly lonelier. With a baby, hiding could not be her focus anymore.

Jennifer shouldn't have moved here at all but Tom, Nathan's father, thought he could get some work with a local silver recovery company who thought they could rape the land without detection and then leave it injured and wound-open. The county was too smart for that and chased the "Silver Thread Mineral Company" away before the sixth monthly payroll could even be calculated. Shortly after that Tom left and Jennifer was home alone with a three and a half month old baby. Jennifer had a job, but helping old people with their chores did not pay for all the necessities. It wasn't until she met Millie Flowers that Jennifer really thought this would be a good place to stay for a while.

Millie had come with Rusty on one of his dinner deliveries during the holidays. She had made pecan pie from the pecans her sister sent her from Houston and was in holiday cheer so had joined in the deliveries for the first time ever, kind of like going to church only for midnight mass. Rusty was not much of a talker and his conversation consisted of mumbled house numbers before they grabbed the cardboard box topped meals and headed for the doors. Millie was reaching her irritation point with him when they got to Jennifer's trailer. He was not only, not a talker, he was not a listener. Millie discovered this when half way through an interesting story, she asked a question. Rusty looked straight ahead gripping both hands on the wheel ten and two.

"Are you listening to me?" Millie blared.

"Space A19" was his response. She had never particularly liked Rusty because he kept to himself too much. She now wondered if anyone really did like him other than desperate widows.

Millie charged up the ripped astro-turf covered concrete steps thinking about giving Rusty a piece of her mind when she returned including to attack his name, hell he may have had red hair up to his thirties but he was an old man now and mainly bald. Rusty her ass. Maybe he was named for his personality. There wasn't much of one, but it was rusty.

Jennifer answered the door with Nathan on her hip and the sound of water slowly filling a bathtub in the background. She quickly took the cardboard box realizing it was the old lady from The Rusty Nail, and began to close the door, with a quiet "thank you," she didn't want her lectures. When Millie noticed that the young baby was very pale and his lips looked as if he had played in his mother's lipstick, she pushed the door back toward her but gently.

"Your baby has a fever." Millie said directly.

Jennifer looked at her and nodded. "I'm about to try to cool him off, it's up to 102." Her voice sounded weak and muffled. It was fear. It closes the throat.

Rusty was already backing up the car. This was the young mother Millie had met a month or so back-well not really met rather ran into at the bar with her overbearing boyfriend. She looked around as best she could and didn't hear nor see the man. Good maybe he was gone, maybe she had everything under control, or did she? She was in fact surprised when she had opened the door and accepted the food. Maybe there was someone else with her; an elderly grandmother in the house she was helping out? Rusty of course had not said anything. But even through the small crack in the door Millie now knew. This girl was on her own, poor and her baby was sick.

"You alone?" Milles asked.

"Yes." Jennifer answered.

Millie turned to Rusty through the open passenger window, "I'll call Grover - you go on." She motioned to Rusty with a flash of red squared nails.

Rusty waved his hand in acceptance and noticeable relief. Reversing the car to do the rest of the deliveries without her he would remember to reread his horoscope this evening. He seemed to remember that one of his lucky numbers was 19, the number of the trailer he was pulling away from.

Millie turned to Jennifer who still stood at the door, having put down the food next to her in the doorway. There was no table to put it. Millie opened the door wider and opened her arms.

"Let's get this baby in the bath, why don't we?" Jennifer who was overprotective with Nathan allowed him to go with this woman with the dyed red hair and heavy bangles on her wrist.

Nathan began to sleep calmly about an hour after Millie had sponged him down. She had prevented Jennifer from bundling him up in thick pajamas she had set out and instead he slept soundly with a sleeveless t-shirt and diapers allowing his body's temperature to regulate itself back to normal.

"When he wakes up just give him some more of the Tylenol. He'll hate it but feed it to him anyways." Jennifer nodded mutely. "Now let's get you something to eat." Millie walked past Jennifer into the narrow hallway and made her way to the kitchen reheating the turkey and dressing and spooning out the corn onto what appeared to be the only plate in the house.

"Do you have many kids?" Jennifer questioned, agreeing to "just go sit down and let me do this." Maybe she should have asked about grandchildren.

"No I don't have any. But I have a younger brother and well I was home a lot with him and now he and my sister have kids and their kids have kids and so on and so on..." Millie poured a tall glass of milk and set it in front of Jennifer. Jennifer didn't have the courage to tell her she despised milk and tried to sip it between mouthfuls using it more as a swallowing lubricant than a beverage.

It was there that night that Jennifer found a true friend in this old woman and decided she would try to stay here in Abbott until courage or circumstances took her elsewhere.

CHAPTER TWENTY

Rusty and Ralph

How Grover tolerated Millie Flowers, was beyond Rusty; way beyond. Seemed she never stopped talking. Nor for that matter did her best friend Rosie. He would say he appreciated the help with the deliveries if he was asked but later he would tell his brother-in-law the truth.

Rusty lived off of Elm not far from Millie and Grover with his widowed brother-in-law Ralph. They had moved down to Abbott together when Jackie passed away three years ago. He had not been very close to his sister growing up, as there were eight kids in the family, seven out of eight girls – he could barely keep them straight. He had been good friends though with Ralph who lived three houses down from them in their childhood Denver neighborhood. They were close in age, two years difference, so played a lot of street games together and then both played football for South High Varsity and Junior Varsity – neither were very good. Since Rusty stayed in the Denver area and Ralph and Jackie Denver-proper they spent a lot of time together as adults; and since Rusty never married, as they got older they spent even more time together. Rusty retired as an Accounting Manager with Shell Oil Company with 36 years under his belt and after ten more years of shoveling snow had enough and made plans to move to Arizona. He didn't care about how hot it got in the summer, he never wanted to see snow again. Ralph was preparing himself to miss his brother-in-law and good friend when Jackie slid on some black ice and hit oncoming traffic. Thirty-five years of marriage was over in an instant.

Ralph was lost. He had retired two years earlier but Jackie had kept on teaching; elementary school. Months after her death he still received the pitied stares and "Sorry for your loss." It all made sense, she was a beloved teacher in the community with students, parents of students and parents who had been her students. Ralph stopped going to the store ever, filled his car with gas late at night and drove up to Evergreen just to avoid Jackie's mourners.

Rusty knew he was having a difficult time but who wouldn't be. He even understood the late night escapes. Rusty enjoyed solitude himself. But as Rusty finalized particulars with the moving company on when to pick up and pack up, he added Ralph's address to their work order. Waiting one night in Ralph's driveway, he met him as the garage door was raised when Ralph made the turn into the long drive. Rusty got out of his own car and followed him into the garage meeting him at the driver's side. Ralph stayed seated for a minute; he had seen his brother-in-law but was feeling vulnerable and not ready to carry a conversation even with him. Rusty finally opened the door for him.

"How're the mountains?" he asked.

"Fine," he rolled his heavy body out of the old Scout. Rusty closed the door and followed Ralph into the kitchen.

Over the clatter of Ralph's keys hitting the counter, Rusty advised, "Been thinking."

"Yeah?" Ralph answered.

Repeating, "Been thinking, " then "you should join me in Arizona." He hadn't adequately thought about how he was going to approach Ralph on this. "There is Flagstaff if you miss the mountain drives."

Ralph smiled, sadly. "I'd like that Rusty."

"Well good cuz' the truck is coming at the end of the week. The kids are coming over tomorrow to help with Jackie's stuff."

What he had thought about was how Ralph needed to go through Jackie's things. It was a delicate situation he'd left to Ralph and his adult kids, Marisela and Ivan, and his other sisters, but with the move they needed to do it now. It was better this way-just get it done.

"Tomorrow?" Ralph sat down on one of the bar stools at the kitchen counter. Rusty stood at the opposite end like a bartender facing him and watched as the big man's shoulders started to fold-in and his breath heaved. In a slow forward lean he took his brother-in-law in his arms and held him even when the counter cut off the circulation to his gut.

Rusty and Ralph now lived like the town bachelors, more physically fit than most of the men their age they seemed to be flirted with wherever they went in Abbott. Rusty acted reluctant, most of the time. For the first few years Ralph was just too sad but as the three year mark hit in April he seemed to enjoy in the attention and was now "going' steady" with Kezia Mallory an old Irish woman from Chicago. He seemed content and so did Rusty, especially on the nights he delivered Meals-on-Wheels alone.

TWENTY-ONE

Day Two at Millie Flowers'

illie laid out from his duffle bag what he was to wear. When not finding a "good" shirt, Patrick did stop her at her suggestion that he wear one of Grover's golf shirts instead of the concert t-shirt that was from Boston when they played back in Boston. She ironed his jeans, he had never seen this done before, and laundered all the rest of his clothes though some of them were clean. "Take advantage of your circumstances," she told him as she rewashed the rest of his socks adding some baking soda into the mix to "soften those stiff toes and heels."

Precisely at 6 Jennifer appeared at the door with Nathan in tow. Grover answered and gave her a peck on the cheek as if greeting a beloved granddaughter. Nathan pulled to get down and Jennifer let him scurry off on all fours in the direction of the kitchen to where he attached himself to the rapidly moving leg of Millie doing final dinner preparations. Millie launched commands at Rosie, as she in her flowing floral moo-moo pulled pots from the stove and poured tall glasses of iced teas.

Patrick wasn't sure exactly what to do with himself. He stood in the living room and drew the shade as Millie instructed from the kitchen. He needed the task. Grover went to retrieve a larger trash bag, "because you know that tall kitchen one will not hold my chicken bone tailings." Suddenly Patrick and Jennifer were left in the room alone. Something they both feared.

"So have you known Millie and Grover long?" he asked, "though trying to remember if they had covered this before.

"Almost a year, or a bit more," Jennifer said and still trying to escape yelled to Millie to see if she needed help. She was told "no."

"Is Nathan being a pest?" Jennifer called.

"Not at all. I need you to entertain the young man while I boil some more potatoes. Don't think we have enough."

Jennifer sighed a little too loudly, and Patrick laughed, "Can't escape. Trapped." He ventured, "Does she do this to you often?"

"What?" Jennifer asked, innocently, but not pulling it off.

"Fix you up. I mean invite you to dinner to meet someone."

"No." Jennifer blushed and Patrick saw that though olive-skinned she reddened high on her checks like a fair-skinned person. "Not many men even close to my age live here, so no not often." Jennifer added nervously. "Anyways she's not fixing us up."

Patrick felt immediately embarrassed, realizing he had made an assumption openly, one he should have held to himself.

"Course she is Jenny," Grover grumbled as he met them back in the living room his chore complete. "She'd do it to anyone else if anyone else here in Abbott were under seventy." Grover winked at Jennifer and raised an eyebrow back at Patrick.

"He's a good catch, except he murdered someone." Grover moved to his chair.

"What!?" Patrick startled a yell.

"You have?" Jennifer questioned amused at the game. "Crime of passion or drive by? I might have an issue with a random killing but due to passion could be intriguing." It was easy to see that Jennifer loved the banter Grover provided, and the break from the awkwardness.

Patrick grinned at her somewhat disturbing humor, liking the fact that she was joining in the game so quickly. An ability to recover; impressive.

"Maybe it wasn't murder, maybe it was grand theft auto. No wouldn't be that either, since he came in on a train." Grover smiled broadly.

Patrick found himself mute wanting to join the banter but not quick enough to.

"Don't take yourself so seriously Patrick, they got you too full of mess in your head at that law school." Grover got more comfortable in his chair.

Jennifer's smile faded and she stood up to retrieve Nathan who had now migrated down the hallway, scooting right past them. She scooped him up, "I think I'll help Millie."

"So, you met Jennifer yesterday? Guess that's not hard to do in this town." Grover motioned him over to the recliners.

"Yeah, she was strolling with Nathan."

"Nice girl, Jennifer Mullen. You don't have to marry her to make Millie happy though, OK?" Lowering his voice, "But you should know that Jennifer hasn't been too lucky in love. The father is a real piece of work. What kind of man leaves his young wife and newborn child?" Grover said.

Patrick shook his head agreeing, he had been told this. He didn't want to go any further down this road, but he didn't want to shut Grover down either. He felt he was still treading on thin ice with his earlier fumble. He wanted to be a good kid.

Patrick was just passing what appeared to be corn and peas mixed together to Jennifer on his right, when there was a knock at the door and Millie's thin sharp elbow nudged him.

"Can you get that Patrick? That will be Manuel." Patrick rose, not knowing who Manuel was and silently wondering why he was the one retrieving him when he was the farthest from the door. Millie's moves were calculated so there was a reason.

Manuel stood at the door shyly a grey felt cowboy hat in his hands. "Good evening." he greeted.

"Hello." Patrick answered in return.

"You must be Millie's young friend." Manuel said but didn't move from the step.

"Yes," he extended his hand "Patrick Emery."

"Manuel Rodriguez, pleased to meet you." Still, he didn't make a move to enter.

"Would you like to come in?" Patrick questioned.

"Yes, very much." Manuel seemed truly grateful. But when he entered he was met with a growling stare. Though it took a tug at the back of the chair to make the turn, Rosie turned to face him.

"One hour ago. I asked you to be here one hour ago." Rosie refolded the napkin on to her large lap.

Manuel nodded acknowledgement and gently greeted Grover and Millie with a bow, then a small wave to Jennifer; and a grin to Nathan.

Jennifer waved back amused.

Rosie huffed and scooped another pile of potatoes on to her plate. There may not be enough. Though Patrick believed they were husband and wife, neither did anything more to acknowledge each other, other than the smoldering scowl on Rosie's part. Manuel took his seat next to her and accepted the vegetable mix from Grover. He looked at the mix carefully before scooping it onto his dish. Then, he carefully separated the three vegetables before taking a bite.

Jennifer told Patrick later that, "Manuel is the sweetest man on earth. But he can't stand his wife. He would never leave her or cause her any true grief, so what he has chosen to do is be consistently late to everything." Patrick thought, that had to be admired.

Patrick and Jennifer were able to talk a bit through the meal once they got over the fact that the other four people would be listening intently. Patrick brought up school a few times, just because it was a familiar topic of discussion for him; something easy to fall back on when you don't know what else to say. Though if truth be told law school was of little interest to him.

Jennifer asked more about growing up in Massachusetts and what that was like. She was from Flagstaff, Arizona, which was apparently very different than the other parts of Arizona and told him it was there in the winter she had dreams of moving to some place like Maine or even Massachusetts. Jennifer's expressions were fresh and animated and Patrick admired the way she handled a restless young toddler without having to stop a conversation. Nathan looked like her, with her black hair and delicate green eyes. Patrick imagined that she didn't lose the chubbiness of her cheeks until she was in at least her late teens like one of his sisters.

Nathan made flat layers of the whipped potatoes on his plate, Grover playfully added peas to his spread. Nathan giggled through the challenge of finding the green within the white and mushing the lumpy balls into the smooth surface.

"Only way I could get Charlotte to eat the peas," Grover shared.

"It works." Jennifer said gratefully.

In the lull between dinner and dessert Patrick decided to talk about school again. "Did you go to college?" he asked. Trying to find a subject, which would allow more than a few sentences of exchange.

"No," Jennifer replied politely. "I've never done much really."

Patrick felt uncomfortable with the measure he had insinuated. "Well I wonder why I'm bothering, I'm a little tired of it." he stated dismissively.

"Why did you go to law school then?" Nathan spit/coughed out a pea and Jennifer caught it in her palm.

"I didn't know what else to do." Patrick was shocked at his own admission; he didn't know where it came from.

Jennifer looked at him curiously, "but there's so much to do." It was such a contradiction to her own defeating comments.

Patrick examined her features as she turned to address a question from Grover who was now bouncing Nathan on his leg. She was truly beautiful. Her eyes squinted when she smiled which was often. There was an even sprinkling of freckles on her tanned cheeks and her chin. She was maybe 4 to 5 years younger than Patrick, and looked like such a child when she told him "there's so much to do," and yet she spoke with an older, knowing voice when she had stated "I've never done much really."

Millie presented the guests with her pecan pie a la' mode. Along with the pie she set out little Dixie cups with pecans, "just in case you want to snack between bites or add them to the top." When Millie talked about the pie her Texas drawl was revealed, not that it wasn't always there it just became more noticeable when she talked of anything Southern.

Even "potatoes" held the "os" too long. "Iced tea", emphasized the hard "I", "fried chicken" the "fry" and when she called you "honey" the word spread out over a few sentences.

During the evening Rosie and Millie had been constantly picking at how each of them performed a task, "Don't put the bowls away until they are completely dry, or they'll never dry stacked in that cabinet," Rosie complained to Millie though they were Millie's dishes.

"Onions should be diced, not left in long strips that sting your teeth when you bite into them," Millie barked as she hovered over the salad preparation.

When everyone was stuffed full, Manuel and Grover retreated to the back porch, to "take a nip." The two old men made a show of sneaking out the door with a small bottle of whiskey hardly hidden.

Nathan had fallen asleep in Millie's arms, almost as soon as Jennifer had passed him to her.

"He never does that with me," Jennifer said, but looked relieved watching the pulsing lids of her son.

Millie smiled content, rolling Nathan in closer toward her.

"Why don't you two take a walk into town, I'll put Nathan down. When he's ready to commit."

"Into town?" Patrick started to laugh.

"Hey, it's Saturday night in Abbott, Arizona, you'd be surprised." Jennifer nudged him playfully with her slim shoulder.

Patrick couldn't imagine that the streets didn't roll up at sunset, an expression he had never much thought of until now as he watched in his mind's eye The Trading Post shades drawn, the building itself turning on to its side and rolling up into the gas station with the gas pumps sticking up and out of the roll like bad teeth.

Jennifer nodded to Millie who pushed herself farther back into the couch so that Nathan's legs fell over her arm and onto the seat. His cheeks rumble in a simulated suck. "Leave a bottle and be gone," she said resolutely, almost rudely Patrick thought until he looked at how happy this old woman was with a baby in her lap. She was not rude she was begging for time to spend with a new life.

CHAPTER TWENTY-TWO

Seeds

He was known in Abbott as the Melon King. As long as he could remember Manuel loved to have his hands in the dirt. The cool chopped-up dirt of a cultivated field, or the cracked dry land of the desert floor with wisps of powdery mist, all presented possibilities to him, literal layers of other worlds. He loved it here, with all the dust and challenges of water it was still fertile ground for his work and it was work he could see in all its stages. Growing things was Manny's passion. The top dirt provided surface, but just below it, were the possibilities of life.

His young life in Tartan pueblo in Michoacán, Mexico was surrounded by harsh and sultry truths and the sheer possibilities of the earth. His father was a farmer who grew squash and melons. He had done so decades before Manny was born. The varieties changed with the seasons but always there was a steady cycle of planting and harvesting. These cycles gave him his own life cycle - he liked the rhythm. There was order and predictability, but with a bit of risk. In Mexico, it was what they called sustainable farming. At each harvest select bountiful fruits were set aside for their seeds alone. The seeds carefully attended to, wrapped for preservation in cheesecloth, catalogued with variety names and dates, and then placed in the dug-down earthen shed whose temperature while protecting the seeds did not get them comfortable enough to sprout. It was a delicate balance. Manuel had helped with the catalogue tags, carefully writing the information in Spanish, English and Latin, swaddling them attentively and shelving them for the next

season's planting. The Rodriguez family had
lived this way for centuries as far as the stories
went, planting, harvesting and cataloguing. They
were not poor, but working poor. His mother sold
the squash or other produce grown, by the
roadside and to small vendors in town. Later the
family sold to brokers who then shipped the fruit
to the United States. In U.S, supermarkets,
Manuel still looked for "grown in Mexico"
stickers, thumped and sniffed the produce for
good measure and smiled. Available evidence of
his life's work. He had chosen his profession well.
He may have married the wrong woman, but at
least he had the dirt.

Living on the family farm was the life Manuel
thought he was to have, but his mother Marta,
thought differently. Marta watched her son in
the fields, tasting dirt to determine iron content,
running his boots gently over a berm to loosen
pebbles around honeydew plants, his heart not
just his head was in the work. That would
suggest he become a successful farmer, his father
was and those before him, but there was more for
Manuel.

When he was about fifteen years old Manuel sat on the tripod leather stool at the vegetable roadside stand one June day. He held in his hand a summer squash, rubbing it with his right hand and then patting it lightly. Marta watched him all his senses dedicated to the specimen, and asked him in Spanish, "What are you thinking Mijo?"

There had not been a customer in the last 30 minutes, "Why this squash stopped growing."

"Stopped growing?" she reached for the fruit and Manny easily handed it over to her, "it grew until it was ready."

"No Mama," Manny pointed to the belly of the squash, it could have grown three more centimeters." He demonstrated the distance with his thumb and index finger.

"They are always this size." His mother said.

"That's because there are not enough nutrients in the soil," his faced scrunched either from the sun he was staring into or the belief he had just spoken of so strongly.

"Manny, your Papa is very careful with the soil, you know that."

"I know Mama, but maybe he doesn't know. This valley is missing nitrogen and potassium those would help the squash grow bigger." He takes back the fruit from his mother's hand, "and they want to grow bigger, if they do there are more seeds. More to replant."

Marta Rodriguez looked at her son. He spoke of the vegetables as beings.

"Where did you hear about this?"

Manny carefully pulled out a small booklet from his back pocket and steadied himself back on the stool. In fancy script with pictures behind the booklet reads "Farmers Almanac."

"Mijo your Papa knows about all that. That is the bible of the farmer." Marta looked up for silent permission to make such a comparison. It was a truth so she looked back down.

Manny ran his finger down a Table of Contents on one of the first few pages, stopped and then read, "Central Mexico Farming in the 1880s and Soil Health." Before Marta could protest that they are into the next century and the information is old, Manny continues. "This valley of Tzirondaro once rich with nitrogen was stripped of the key nutrient due to farmer's previous practice of single crop farming." He looked up, "See Mama, farmers didn't know that when you farm one crop you use up some of the soil's nutrient. They don't come back unless you plant a crop that is its opposite-there's a word for it." Manny struggled to recall but didn't want to delay the story, "You have to reintroduce it through another crop or give vitamins to the soil and ready for tilth."

Marta could not help but grin, "Vitamins for the soil? That's what fertilizers and manure do Mijo."

"Not always." Manny looked at the article again with a tightened brow.

Marta looked at the cover this is a very old edition of the Almanac. "Manny is this from Mr. Garza's library?"

Mr. Garza was the town "historian" who kept just about every publication of everything he could get his hands on. Manny loved spending time going through the piles of newspapers, magazines and journals. Others in the small pueblo were not as respectful and considered Jaime Garza a pack rat, and a fire hazard.

"Yes and just because it's old doesn't mean it's not true. It is." Manny looked off toward the road with the squash still cradled in his hands like a baby, like a being.

Marta studied his face. His gaze gives her the opportunity.

"Did you know there are plant breeders?" he looked as his mother, focused on her still troubled face, "They come up with new varieties of vegetables and fruits." Marta has heard of this, but never really thought about it. She knew about farming from seed to harvest, but not that much of the science behind it.

"They do? What do these breeders do exactly?" she asked.

"They are like gods, Mama, they put cells together with the characteristics they want and make new plants. Stronger and bigger ones. Ones that don't need nutrients not in the soil."

"Gods?" Marta wasn't sure about this and made the sign of the cross and kissed her hand. There would be no permission granted here. If this is what they did, were they disturbing God's order? Marta did not look-up this time. Years later Marta thought back on this and was glad she hadn't voiced this fear. Manuel was still an observant man in his adult years, yet he was a very clever scientist.

From that point on with the urgings and support of his parents, Manuel worked toward understanding every biologic science related to growing vegetables both from on-the-farm experience, his small pueblo based school and his readings from Mr. Garza's library. His parents could not ignore the passion when he spoke of the science of breeding, higher yielding, more resistant varieties. With the help of the town, his parents, and from perseverance at nineteen he received a scholarship to the University of California, Davis in the States to study agriculture. It was the premier agricultural school for such studies and this young boy from the pueblo of Tartan in the state of Michoacán had been asked to study there.

CHAPTER TWENTY-THREE

Swing Jazz

The I Street Music Store was in downtown Sacramento, wedged between a deli with great kosher pickles and a fabric store. Rosie worked all day Saturday and from 3:30 to closing at 7:00 Monday through Friday, except when there was orchestra practice which was to be Thursdays but many times was canceled due to Mr. Morris' health, or rather his love of the gin bottle. The owner, Mr. Kowalski let Rosie work even when she wasn't scheduled on Thursdays just because he liked her company and knew idol time of a teenager could be dangerous. He certainly preferred her company over Shaina Owens who stiff-backed and click-heeled was good at keeping inventory but talking about music was not her forte. She lacked the passion Rosie had in abundance.

Rosie had not known Manuel when she was a growing up in her tight knit family of five. No, she had not grown up in Mexico like him, but was born following her own parent's crossing into the California desert. She was a citizen but she did not have a birth certificate, which proved to be a problem as she got older - being born at home outside of the visibility of the authorities. When Rosie was a teenager she worked wherever she could, places that wouldn't ask for the proper papers. It was known in the tight-knit immigrant community who would turn an eye to the legal requirements and who would turn their backs on illegals. Since there was no proof of her actual citizenship she fell into that category of uncertainty. Many of the positions available were what was to be imagined, maid work, work in the fields, but at sixteen she was finally lucky to get a job at the small record store downtown. Mr.

Kowalski was an immigrant himself, but not from Mexico, but Poland far away and tucked into the communist block. Rosie knew little of Europe and even less of Eastern Europe, and honestly would tell her family she only cared that Serge Kowalski did not notice she had left the section on "right to work in the U.S." blank. She was proud she hadn't lied and happy he hadn't asked.

In school Rosie played the violin. She was not particularly talented and was second chair, barely, but she loved the music. Everything about it, the complexity of an arrangement, figuring out where she came in and the other instruments met and made music together. Learning to read music had been challenging for her but she had done it. It had been like learning a new math equation. She did not have one form of music that she liked over the other. Classical was what she played in school, but she also like country and folk in which the violin became a fiddle. That would be an act of heartless favoritism. But she would admit that some of her favorite fiddling came out of Nova Scotia, some far away place in Canada. They did reels there and moved their feet to the music. If she was forced to choose maybe she liked that the best, for her instrument at least. But for the other instruments of music she loved big band. Tommy Dorsey, Glen Miller were gods to her - something she didn't share with her devout mother. Maybe that's why Mr. Kowalski ignored that box. They would spend what amounted to hours each week talking music. He loved to expand her world of musical knowledge with new talent and new genres and many a time motioned her to join him in a listening booth. She loved his passion and thought he was a man who had truly found his calling; though he admitted to her he had no actual musical talent "couldn't play a darn instrument, not even the triangle." In his more somber moments he confided, "music brings him home."

Joining in with Nat King Cole one afternoon, as it hummed from one of the listening rooms, and counting change from the register to balance the till, a young man came through the door looking very focused but a bit out of place. He was clearly Mexican and bore the stripe of a fieldworker with a line of lighter skin exposing past his half sleeves as he walked. But curiously his shoulders were not rolled into his chest from the low pulling of plants rather seemed to have an unusual tightness to them that pulled them back. He moved toward the big band section of the store and started to finger through the artists. Rosie tried to see where he was pausing. He looked to be in the "H"s. Woody Herman, interesting. Al Hirt, a favorite. Suddenly he looked up and straight at Rosie. She looked down and out loud counted, "twenty-one" which was not where she was at all. "Darn it," she said under her breath. Concentrating again, she began to re-count the change in the till.

Mr. Kowalski came out of a listening booth with Nat, clicking off the light inside and started to head to the back of the store to his office. They were closing soon and he would want the drawer count from her. But he stopped midway and approached the young man.

"Help you with anything son?"

The young man kept one hand in the record bin to keep his place, "Just browsing sir. Thank you."

Kowalski nodded, "Let us know if you have questions. We are closing in a few minutes but no rush. Rosie can help you." He smiled and headed to the back.

Rosie looked up and nodded to acknowledge she was Rosie, the young man smiled and returned to his search.

As Rosie put the last tick on the register sheet and closed the drawer, the young man left. "Have a good evening," Rosie called out.

"Thank you, you too." He returned politely.

It wasn't until about two weeks later that Rosie saw him again. He walked into the store and went directly to the big band bins or what Mr. Kowalski has recently labeled "Swing Jazz" in his artful attempt at category signage. He filed through the selection but this time approached the counter within minutes where Rosie was sorting LP needles delicately, placing them in their protective packaging.

"Afternoon miss, I'm looking for a Al Hirt record. There was an album a few weeks ago. Do you know has it been sold?"

Rosie, put down the bundle of small envelopes, "Let me see." She stepped down off of the platform. Ms. Owens would know off the top of her head but Rosie did not catalogue every sale as they happened.

Rosie and Manuel walked together to the bins and looking through the H's and G's and I's just to be sure, confirming the album had been sold. "Sorry but we do get shipments in weekly."

"OK, thank you," the young man tried not to look defeated, but had a hard time hiding his dismay.

"If you like big band, how about Glen Miller or The Dorsey Brothers," she added.

"I like the trumpet, I think Glen Miller is only the trombone."

"Actually he also plays the clarinet and some strings, mandolin I think, he's just known for the trombone." Rosie offered enthusiastically, she turned to pull some albums and found a Glen Miller album with some clarinet music.

Manuel paused and then connected eyes with Rosie for the first time, it was unclear whether he was really interested in other instruments Glen Miller played or maybe just interested in the conversation. Not being able to detect which, Rosie started walking to a listening booth with the record in hand and surprisingly he followed.

Given the length of time he was in the booth, the young man had clearly listened to both sides of the record. Rosie had hoped he would, but as it always put the condition of the album at risk when someone listened to it all the way through. Really the booths were just for sampling. She hoped Ms. Owens had cleaned the needles like she was supposed to upon opening the store each morning- one scratch could be her paycheck.

With a click of the booth light switch and a gentle closing of the door, he walked toward her with the record in his hand.

"This is quite good. I'll take it." and put it on the counter as Rosie rang him up.

Before taking the bagged record and receipt from her, he commented, "I'll check back for that Al Hirt. Really need that one." "Need," Rosie liked that. "What day do you get your shipments?"

"Thursdays, every week. So if it is not in this week, you can always keep checking."

Manuel nodded, smiled and wished her a good evening, as once again it was closing time.

On Thursday she made her way to orchestra practice arriving about 3:30 after Civics class and on this particular Thursday Mr. Morris decided to show. She should be happy, he had missed the last few weeks and she had missed playing Wagner, which was now the composer of choice for Mr. Morris. But why did he have to be there on this Thursday? Rosie found it hard to concentrate. Where the harshness of Wagner's compositions usually swept her away, today they throbbed her temples pressing in like a headache.

When Rosie got to the shop on Friday, she asked about the shipment. Ms. Owens of course had checked everything in and all stock that needed to be out was now in its proper bins. Rosie didn't see Al Hirt in the H's, and through futile checked the packing sheet properly placed in the received file. No, no Al Hirt had been received – she smiled and folded the paper replacing it.

It was not for another few weeks that the young man would come in again. Rosie had practice on the next few Thursdays, but saw when she arrived on a Friday the Al Hirt record, received had not yet been claimed.

About 6:45 the door chimed and Manuel entered. He saw Rosie at the counter and without checking the bin approached her, "Hello, wanted to see if you got that Hirt album in?"

"Actually we did," she smiled warmly and rounded the counter. She counted her blessings it had not been sold the weeks that followed its arrival.

"How are you enjoying the Glen Miller?" she asked as she rung up the sale.

The young man shuffled his feet a bit, "I think I prefer the trumpet," he looked up tentatively.

"Oh, I hope you don't regret the purchase?"

"No, no but I have been excited about this one," he patted the record to his chest affectionately as Rosie handed it to him.

"Do you play?" she asked.

"No, I don't, my family is very musical though. I was the only one without ability so my ability is the love of music." His grin had some humor to it. Humor, humility this attracted Rosie Chacon to Manuel Rodriguez.

At the time they met he was a student at UC Davis, 19 and full of an inward ambition that was visible to everyone. He studied botany and in his upper classman years focused on plant breeding. He liked Cucurbita and Cucurbitaceaes, which

Rosie came to understand where squash and melons. His family lived in a small pueblo in Mexico the largest big city being Guadalajara but neither of his parents had ever been there; to the big city that is. He had two older brothers who had farms nearby his parents. His grandparents, both sets still alive, lived with his parents in a small house on their shared land.

Rosie's parents liked that Manuel came from a traditional Mexican family, but her father voiced why had they never wanted to come to the U.S.? That had been such a driving force in her own father's life that he couldn't understand why it wasn't for others. Manuel explained, as best he could, "he owns his land." Rosie's father paused and looked across the room and slowly nodded. It was now understood. What was not understood was what Manny studied. Rosie called him a plant scientist who many times picked her up for dates sweating manure and never seemed able to clean all the dirt from under his fingernails. Once when she met him on campus, she had wanted to see where he went to school, he met her in the Quad with round imprints of dirt embedded around his eyes. "Microscope", he answered casually. He was an intense student.

Manuel brought produce from the university greenhouses to Rosie's mother. Much of it was the standard fare varieties but a few were some of the breeding experiments. Manuel was a rule follower, and they were not supposed to take experimental varieties out of the greenhouses but he felt it was such a waste and was rather proud of some of them so bent the rules a bit. Mrs. Chacon loved it and was always coming up with recipes to incorporate the vegetables, though Mr. Chacon was tiring of squashes. A chutney mix with jalapeño and yellow squash was the favorite of everyone else. Mrs. Chacon started making it and giving it away as small gifts, which Mr. Chacon supported, less for him.

CHAPTER TWENTY-FOUR

A Lack of

Choices

The Rusty Nail was the place to be on a Saturday night and Patrick and Jennifer had to wait for a table to come available. This was one of the two restaurants in the town of Abbott "proper", and if you wanted an evening out, this is where you went since the other eating establishment closed at two in the afternoon. Patrick looked inside as they waited their turn, sitting on the narrow sagging wooden porch. At one table sat a small, hump-backed man by himself though four chairs made up his table's entire seating. Most of the other occupants were younger than Millie and Grover, but not by much. Two old men sat at the small bar smoking cigarettes and drinking beer. Beside them were three women, about ten years younger than the men, enjoying what appeared to be wine coolers from tapered glass bottles. One of the women was Esther Begay, who appeared cheery and more lively than she had at The Post even raising her bottle to Jennifer with a smile. When she looked to Patrick she seemed to recognize him, but didn't offer him a similar toast. Instead she gave him a deep examination that seemed to go from serious furrow to a slight abiding smile. Not ready to pass full judgment yet, but developing an opinion. The five tables that made up the entire eating area were all full of people eating meals or just drinking and talking.

"In Boston we would just go in and join him." Patrick commented pointing to the old solitary man with his nose.

Jennifer looked over in the direction his nose-point led, "Then people in Boston are braver than me," she turned back to face the street.

The man's mouth seemed to move in active conversation. He moved his head to the other side as if to address the chair to his left equally as to the one on his right. The one in front of him was being ignored. At right arm's length was a half-consumed beer, a bowl of pretzels down to the dregs and three glasses of water centered on each rim of the table.

"Who is he?" Patrick asked.

Jennifer reluctantly bowed her head toward Patrick, "Chuck Love." She was about to say something more but didn't and shoved her hands into her pants pockets sliding her legs straight out to do so, something Patrick did himself when he was uncomfortable and didn't know what to do with his hands, or a conversation.

"Someone, or three, seems to have already joined him." Patrick looked toward him again.

"He's crazy Patrick. No, no one will be joining him and no one will ask to sit in those seats or borrow a chair here or if we were in Boston." She paused, "He thinks they're with him and he'll freak out if anyone claims they can't actually see them."

"Who?"

"Aliens."

"From outer space?"

"No, Mexico. Yes, from outer space. He believes he was abducted some twenty years ago and instead of taking him with them, they joined him here on earth." Jennifer got up crossed over to Patrick's left side as a couple of retirees vacated the small two-top table. They saw a signal from a waitress and sat down at the table in front.

"The creepy thing is," Jennifer said as she took her seat across from him because the jukebox music was surprisingly loud, "he can tell the future."

"The aliens gave him that ability?" Patrick asked a bit sarcastically.

"Yeah, supposedly. I guess."

A rusty-haired woman appeared between them blocking any further view of Chuck Love.

"Well Jen, haven't seen you venture out in awhile."

"Hi, Mona," Jennifer greeted her with an uncomfortable wrist-flip wave. Mona looked at Patrick as if he would confess what his connection was with Jennifer.

"We'd just like some drinks, Mona."

"OK Sugar." Mona tapped her order pad as if she was Flo in Mel's Diner. It was remarkable how many Flos inhabited this town and all seemed to have the same shade of red hair. Maybe hair dye choices were limited.

"I'll have a tap beer."

"Same here please. Whatever you have." Patrick added.

"I have some cobbler left and some ribs if you're hungry at all. It'll all be gone by the time that next table fills up." Mona said but it was not out of generosity, rather a further attempt to find out who this boy was with Jennifer Mullen.

"Thanks, but we just came from Millie's." Jennifer offered up too much. Patrick saw Jennifer flinch at the revelation.

"Ah. Friend of Millie's?" Mona inquired allowing her hip to roll to one side and rest her arms on it in a too dramatic fashion.

"Well kind of." Patrick wasn't sure of his place and got the feeling from Jennifer that he didn't want to say much to this woman.

"Friend of mine." Jennifer offered, possibly maybe it would be enough.

"Ah." Mona motioned the two men who hovered in the doorway to take the vacated seats at the table in the middle of the restaurant.

"You waste no time," and she was off to retrieve their beers.

Patrick tried to read Jennifer. This time he couldn't. Why had she associated him with her? What was that "time" comment? But Jennifer's attention didn't linger on Mona instead it was again on Chuck Love who bellowed a laugh that could be heard over the croon of Waylon Jennings on the jukebox. He pointed a skinny index finger to the air that inhabited the chair to the left and blew his nose on a cocktail napkin. Patrick watched with amusement but Jennifer's expression was something else.

"Jennifer, you OK?" Patrick ventured after her look of pity turned quickly.

"Yeah. It's just sad not to have anyone to talk to but empty chairs."

Mona arrived with their drinks and two dishes of cobbler for the newly seated bar men, who clearly did not ask for it but thanked her anyways.

"Well you missed the cobbler." Mona grumbled as she delivered their drinks and went to replace the pretzel bowl at Chuck Love's table.

Jennifer looked at her watch. "She doesn't have a freezer so she has to throw out the food she doesn't sell in a night. She got busted by the health department for keeping the leftovers in the bar ice. That's why you never order something on the rocks at The Rusty Nail," Jennifer advised with a smirk.

After thirty minutes of watching Mona distribute the remaining food to the room, she arrived in front of Chuck Love as he was paying his bill and placed in his hands Styrofoam containers and foil wrapped leftovers. Chuck made room for his alien friends to walk out before him and they left the bar. Through the window Patrick watched as the old man walked the middle of the street toward the mountains' silhouette appearing to chuckle along the way at some new joke the air around him had delivered.

"She doesn't like me." Jennifer finally confessed to Patrick as she avoided another one of Mona's glances. She sounded like a schoolgirl who had been shunned by the "cool kids."

"Why?" Patrick asked.

"Well she liked Tom. He drank here all the time."

"Tom?"

"I would have thought Millie told you my whole past. She certainly knows it all." Jennifer took a slow sip of her beer and then positioned the bottle back on to the damp cocktail napkin turning it squarely. "Tom is Nathan's dad. We moved to Abbott together, he left oh about five months ago, moved to Tempe I think. Anyways Mona and Tom used to stay up and drink here all night. She took his side on everything even on raising Nathan - not that Tom had any valuable opinion on that." Jennifer's voice started to swell in resentment. Her voice had changed away from schoolgirl.

Looking at Mona across the restaurant, "Why did we come here then?" Patrick meant for it to be a casual question but it wasn't exactly delivered that way.

Jennifer's voice changed now to scratchy and raw, "because there's nowhere else to go Patrick. This is Abbott." She ripped at the wet napkin.

Patrick felt a wave of uncomfortable sympathy for Jennifer, young mother, who had obviously no reason to live in this desert retirement other than she didn't have the means to leave. Patrick speculated that she could not return home after the debacle of fleeing with a drunk and had to suffer the scrutiny of a nosey lopsided waitress and a town who either viewed her with pity or resented her youth.

Patrick looked over at Mona again knowing Mona was now looking at Jennifer directly having heard the emotional rise in her voice. This was easy material for Mona. Without knowing anything more about her he knew that she would needle Jennifer over this "scene."

Jennifer's face reddened as she held back her tears. Patrick reached toward her with his reserve cocktail napkin in his hand and with his right hand he cupped her elbow, and from close range wiped her eyes. She was not the least bit startled and watched his eyes as he took care to follow the trail her tears had left. He brought down his hand and squeezed her hand but still didn't say a word. Slowly he sat back in his chair pulling her clasped hands toward him.

"Let's go," he said quietly. She couldn't hear him over the music but she could read his lips.

Passing Mona, Patrick plopped a twenty-dollar bill on her tray.

"Good Night," he said rounding Jennifer's back so that Mona would not have a chance to further comment.

They walked quietly down the street together, closer than before but not openly intimate to anyone watching.

"I'm sorry." Jennifer mumbled chewing her lips.

"For what? You have nothing to be sorry for." Jennifer seemed to consider.

"Why do people apologize so quickly?" Patrick was going to say more but didn't want it to sound like he was criticizing her in particular.

"People don't, women do." Jennifer said.

Patrick thought of Ellen. Putting on her makeup in her own passenger side mirror, pretending she was returning from a date of dinner and a movie with someone who respected her. He thought of his mother saying, "I'm sorry" as his father shuffled off.

Nathan was up and fussy when they got home.

"He woke the minute you left." Grover confessed over Millie's shushing. Rosie and Manuel were still there sitting next to each other on the couch watching an episode $10,000 Pyramid and arguing with each other in Spanish. Rosie, loudly, Manuel quietly looking away, but obviously making some counterpoints.

Jennifer took Nathan into her arms and accepted a bottle from Millie. She laid back in the Lazy Boy chair and fed her son. Grover stood next to her and watched, really wanting his chair to watch the rest of a game show but wanting Nathan to fall asleep even more. Patrick offered him the last seat on the couch and sat down on the floor beside Manny.

Before Rosie had a chance to ask, Jennifer moved her back pocket up with a lift of her hip to retrieve a small packet of Red Vine licorice and threw aptly at Rosie's open palm.

"You're such a good girl." Rosie commented and went back to giving answers to the TV host, this time in English. It didn't take long for the candy to make its way to her mouth. Manny always wondered how a woman he married liked artificial food so much. How was that possible, just like how was that red color possible? His stomach lurched.

"The gas station was open?" Millie looked at the bulky jeweled watch on her wrist. Answering herself, "Guess so seems like it's midnight."

"Babies will do that to you. I lose track of time every day." Jennifer smiled, tipping the bottle up at more of an angle as the baby's cheeks pulled it in harder.

"Josh Kenton is in town next week. Think he'll probably be needing some shopping done." Millie offered Jennifer rubbing her arms.

"Jeez, guess he survived his hip replacement." Jennifer retorted. She set the bottle down on the tray next to the chair as Nathan's eyelids hovered down and she placed him over her shoulder.

"Yep, all piss and vinegar. The surgeons couldn't do anything about that."

"Who you got next week?" Millie inquired, struggling to find the mute button on the remote.

"Hey." Rosie yelled chomping down on a strip of candy, which seemed to cement her teeth making her words come out sticky.

"Jesus, it's a commercial Rosie." Millie snapped.

"I like this one. It has that cute guy giving her water." Rosie grinned.

Millie kept the volume muted you didn't need sound to enjoy that. Rosie seemed to agree and tore at another vine.

"Oscar and Alice need to be driven to Scottsdale on Wednesday." Jennifer padded Nathan's back a bit harder and he expelled a loud-gurgling burp but didn't appear to wake up. "Emma needs to go to Cut-n-Curl and Randall wants to start taking walks around the trailer park again."

Millie nodded, "That Danish woman on Hopi mentioned to me the other day she could use some help bathing her husband. He's a little guy shouldn't be too hard."

Jennifer, nodded, "OK, thanks."

"Oh please." Grover growled, "let's not talk about old men bathing again."

"Grover some day you may need help and believe me you'd be happy to lay naked in a warm tub with Jennifer sponging you." "Naked" came out with three "a's."

"You make us men sound like old perverts."

"Well most of you are." Millie brought her glasses back up on her nose to find the mute button again. Someone who looked like they hadn't taken a shower in months was on the screen. She assumed it was the ridiculous show Rosie and Manuel, and Grover were watching. She hated reality TV. Rosie didn't seem to notice that Millie hit the volume but adjusted it down she was more concentrated on eating the rest of the candy. Manny looked to be nodding off.

Next commercial Jennifer spoke to Millie quietly about Chuck Love. "Didn't think he went out much anymore?"

"I think he comes for the 9:00 left-overs," Jennifer advised. "Haven't seen him in quite awhile though."

"Not since he told you you'd lose your head, huh?" Millie giggled. Jennifer didn't respond equally and with the commercial over pretended to turn her attention to a conflict between a corn rowed blond woman and petite brunette.

Patrick had been sitting quietly, "He what?"

"Nothing," Jennifer shifted Nathan back down into a cradle. He punched the air in continued sleep.

Millie leaned up from the couch blocking Grover's view over his protest. "Oh he was drunk one night at The Nail and told Jennifer that he saw a dark space over her head. But then corrected himself and said he saw her without a head."

"Without a head?" Patrick was intrigued.

"Yeah, said it looked as if it had been chopped off."

"Millie please, the man is crazy. He's still walking around town with three aliens."

"Three, what happened to the fourth?" Millie questioned.

"They had a fight," Grover answered as if they were speaking of a normal relationship.

"Pity too, he was the nice one." Rosie chimed in with a red-teeth grin.

Patrick and Millie laughed, but the others were too preoccupied, except Jennifer who pushed herself up from the chair cradling her sleeping baby.

"Grover chairs back to you. I need to get Nathan down at home or he'll keep waking up and never get in a full night's sleep." Grover didn't hesitate and settled himself into the chair. Patrick rose with her as did Millie.

"OK, dear, I boxed you up some leftovers and they're tasty not Like Ol' Mona Morton Salt's. Patrick can you help me with it?"

Patrick followed Millie to the kitchen while Rosie helped Jennifer gather all the baby belongings.

As Millie loaded foiled plates on top of one another, Patrick realized that the left-overs she was sending on where not only from this evening's meal. There was a mix of entrees and sides. It looked like the sides were loaded with vegetables and varieties of fruit salads.

"She's a good girl Patrick." Millie sealed a container of pineapple rings with floating half cherries.

Patrick felt indifferent, or maybe just tired or maybe irritated that she was also referred to as "good". "She's OK."

Patrick heard the car door open outside and assumed Jennifer was loading Nathan into his car seat. "She just suffers from lack of choices, can't hop a train when she needs to escape." Millie plopped a Tupperware dish on top of what looked to be fried chicken and a lot of it. The comment was to sting his apparent indifference and his contradicting affluence.

"I wasn't escaping." Patrick said.

Millie put her hands on her hips, "Oh sure you were. But no true harm in that son."

She steered him out of the kitchen but stopped before Rosie was back in listening range. "Actually it was a show of bravery if you think about it. You just need to appreciate that many of us can't or don't have the courage to, that's all."

"I just needed a break." Patrick pleaded.

Millie adjusted the load in Patrick's hands and wiped her acrylic nails on a dishtowel.

"From what Patrick? School and a job? Ever not have neither?" This time there was some accusation and it stung.

Millie left the kitchen calling to Grover and Manuel to "get off your lazy butts and take some of that stuff to the car," clicking the T.V. off as she passed. Patrick followed, not able to enter another word in his defense. He didn't quite understand what he was defending, but he would lose regardless.

Jennifer having secured Nathan in the backseat, Patrick loaded the food onto the opposite passenger seat of the car, and she now sat behind the wheel. They exchanged a nod and a soft "goodbye." Millie leaned in and whispered something to Jennifer; she nodded closing the door and pulled out of the narrow drive. The tires popped with the heavy gravel and when she shifted into drive a handful shot up and over into small pile next to the driveway. Grover smoothed them out with this foot and made his way back into the house. The others followed including Millie, but Patrick remained outside. He listened beyond the gravel talk, though he didn't know what he was listening for. In front of him was a small narrow dirt road that led from the string of six or so houses toward the main part of town. Had he been escaping his choices when he jumped on that train? All he knew is that he was escaping when he jumped off. Brushing his foot over the section of the gravel Grover had smoothed he shoved his hands in his pants pockets and made his way back toward Millie Flowers' house.

CHAPTER TWENTY-FIVE

Buy Time

Jennifer didn't notice the Ford truck that was parked in front of her trailer, instead focusing on getting Nathan out of the car seat and into bed without too much disturbance before she unloaded the car. Not in a spot per se, but rather the truck was parked as if the driver was just going to run in and pick up a forgotten coat.

She should be tired, but she surprisingly wasn't. It was not many nights that she was up past 10:00, and let alone out of her trailer. On the drive Nathan had continued to sleep soundly though he tugged at the belts that tied him into his seat. What was he dreaming? She always knew her dreams, the moment she woke in the mornings, but wished she didn't. Hopefully it wasn't yet that way for her son.

Tom met Jennifer at the door, standing centered in the doorway, proud of the proof that he had let himself in. Jennifer held Nathan tightly, afraid that her own fear would startle him. She was right, as soon as Jennifer was able to get out "What are you doing here?" Nathan started to cry, first still in sleep and then wide-eyed, frightened and wailing.

"Well hello." Tom offered back at Jennifer. "and how the hell are you? I'm doing fine. Thank you."

Jennifer continued to stand though Nathan was now trying to force himself down.

"Why are you here and why are you in my house?" She demanded, with all the fervor she could though her voice was difficult to hear over the baby's crying.

"Why it's both our house." He leaned on the door and nearly fell into it. "And I'm just here."

He was drunk and Jennifer wondered if he had hooked up with his old friend at The Nail and talked over what Jennifer's evening had entailed. Had Mona known he was here when she made a scene of praising him?

"Welcome home honey would be nice." Tom backed into the trailer as Jennifer moved in, unable to hold the scrambling infant any longer.

"You're drunk and I need to settle Nathan down." Jennifer moved past the short love seat that occupied the living room and made a straight line to the bedroom, picking up Nathan again since his crawl was heading toward the kitchen. Her heart beat loudly and her fear was making Nathan worse. She should let him make his own way to the hallway, away from her infectious fear, but panic was controlling her decisions. If she could get him down he would fall back to sleep and she could deal with Tom without concern over her baby.

What Jennifer realized then was that she had made a mistake entering the house. She had made a mistake not telling him to leave, or making him. She had made a mistake in being polite and not wanting to have the neighbors hear or view a fight outside her trailer. Thinking her son would be safe if he could just sleep was naive and too hopeful for the circumstances.

Tom was not just buzzed, he was a torrent drunk, which added up to a combination of anger, hostility and passion. With Nathan screaming in his small bedroom, Jennifer tried at first to bully him out of the house. When that achieved even more heightened anger she tried to reason with him to sleep off his drunk and they would talk in the morning. "Buy time, buy time," she told herself. But it was morning before the screaming stopped and when Jennifer woke up in the bathroom, her aching face level to the floor she knew she was trapped.

CHAPTER TWENTY-SIX

Exactitude

When Grover began to stir it was only 4:30 or so. He tried to turnover and face the window with hopes of drifting back to sleep, he didn't need to be up this early. Sometimes when he did this he was able to focus on some object outside the house that would turn fuzzy and cause his eyes to curtain. He stared at the tree stump that was on the east corner of his property line. It was about two feet high if at level with Grover's vision when he lay with his head solidly on the pillow. He couldn't see the dandelions and weeds that grew around the base of the stump only the midsection to the roughly sheared top. He was glad he couldn't see the weeds, they would only be a distraction and prevent him from falling back to sleep. Seemed the small amount of rain they had gotten this late summer made weeds grow, but nothing else. When Grover started trying to determine again what type of tree the stump had once been since he hadn't been the one to cut it, he got up, abandoning the chance of being able to drop off to sleep again this morning.

He did like the mornings in Arizona. He had never been fond of the heat when he was younger, probably because he had to play ball in it. But now he liked the mornings with the quiet blue skies and the dirt not cool but not yet hot on his feet and hands. As Grover pushed the soil around his tomatoes he was careful not to make too much noise under Charlotte's window remembering that Patrick slept in there, their visitor from the East Coast. Grover was always amazed at who Millie took in and how often. Charlotte's room was room to strangers more than Charlotte or her family. Once it had been monks; that had been an interesting few days.

When they had lived in Vegas, Millie hated the gamblers would have no sympathy when it came to those type of vagabonds who had bet it all, and much of what they didn't have, and lost it. She could care less if they didn't have a place to live. But it was the others, the workers of Vegas, much like herself really, that she inevitably took in. Those ones who at one time thought Las Vegas would be their answer to high and steady pay; it never was. To this day Vegas was a place of poverty.

When they lived in the two-bedroom apartment off of Sahara before moving here, Grover swore she was running a halfway house for downtrodden showgirls. She was like a mom, spooning advise into their scrawny hungry mouths. Grover always kept to himself, not really having that unselfish spirit about him. Except maybe for young ball players, maybe he wasn't so different from Millie.

He had come to Las Vegas when his carpentry work led him there. His baseball days had long-ended when he threw out his arm back in the thirties. He was in his late twenties with no skills at all other than throwing a ball and that he couldn't do any longer. But he was still strong, fit and he figured he could still do manual labor. He also knew himself well enough to know he needed the physical distraction of hard work and would never fit behind any stationary desk job. His skills also lent to precision so carpentry seemed to fit the bill.

During that first year off baseball his marriage had been strained, though truthfully it had been strained previous to that time. When living in the small house on Santa Cruz Street in Ventura, California, with Charlotte and Adele, he served as a carpenter's apprentice for nearly eight months before being allowed to bid jobs on his own. He liked the work. As he anticipated, he liked the exactitude of it and the sweat. Both reminding him of baseball for which he longed and grieved. Adele also began to work since Charlotte was now in elementary school. She worked as a teacher's aid and began to develop a close circle of friends, or a triangle actually. Adele and her fellow aids, Mary and Rae spent every other Saturday morning drinking coffee and reviewing their weeks' activities. Grover liked Rae, she was a short squat Italian woman who pin-curled her hair tightly around her head. She was direct and never spent any time considering the "right" things to say, she just spoke. Mary on the other hand was a devout Catholic and had been raised to be always obedient. Grover didn't necessarily dislike Mary, but he didn't like that Adele focused so much of her time on her. It seemed Adele felt she was somewhere in between the personalities of the two friends, preferred Rae but felt the need to take care of Mary. Adele had decided her place.

But it had been Mary that ultimately years later convinced Adele that Grover was not the proper choice in spouses and though divorce was of course against the Catholic belief system, felt she "had" to convince Adele to go down that route. Mary herself never married as far as Grover knew, though he didn't really know since he had not seen nor heard from her since the separation. Rae on the other hand married twice or three times and it was during her second marriage that she and Grover had an affair. The affair was shortly after Adele had left him. It had been a splendid, torrid two months helping him ease his pain. All the enjoyable activity seemed to be attempts to mask his loss of Adele. He had failed at baseball and now marriage.

CHAPTER TWENTY-SEVEN

Adele Gilbert

Pendrell

Adele Gilbert had been a young redheaded beauty working at a local soda shop when high school baseball star Grover Pendrell began spending more than weekends eating there. She was such a contrast to the other girls he knew. Funny when they got to talking because they both went to Ventura

High but hadn't ever talked to each other on campus. In fact, because she was so striking, Grover couldn't figure out why he hadn't noticed her before. Their lockers were across the quad, but still.

Grover found himself sitting at the counter after school when he could. It was winter when they met, when he didn't have afterschool practice so he was able to spend time drinking soda after soda, lemon and cherry were his favorites, but he would drink anything Adele was pouring. This arrangement became a target for teasing by his friends and especially by his younger brother Mick when he could sit beside him. Mick was a freshman in high school to Grover's senior status but they were close and remained so throughout their lives. When Mick visited Abbott from Florida once a year they sat side by side at The Trading Post drinking coffee because soda now had too much sugar for them anymore.

The teasing was tolerable in its subtlety. A poke in the ribs - a side-angled grin. When Grover started spending every afternoon at Wilkins Soda Shoppe, Mick dropped off.

Adele had not thought much of Grover upon meeting him. He was a bit of an embarrassment. He got there shortly after she did and hung out for hours, easily half of her shift. This was a job for Adele, and important one for her family. She brought in little but enough to keep the household coffers full in times when her father could not find work as a tradesman in the nearby oil fields.

Grover had a small build, for a ball player was maybe 5.7", though big hands that wrapped fully around the soda glasses. He had deep set brown eyes, but the kind that smile even when his mouth wasn't; and a rather big nose. Many times while sitting at the counter he read books. They were beat-up books from the Ventura Library, not the school. The lateral pages bore the inked markings. The one he talked about most was "Geronimo's Story of His Life." It was a biography written with a dedication to none other than President Teddy Roosevelt. Adele never connected the two and found it a bit hard to understand the friendship. In her town only like people hung out with like people. It wasn't that either was the way to exist but such a friendship was just hard for her to fathom. An Indian Chief and the Chief of the United States; maybe that was the connection, Grover was close to "like" her but he was technically from Casitas Springs up to road from Ventura. Some ten miles away, it was still a one street town with a few small streets that branched off to provide space for small homes. One of those clapboard homes was the Pendrell house; two bedroom with a screened in porch where Grover slept. There Grover lived with his parents, and young brother Mick, much younger Jack and older sister Errin who close to getting married was ready to leave the home. His father had moved the family from Long Beach and worked as a janitor in the local schools, including Ventura High. During baseball season this allowed him to watch home games though he tried not to cross paths with his kids during school hours to avoid embarrassment.

Adele had two younger sisters Issy (Isabella) and Margaret (never Maggie). They were as close to twins as could be, being born only 13 months apart. But more different than strangers. Issy was outgoing, rambunctious, adventurous and at fourteen had broken three bones in her body.

Margaret was quiet and would rather read in a corner than be noticed. Adele was somewhere in between. Openly friendly, but truth be known she did not particularly care to be a center of attention nor really hold conversations of any length. The daily appearance of Grover caused her discomfort in the requirement to converse and find subjects they had not already discussed. Both were a struggle for her. But books was a good one. Adele had not attended any of the school games so she could listen to these stories but really had nothing to add. He spoke to her about the dynamics of a team, your home team and the opposing. There were positioning struggles for the former, jockeying for playtime and Grover had to deal with rotations. He was a starter not great at relief so the roster dictated whether he played in any given game. If not on it, it would be a day of sitting, or pacing back and forth the length of the dugout until Keith hit him on the shoulder with his glove before the rest of the team reached their irritation boiling point. Keith was a fielder so many times he was in and out of the dugout pretty quickly depending on the need for a deep or shallow field.

When the spring rolled around Adele attended some games. Grover's expectations for a good season had made her curious. Sitting in the stands watching not only the game but also the activity around her she surprisingly found a community. A loud dedicated one with a language she had to learn. Families and younger siblings were the main composition of the gatherings. The shouting of support and disappointment mainly from the parents rippling down through the younger extensions. Adele had not been exposed to the rough language before, though hidden from view, was there in prominence.

"Dirt bag" was tossed out when the other side's pitcher came too close to the Cougar's batter.

"Bum," for just about any other infraction.

Adele loved the volatile explosions when big plays happened, though the in between was pretty slow. She spent those times trying to grab view of Grover beyond the fence dugout. He appeared so focused even when the activities in the field didn't seem to warrant it, but maybe she just didn't understand the nuances of the game.

CHAPTER TWENTY-EIGHT

Safety Glances

Grover picked two tomatoes he considered slicing for sandwiches later and went back into the house for the morning's coffee. He was surprised to see Patrick sitting at the kitchen table in shorts and a tank top rubbing his eyes and yawning with long intakes of air.

"Did I wake you?" He questioned with some slight guilt. Had he been whistling? Maybe, when he was adding mulch to the zucchini beds?

"Oh, no," Patrick was able to yawn it out. "Just ready to get up."

"Coffee?" Grover suggested as he placed the tomatoes on the sill and filled up the coffeepot. "Millie will be up and demanding you eat eggs soon. I personally can't face an egg without caffeine. Even when Millie insists."

"Coffee would be great, thanks." Patrick managed to say after yet another yawn though this one was minor and he swallowed it. It certainly didn't look like he was ready to be up.

"Got any plans today?" Grover inquired over the stream pushing through the coffee grounds.

"Plans, no." Patrick considered. He looked out the window in case there was an answer there. Something he should be considering.

"Guess not huh? Why did you jump off the train though if you were headed to California? Nice place, ya know that's where I'm from."

"I was going there," Patrick confessed. "Just didn't want to ride with who I was riding with." Patrick again looked out the window, "I'll still make it there." He decided.

"Got ya," Grover answered. "Nothing worse than having to spend time with people that are disagreeable. I went a whole season bunking with a right fielder who had terrible habits. Snored, well that you can live with, but ate garlic and spicy food all the time and did not have the stomach for it if you know what I mean." Thinking of the familiar list of complaints in his head. "Also a smoker." Grover shakes his head at the memory.

"A baseball player who smoked?" Patrick asks prepping his coffee cup with a bottom layer of milk and sugar.

"Oh, hell yeah. We didn't just do chewing tobacco. Everyone smoked. I smoked but didn't like it too much, but hell half my teams smoked, more than half. But Buddy Brew was a human chimney. Coach finally forbid him from smoking in the dugout, but that made every other place he could smoke worse. Bathroom. Bus." Grover poured the hot coffee into both cups.

"He had a foul temper. Not like mine, I mean really foul."

"Who'd you play for then?" Patrick asked wanting more.

"Oh, let's see that would have been an Iowa team. Hawks. Played with them one season in

1929. Had a good season though I had that crumby bunk-mate." Grover looked over his lifted coffee cup. Then a tentative sip like he was tasting whiskey his mouth drew in at the corners.

"Those guys you were on the train with, friends?" Grover asks and pulls up the chair next to Patrick. It was remarkable how long his legs were and they bumped knees when he slid in; but he was not tall.

"Well yeah, roommates and friends. We share a group house not far from campus with two other guys."

"How is this going to go over come fall?"

Patrick hadn't really thought about it to the extent of September. He'd only been off the train a few days, two, three? He hadn't even considered what he would do today or how he was going to get back to Boston, or whether he could really make it to California alone. He didn't want to have to talk to his mom about an exit plan to officially end his trip.

"Don't know," was all that he could come up with as inadequate as it was.

"Well don't sweat it. Some things are worth suffering through, some things aren't."

They heard the clap of plastic soles and Millie arrived in the kitchen in her short robe with the pink-feathered trim.

"Morning boys." She called to them as if they were sailors and proceeded to pull out a carton from the fridge and fix eggs for both of them without asking if they wanted them or had an opinion on how they wanted them. "Fried." She told them with her Texas drawl coming through with a hard and long "I."

"Today is shopping day," Millie announced as Patrick helped wash the dishes in the soapy sink water, which was later used to water the tomatoes. She looked very plain without her make-up, but her skin looked softer, younger without. He thought of telling her that but didn't.

"Darlin' need you and Grover both today. Told Jennifer I'd pick up Josh's rations for the week so she can spend the day with Nathan, also because she will never be able to get through the store with Nathan in tow, their own groceries and Josh's its just too much."

Grover said nothing to that and retreated to the living room to read the paper. What was

Patrick going to say, he didn't have anything to do and Millie would tell him that if he objected.

The grocery store, was in Elk Cliff, twenty miles away. The town wasn't much bigger than Abbott but as Grover explained they were governed by an aggressive mayor who courted all the retail chains to take a try in the Arizona desert. This meant that there was a Safeway, a Payless shoes a block down and a Discount Tire, Dairy Queen on the corner of State and Mound. They also had the only hospital in the area.

The Safeway was much the same as in every other city, but brighter and cleaner. "People take care of what they have here," was Millie's explanation, "Cuz there's not much."

Patrick realized that as Grover dropped back from the cart, feigning to read a Sports Illustrated he had nabbed from the magazine stand on the way in this trip was all social gossip to Millie. Patrick hung at the back-end of the cart pushing and stopping as Millie introduced him to each of the aisle inhabitants and spent time telling him their personal details in loud whispers as they headed to the toiletries aisle that was unoccupied.

"Rema LaRance is cousins with the Begays that run The Trading Post, except she's likable unlike Esther." Millie explained. "The Moore's moved here after their down syndrome daughter died. Raised her until she was forty-five. Can you imagine? So sad." Millie padded down the aisle of fabric cleaners and detergents. "Araceli Munoz was Ms. New Mexico, something happened after her reign though and she came to live with her aunt who raises ostriches. Kind of young to the be doing that."

"Oh sweet Jesus" Millie breathed out the words more than saying them. In front of them, circling around the bakery table of week's old leftover Fourth of July inspired cookies was Mona from The Rusty Nail. Her hair was wrapped in a large print floral scarf and she wore a one-piece denim jumper with rhinestones. "Something I wouldn't be caught dead in," Millie commented later, though, Patrick could easily see Millie wearing such a get-up.

"Well, there's Jennifer's man." Mona called and waved as if Patrick were one of her after-hours drinking buddies. "Hello there," she sashayed.

Millie was not pleased that Mona had made, or pretended, to make this connection. Some form of camaraderie.

The wheel on Mona's cart pulled to the right crashing into the shelves every two feet or so, but regardless, she made her way to them.

"Mona, how are you?" Millie managed, though the sarcastic lilt in her voice could not be disguised even for someone who didn't know her well.

"Oh, well you know aches here and there but I manage." She mimicked an aching back by putting her hand to the small of her back, " How are you?" Not waiting for an answer she looked to the side of Millie and far behind, "Hey Grover."

"Hey." Grover didn't look up and almost ran into the now stopped cart.

"So you're not just a friend of Jen's you're a friend of Millie's?" Mona directed to Patrick. Patrick tried to remember what he had said to her the night before, but realized even if he had remembered he could not signal any kind of necessary response to Millie.

"Yes, friend of the family, from Boston. Spending a few days with us." Millie answered and Patrick nodded not sure he was understanding the dynamics of the relationships.

"Great, well you going to be seeing more of Jennifer?" She asked pointedly. This time her stare squarely on Patrick.

"Now Mona Garrett what in the hell business is it of your's?" Millie retorted. Grover sighed happily and turned a page, this will be a long stop; he could read the whole article, possibly.

"Well just that Tom is back, stopped by to give me a sweet hug last night when he pulled into town." Mona smiled as if this was some victory. Again her hand going to the small of her back but this time to support her standing up straighter.

Millie had taken care to properly powder her face and apply her lipstick and of course pencil her brows, "You can go out without your lipstick, but never without your eyebrows." She had advised that morning as they had waited for her to leave, but at this moment the rouge she had brushed-on could not hold the color in her face.

"What?" She questioned.

"Yeah guess he missed his life here, too much activity in that university town." Mona tucked an orange hairpin into her scarf and ran her cart into the canned beets and green beans, recovering, is then off. "See ya."

Millie stood still for a moment to gather herself. She turned and faced Mona's tottling rear-end. "Well he's not staying with Jennifer."

Mona, barely slowed to make a very sharp turn into the paper towel display to retort, "He most certainly is, stayed there last night."

They passed more than a half dozen area residents through the remaining two aisles, including Elbert Begay who surprisingly looked like he wanted to talk, but Millie barely managed a "hello." When others stopped to say "hi" and attempt at conversation, Grover and Patrick found themselves reluctantly holding short conversations as to not appear too rude while Millie walked on faster than usual.

Grover finally addressed the situation when they had successfully loaded the last bag into the gold Impala.

"Millie she'll be fine. We'll call her when we get home."

"With what Grover Pendrell, she doesn't have a phone." Millie's face started to unravel now that they are in the car and a few blocks from the Safeway.

"That bastard. I knew she should have left with that baby before he could find them. That son of a bitch." Millie's lipstick smeared as she bit her lip.

Millie could not seem to settle herself down and this in turn unsettled both Grover and Patrick. When Mona had said that jerk's name for a moment she was going to laugh and act like it was not a big deal. News like that coming from such a bitch was almost cause to laugh. But Mona had told her and though she should be glad she knew, that emotion was strangled by the fear that now welled up in her chest. It was as if her lungs would pop.

Tom Wheeler was one of those young men who began mean, Millie was sure of it. If she ever wanted to spend time in a room with someone's mother it would be Tom's.

"What went wrong? What did you feed him? What desires did you or his father deny or allow him so that he grew up to hate so much?" He also fueled his hate through alcohol or vice versa. She wasn't sure which and wasn't sure it mattered. He was mean.

Tom was a man who drank too much and all those around him suffered for it. Millie had not known him very long, having met Jennifer a few months or so before the silver recovery operation he had worked for was closed. She was surprised she had not meet Jennifer sooner, until she met Tom. Jennifer didn't look up when Tom was around, never inter-acted and spent all her attention on her baby unless Tom asked a question she was expected to respond to. That is what she had seen at The Rusty Nail, the night Grover took her there for their four-year anniversary. The young couple had caught Millie's attention because they were just that, young in a town of old people. Millie's attention stayed on her because of the way Jennifer did not engage herself with the room. Tom on the contrary, he was a rooster, he was animated and openly talked with the other occupants of the bar trying to get tips from everything from new drinks to leads on jobs since "the silver thing ain't workin' out." It was during one of these performances, Tom at the bar shooting quarters, the silly college drinking game, that Millie made her way over to Jennifer despite Grover's objections, "Leave them be" was his embarrassed instruction. An objection that was entirely ignored.

Millie made the excuse to come see a baby and cooed for a bit while Jennifer seemed to get her courage to look at her.

"He's beautiful," Millie assured her. "How old?"

"Three months," Jennifer answered.

With no kids of her own and the kids she was around were always in bars so she didn't want to scold Jennifer for bringing a three month old to a loud smoky bar with a drunk obnoxious man, for sure the father.

"Millie, Millie Flowers," she extended her bejeweled hand.

Looking up through her long bangs, Jennifer did not know what to do in response to the hand in front of her. She did know, finally she shook it awkwardly. Millie's appearance shocked her not only in her willingness to approach a stranger but she was a woman clearly in her seventies with a make-up style of a younger woman, a tall one at that. Her hair was a bright crayon burnt orange, yet her lipstick in the light of the bar appeared to be red. Between the thick lashes her eyes were kind and this is what showed through most of all.

"Jennifer Mullen." Jennifer answered back reluctantly and looked over to Tom but he was still involved in the drinking game.

"Do you live here?" Millie knew everyone.

"I don't think I've seen you before" she said.

Jennifer looked over at Tom again. This "checking in," irritated Millie, but she needed to ease into this conversation gently, which was not her nature. With a swish of her hips she leaned in a way to block Jennifer's fearful glances to the man at the bar.

"Is he the father and the husband, or just the father?"

"Father," Jennifer replied. Tom would be there in a moment horning in to make sure no outside influences infiltrated his control of her.

"Well, glad to hear that." Millie smiled. "It will make it easier."

"Make what easier ma'am?"

"Leaving him dear, leaving him." Millie winked at her. "And you can do it. You got on this bus, you can get off this bus." Millie grabbed a pen from a passing waitress and scribbled her name and number on a napkin.

"Millie Flowers 555-1234. Call me. And soon." The last word added to make sure this directive was not missed.

Millie pulled herself up to a full stand but still blocked the bar. "I'll look forward to hearing from you honey." She smiled, patted Jennifer's arm, which seemed too elderly of a gesture for her, and joined the elderly man who appeared to be her husband at the cashier's stand. Jennifer watched her wondering who this woman was and why she was taking a particular interest in her? It must be very apparent how bad things were for her to walk up to her in a bar and tell her to leave Tom.

Jennifer had not been giving safety glances toward Tom for the last couple of minutes, and he appeared next to her as she continued to stare at the old flashy woman now leaving with the old man who appeared to be her opposite in mid-body stature as he took long steps next to her.

"Who in the hell was that?" Tom asked. Jennifer jolted from her trance. "Someone who offered to watch Nathan." She said, her eyes downward.

"Right, like I'd let that old hag watch the baby." Tom scoffed and took a handful of peanuts and tossed them in his mouth. "Just heard about a job in Tempe, pays big bucks."

Jennifer's heart skipped. She looked around the room, Millie wasn't there any longer but she realized she felt safer with Tom in public than in the confines of their trailer.

"You going to take it?" She asked offering him a way out and hoping he'd latch on.

"You asking and you don't know nothing' about it?" Jennifer looked downward again and watched as Nathan's plump foot lifted in his sleep to wrap around his other ankle.

"Well sounds like I should at least head down there to check it out. I'll leave in the morning, Morrie Ellers can give me a ride. Looks like Peterbilt needs wheeler mechanics. Just up my alley."

"Up his alley" was anything Tom wanted to do at the moment, or thought he could do with his overblown confidence. Jennifer just wanted "up his alley" to be away from Abbott and away from the chubby crossed-ankles under the table.

He left that next morning, Jennifer having to rustle him out of bed while Morrie Ellers, some guy who claimed to have "the right connections", honked outside in the narrow strip of dirt beside the trailer. Tom had been too drunk to cause any problems so Jennifer was truly relieved once she heard the door slam and the truck pull away. She squeezed her eyes tightly in a semi-prayer, though she was not religious and asked that he never return, ever.

It was five and a half months since he had left with Morrie stumbling out the trailer door. Five months of understanding who she was and that she would never allow another man like Tom in her life. But that morning, she woke up on her bathroom floor with Tom passed out in her bed. She had made sure to stay away from men like Tom in those months, it had been easy in this town, but she had not protected herself from Tom himself and his inevitable return.

CHAPTER TWENTY-NINE

Day Three at Millie Flowers'

When she walked up the drive to 25 Pine Street, Patrick felt he had betrayed Millie with his doubts.

Millie had paced the kitchen until Grover talked her into laying down with a washcloth on her forehead. Still she called him in time and time again trying to get some kind of assurance.

Patrick unpacked the groceries, and had busied himself setting aside supplies to give to Jennifer "who was due at 2:00 and if she's a minute late I'm calling the cavalry," per Millie.

"No need for that Millie, please," Grover had visibly bristled. Patrick could tell that Grover was losing patience with her. Millie was hard to gauge, hard to determine what was real and what was part of Millie's persona which was apparent in the highs and maybe also in the lows.

Jennifer was careful to try to conceal the wounds, but it was easy to determine without careful examination what her night had been like. Millie met her at the end of the drive and Patrick could tell she was pleading with Millie in some way. Her arms went from her heart to the air on either side of her quickly. He was able to hear some of Jennifer's words since she faced the house, though reluctantly, not knowing where Patrick stood inside.

"Just bring me Josh's..." Jennifer pleaded.

She didn't want to come into the house. She didn't want Patrick to see her black eyes and torn mouth. With this revelation the beating in his chest soared. He ran for the door as if just realizing that a serious accident had just occurred. When he reached her he could hear Millie's words clearly.

"I'm calling the sheriff this time. I won't allow you to be beaten by that scum." "By" contained her drawl but was unnaturally cut short with the force of the words that followed.

"Millie." is all Jennifer could say once she saw Patrick approaching in his dead run.

"Jennifer." He stood between them though there was no room.

"He did this, this Tom guy?"

"It wasn't all him..." she started.

"It wasn't? What the hell are you saying? Who are you defending?" Patrick hadn't realized yet that his voice was harsh and his questions were in rapid fire.

The proximity and intensity of Patrick pushed her toward a stumbling defense.

Jennifer took a noisy gulp, her throat clamping "Who the hell are you? You've known me what, three days?"

Millie moved around to Jennifer's side in line to protect, control the situation. She didn't really know this boy.

"Patrick!" Millie yelled and demanded attendance in the discussion. She was at his shoulder but he was excluding her nonetheless. She cupped his shoulder and Patrick turned to her, "When will the sheriff get here in this town? How will they protect her? Shit." He turned to both sides as if needing to restrain himself from an angered flight.

Patrick's hysteria seemed to detract momentarily from the situation. He took a breath.

"Who is going to stop this? Who is going to say this is not right? Where's Nathan?" Patrick looked past Jennifer now but didn't seem to be able to focus where he was looking and turned at her again.

Millie gripped Patrick's shaking arm and draped her other arm over Jennifer's shoulder. Patrick was explosive but in a way Jennifer didn't understand, but Millie did. His whole body shook and his limbs seemed to flail. He was not the angry Jennifer was used to and she even in her own fear had the urge to comfort him though he had just verbally attacked her.

It was not until Millie had settled them on the screened in porch with iced tea that was way too sweet and the ceiling fan on full blast, that Patrick was able to look Jennifer squarely in the face again and form a question that was not in need of a defense.

"Are you alright?" his attention fell on her bruises.

Jennifer shook her head "yes," battered eyes brimming with tears.

"Again, where is Nathan?" This question was punctuated by a quick inhale.

"He's with Noonie, a friend in town who watches him, when..." Jennifer did not want to continue. "He doesn't know her or where she lives."

"Jennifer," he pleaded.

She rose and entered the kitchen where Grover and Millie were watching them and not hiding that fact.

"I need Josh's groceries, it's getting close to his dinnertime," trying to insert routine. Grover stood stiffly and reaching over to the counter and handed them to her. Millie took Jennifer's cheek in her hand since the young girl had no free hands and whispered, "It will not happen again. You come straight back here after you finish with Josh." When Jennifer responded it was a nod and nothing else. She walked calmly with the groceries through the screen door past a mute Patrick and down the drive to her car parked oddly on the street.

Millie heard Patrick breathe, before she noticed his movement. The intake of his breath was gargled as if he were under water.

"Patrick," Millie called, but before she could reach him he was off the porch and next to Jennifer taking the grocery bags from her and rounding her car to drive.

CHAPTER THIRTY

Cull Down the

Information

Jennifer moved efficiently, placing a can of mixed nuts and a Gatorade on the unfolded T.V. tray next to a wooden chair. Patrick stood watching her but not doing much else. Josh kept eyeing him questioning his presence, but his eyes off of Jennifer whose bruising was still noticeable.

Josh's house was a trailer turned permanent. It looked as if it was melted into a berm of dirt with a ramp coming from the ground covering the stairs. Josh was sitting in his wheelchair in the living room when they arrived and seemed miffed that Jennifer came calling with a "male friend." Patrick could tell from the exterior that he tried to appear gruff, his eyes followed by a series of puffy folds that drooped to his mouth. His voice was a harsh New York version of Detective Columbo. Patrick introduced himself to the cool reception, as Jennifer unloaded the groceries, throwing away food that had been prepared yet not eaten and replacing it with the bundles she had brought. Above Josh's sink, was a cross and draped across it a badge. He had in fact been a beat cop in New York, lower Manhattan. In his retired years he had pushed a mail cart in a corporate office in Phoenix until his knees gave out, "I'm like an old catcher." Grover apparently disputed this comparison whenever it was brought up. There was nothing like crouching for nine innings and taking 145 pitches.

"Astros play Dodgers tonight." She brushed the seat of the chair dislodging misguided nuts from previous games into her hand for disposal.

"Better play better than that last series." Josh said. He turned to look at Patrick directly irritated now that this unauthorized companion was standing mute.

"You a anti-dodger's fan like old Grover?"

Patrick felt amusement even in this state that Josh would refer to a man obviously his own age, or close as "old."

"No sir." Patrick replied.

"Sir?" Josh squared his jaw as Jennifer walked by toward the wide opening of the bathroom doorway with rolls of toilet paper in her hands.

Patrick nodded, not knowing the violation, yet.

"You in the military?" He examined Patrick's physique and considered.

"No, no I'm not."

"Huh. Well, it could pay for your college you know."

"Yes." Patrick hoped this stop was not a long one, but he heard some rummaging in the bathroom that indicated he may not be so lucky.

Jennifer was apparently cleaning as she put the toiletries away.

Patrick had never considered the military as any kind of option and because his emotions were still ragged, he almost told Josh so having resented the carrot the military sticks out for the more economically challenged, but as the old man wheeled toward the canned nuts and offered them to him, he decided he did not need to make any political statements in a trailer in the middle of the Arizona desert.

When Patrick was about eleven, maybe twelve, he had decided he wanted to be a pilot. It was a latent interest really, even though he was young. He had never been the kind of kid that spent time constructing model airplanes, patiently gluing those delicate plastic pieces together, nor did he pick out the cloud embellished wallpaper when his mother re-did his room for his seventh birthday. He did design variations of the paper airplanes in elementary school and prided himself on designing low altitude flyers, mid-range and paper airplanes that arced sharply and then plummeted at ninety-degree angles. But it was when he discovered the complex math equations that were required to determine the path to maneuvering, flying and landing a plane that his interest soared to the puffy cumulus clouds. His train wallpaper seemed to belong to another child.

In his last year of junior high school, Patrick was asked to participate in the end of the year science fair. He was not the best at presentations, no matter which experiment you choose, "the student must present out loud the problem/quandary, the solution-resolution-conclusion." Patrick convinced himself he could do the presentation if he was doing something that related to flying, so he decided to explain the evolution of the airplane to the commercial utilization of the jet engine, but really spending most of the time on how all the problems that previous plagued flying machines had been solved by the jet engine in whatever variation was used.

The night before the fair Patrick realized that he had packed four hours of information into what needed to be of a fifteen-minute speech. Panicky he tried to trim down all the information he had gathered into a shorter, yet complete presentation. At three o'clock in the morning his mother met him in the kitchen re-writing his index cards, trying to reduce a two inch stack to ten maybe twenty cards.

His mother was never a light sleeper, quite the contrary, but seemed to have a sixth sense when one of her children, was sick, had had a bad dream, or was struggling with some crisis that prevented sleep. Patrick felt all three as he sat there pulling cards out and trying to determine which to eliminate. They were all so important. When he heard his Mom's rubber-soled slippers pulling up from the floor in dainty flops, he signed with relief. She talked to him gently, not questioning why he was awake but cautioning that they needed to be very quiet not to wake his father who was a light sleeper and who if awoken would not be happy.

Together they eliminated all the topics that though interesting, were not essential and focused on the main one that centered around the development of the jet engine. When he went to bed an hour later, he felt a confidence in not only his ability to perform the presentation, but that all the work he performed had actually helped him cull down the information so that only the essential remained.

Over ten years later Patrick still used the experience when he didn't know what direction to take in a study project, or more specifically in a moot court competition this last year. In the latter, Patrick knew the whole case backwards and forwards, what the defense may rely on and what evidence needed to be entered to path the facts toward the verdict he advocated. It was just recently that he wondered - had he lost this ability to cull to the important, and now standing in an old man's 6 x 8 living room he tried to remember when he first saw it fading away.

Jennifer made her way back into the living room, following Josh's speech on why military service allowed him to skip the police academy agility tests which he would have certainly struggled with. "Guess they figured if I can kill Japs and Krauts I can chase a purse-snatcher."

Patrick twitched again, and restrained comment. His college years had made him increasingly liberal. Jennifer, looking for distraction or not listening to the men, grabbed Patrick's wrist to view the time.

"OK Josh, let's get you into your chair." She wheeled him closer to the wooden chair, not waiting for him to do it himself. "I set up the rails in the bath. Can you do the bath yourself tonight, or do you need my help?" Apparently assistance required varied with Josh's tolerance level and not necessarily physical need.

Josh positioned his arms on her shoulders as Jennifer eased him into the chair.

"Oh, I can do it. Since you probably have a date tonight." He lingered a glance at Patrick. It was not one of dislike, but more sincere curiosity mixed with some playful teasing.

Jennifer ignored the comment and clicked the T.V. on it was already on ESPN.

"OK then." She leaned into him. "Remember when your back starts hurting you need to go back into your wheelchair." Josh nodded like a child. "There's a Hungry Man thawing on the counter, should be ready to pop into the oven in about an hour. Don't forget to poke the plastic."

Josh nodded again, this time not to her instructions but a routine nod that signaled he was now watching the T.V. and they should leave. Sports Center was on.

Patrick and Jennifer got into her battered Toyota without an exchange of words.

Jennifer drove about a fourth of a mile and pulled over on a stretch of the street that held in its angular arms only one house that had a large fenced yard adjacent to it.

"Just don't lecture me with any feminist crap." Jennifer snapped.

"Millie feeds me enough of it," she began quoting, 'I can be anything I want to be,' 'A women can accomplish a lot on her own these days,' 'Never compromise.'" Patrick listened to the mocking melodic diatribe while also listening to the angry dog on the other side of the fence who was now kicking up dirt as he ran parallel, making tight swift turns as he crossed the yard back and forth. He felt a bit like the dog.

Jennifer ended with, "'You have to think of Nathan now when you make choices in men.'"

"Who calls that feminist crap? It's not crap."

Jennifer's voice had had a sarcastic lilt to it when she was giving the recitation, but the sarcasm failed when Patrick volunteered bravely, the answer, "The man who beats you?"

Jennifer's eyes teared-up. The purple trim of her right eye brimmed with the water. It was a wonder it held; the dam of the eyes were not reinforced.

"Add to your list that, 'you will become what your environment is unless you break free of it.'" Patrick's voice had dropped the anger. But he feared it may rise again. He wanted to make the message ring true but he may be hurrying it too much. He paused forcibly, because audibly words expelled.

Jennifer's voice, held the tininess of a child, "How do you know what my environment is?"

"Everything about you tells me." Her purple eye looked like it was swimming in a glass bowl now, the water unable to slip out. Patrick gently leaned toward her and kissed the corner of her eye, which reacted, to his touch with the release of the liquid. He followed the tears down her check and to her neck with his lips. She was salty and soft. He thought of the expressions, "as soft as a baby's bottom." That expression now needed to be "as a beaten eye."

Jennifer took in air and gulped it down. Patrick felt her relax, his hands where now on her folded hips, and he pulled away from her face, but kept a gaze on her. Jennifer didn't look at him and turned to examine the surface of the road in front of them. Patrick took his index finger and slid it on the outline of her jaw turning her head toward him.

"'Never compromise.'" He said in a volume meant to be a whisper, but clearly stated it was more than that.

CHAPTER THIRTY-ONE

Triangular

Cracks

S he had all but given up hope. He was to have met her at 3:00 and from the kitchen clock it was 3:25 and thirty, forty seconds. Mrs. Madrigal had taught her to read time in the second grade and she loved to count minutes even seconds, it had a secure rhythm to it, groups of five long dashes between the numbers.

Jennifer's mother had bought her a digital clock for her bedside table but she refused to look at it, it was too easy, so when she needed the time she came into the kitchen. Her mother never noticed. By the time Jennifer was in fifth grade she was convinced she had tired her mother out.

Jennifer Mullen was what the school counselor considered a hyperactive child. She had a hard time staying still and sitting in her seat for any length of time. Her transition from kindergarten to first grade had been particularly difficult, confined to a desk that trapped her through the long hours of reading and addition; it was more than Jennifer could stand. When it got to be too difficult she would concentrate on her shoes and swing them in front of her. She could run and skip in her seat and she wouldn't feel so trapped. Her teacher didn't see it that way. That year she spent many lunch hours on the "stump" in front of the principal's office, punishment for not staying in her seat. Just opposite of what she needed, an old chopped piece of a tree, sitting because she couldn't sit.

Jennifer had a faithful friend during those years, Lizzie who would walk by her on her stump and make little signals with her fingers. It was their own sign language. An "O" with the thumb and index finger was a "hello", a crossing of index and middle finger a "only a few more minutes", a clenched fist "Ms. Powers is a grump." Jennifer tried not to laugh when Lizzie walked by, taking care not to look at her face. Lizzie would do it ten times or more during lunch, eating her sandwich as she walked by until one of the teachers noticed and shoed her away. That was true friendship.

Jennifer understood now that it was not her endless movement that tired her mother out, but her mother's own inability to handle even two tasks that may need to be accomplished in one day's time. The inability had progressed slowly to menial tasks causing obvious lethargy. First she was unable to drop Jennifer at school because she had to go buy orange juice. Then she couldn't make the school play because there were dishes in the sink. Jennifer cried openly about her mother's inabilities at home against her pillow to muffle the sounds, but at school she developed stories, not too elaborate, but ones that would help cover her mother's continued absences. Only

Lizzie knew the truth. They had pulled-pinkies in a promise not to let anyone know Jennifer's mother was crazy. Soon Lizzie made up stories to help her friend. One person could only come up with so many and Jennifer had tapped out. Jennifer liked the chef idea the best. Jennifer's mother was a world-renowned chef and had to travel all over the world to discover new recipes and cook for famous people. When she came home, which wasn't very often, she threw elaborate parties; her classmates couldn't come. They needed to understand it was for famous people only. Lizzie of course attended school in tulle skirts and glittery headbands. Jennifer's mother also brought them exotic presents, but they would never risk bringing them to school, they were much too valuable. Jennifer's Aunt Beth who was younger than her mother gave her a simple gold bangle bracelet for her eighth birthday. It had an enameled green trim. It was a treasure from India she told her classmates. They ohhed and ahhed at the gold circle around her wrist since they had been waiting anxiously to see the gifts they only heard about. When the enamel started to wear off, Jennifer reported her mother did not want her to wear such a valuable piece of jewelry to school any longer. She put it in the left shoe of her tap shoes so she could still see it once a week.

It was now 3:31 and ten seconds. With the slam of the screen door, Billy Mullen walked into the living room, scanning as if he had mistakenly chosen the wrong house and was trying to set a scene. He was still dressed in his mechanic's jumpsuit that even when it was not covered with grease smelled of it. His hair was naturally brown, but lightened in the summer when he worked outdoors on his days off. Especially on top with the sides of his hair darker because Billy had a habit of pushing his hair behind his ears and the grease was bound to settle itself in no matter how much shampoo he applied.

"Jen?" he questioned from the front of the house. He walked into the kitchen. She waited a minute to answer him though they we looking directly at each other.

"Yes?" She had wanted to say more. Why her mother, who was sitting in her bedroom, could not take her to tap practice? Why her tap shoes did not bear the same shine as the sides of his head?

"Let's go" he directed. "Lorna?" he called to the back of the house.

"Yes" an anguished voice answered, afraid she would be asked to check the mail or something else that required she come out of her room.

"I'll be back in an hour, but then I got to go back to the shop." He looked to the doorway that led to the bedroom as Jennifer scooted around him making her way through the backdoor of the narrow galley kitchen.

Her father lowered his voice as Jennifer walked down the steps, making sure not to step on a crack, which was difficult because there were many.

"You might be late." He was more remorseful than usual.

Turning back toward the house in the direction of the bedroom, Billy yelled, "Try to feed the girl Lori, if only a sandwich, or something."

Jennifer heard no reply from her mother. Triangular cracks were so hard to miss.

Tap dancing was good for Jennifer. Maybe something a school counselor had recommended. It allowed her to move without restriction and hit the floor loudly, all the things she wanted to do from her confining desk. The louder she hit the floor the more the dance teacher praised her. No one knew she was stomping her mother's inactivity when she did the slide shuffle. If they had she was sure she would have been arrested or at the very least condemned to serve in "bad daughter jail." She made sure she didn't step on a crack but that was all for show to cover up her dance aggressions. She didn't even tell Father Walters the thoughts that filled her mind and poured out her pores when she tap danced, because she was sure he would in turn tell her mother, or God. All he ever said to her, anyways, was "Lorna Mullen's girl" and his head would lower as if in prayer. She never understood why he needed to say those words with such scorn or sorrow when he saw her. Maybe it was because her mother didn't make it to church anymore. Maybe. Maybe she really knew why and wanted to pretend she didn't. People who knew pitied her too openly.

Many times Billy Mullen wished they had had more than one child. Illogical as it was he thought that it would somehow make things easier. Easier to share the burden of his mentally ill wife. It was a heavy burden. But just a few years into their marriage, Billy realized he would not have the large family like the one he had come from and instead would have to be two parents for his only daughter. By the time Jennifer was sixteen, her mother had not left the house in five years, she had asked her father why he didn't just divorce her mother and marry someone "normal." Her father had slapped her and returned back some Catholic reasoning that she had heard in the few catechism classes she had attended. "Marriage was a sacred bond...etc." But it wasn't love or commitment that kept her father there but some fear that caused him to stay with his demented wife, yet strike his only daughter. She had never told her father she hated him until that day when she realized she did. His inabilities became hers.

At sixteen Jennifer made a number of decisions in her life. One, that she would never commit herself to any religion that would trap her in a bad relationship. Two, that she would leave home when she was eighteen, and three that she would have a child. She wanted someone to love and believed that that was what was missing in her life. A child would have to love her, she reasoned though the selfishness of such thought embarrassed her. On June 21st, the first day of summer 1982 Jennifer left Flagstaff, Arizona with Tom Wheeler and a baby in her womb. It was not that she had felt he was the one, but he was the means. She didn't know then the danger of choosing the wrong exit ticket. Only that at eighteen and a half she had met two of her goals.

Lizzie was still her friend up until the day she left but had wanted something different. She had been accepted to college and was busy planning her departure in the fall. Jennifer had not even applied, not even taken the entrance exams. That was not to be her future. But there was no resentment of Lizzie. True Lizzie had two "normal" parents, a house with a green lawn in front, with no cars parked on it, and a mother who could pick her up from school on the same day she grocery shopped. She had faithfully held

Jennifer's secrets since elementary school. The intricate stories to cover up her mother's absence had stopped in high school when no one really cared if you had troubles at home.

CHAPTER THIRTY-TWO

Two Goals

Won; One Lost

Tom's abuse had started slowly, almost methodically ticking, if he was capable of that, and his MO became controlling everything Jennifer did. Though they had no money, he would not allow her to work. Instead he watched. She spent her days being eyed. Every step monitored. She could not even go to the store by herself, he would accompany her on the trips to her doctor. Making sure she didn't strike up any conversation with "someone who wanted to just get in your pants." When he had first said this she had commented, "Like you?" What she thought was an appropriate and clever retort became the first time he struck her. His fist had hit squarely on her chin and taken her to the ground. It wasn't a slap like her father had delivered when she complained about her mother too directly. It was a punch. Jennifer had never been punched before, not even in a playground scuffle. The intensity of the blow not only physically hurt with a welt grew into an off-center lump; it unsettled her to the core. Someone could hurt her. She was vulnerable; she could be knocked to the ground.

When Jennifer first arrived in Abbott she didn't have many expectations. Tom though had many, but Jennifer knew not to put too much faith into that. They had already lived in several places, several towns in the months they were together. Now they were in the middle of the Arizona desert, a po'dunk town with old people. They set-up house in the trailer they had rented from, what else, an elderly man who was hesitant to lease to an unmarried couple, but needed the money, "Social Security just didn't stretch too far," they had been advised them without much eye-contact. Within months in Abbott the mining opportunity collapsed and so did any of the slim expectations Jennifer had of a healthy relationship with Tom. At least she hadn't married him. But surprisingly what she thought would be an easy exit from a five-month relationship was not so easy.

She had landed next to rusted railing that was meant as support to lead people into their trailers. Her increasingly large belly barely missed the concrete block of the first step. It had not even mattered to Tom that she was carrying his baby when he hit her. He also hadn't even waited until they were inside before striking her. Instead of apologizing or helping her up as she held her belly with one hand and pulling up with the other, Tom walked past her. He went into the trailer and opened a beer, turning on the small grainy T.V. that sat on the kitchen counter.

Jennifer looked around the trailer park, brushing off the arm that had landed in the dirt trough next to the stairs. She was nauseous and light-headed. Her jaw felt as if it was unhinged at one end, her chin hot to the touch. She tried to stand but found herself holding onto the rail and puking into the same trough that had held her a few seconds earlier.

"Don't stand there and puke," Tom ordered from inside the trailer. Jennifer could see him leaning on the counter trying to find a channel that could distract him from what he had just done. She wouldn't stand fully until she saw him facing a loud football game.

"What do you expect me to do?" "You son of bitch" she said in a quieter voice. But he heard her and when she entered the house, this time he beat her out of the view of the neighboring trailers. But she was certain they could hear the sounds.

Six months later when Tom had left Jennifer, she found herself grateful for a number of things. First and foremost that she had had experience nursing her mother all those years and was able to make some money helping out some of the local senior citizens. Helping people clean themselves did not embarrass her and her comfort with these tasks made her clients feel equally as comfortable. When caring for some of the dementia patients, Jennifer was reminded of her mother. She eased into their disjointed, almost intelligible conversations and joined them on their journeys from the past, leading them through the routines of short-term memory that they could no longer maneuver.

And there was of course the overwhelming gratitude for Tom leaving. The last months with him had been a paralyzing dream in which she could not move her limbs, stir her chest to take in the enough air. In the last month of her pregnancy he had not been around for any substantial amount of time. He had gotten a temporary job down the road about fifteen miles at a muffler shop in Tree Limb, which was right next to the neighborhood bar. He typically had a few drinks there at "Mollie's" and then headed south as if he was headed toward home but had a few more drinks at The Rusty Nail in Abbott, developing his waitress/drunk friendship with Mona the owner. Jennifer could not say that she missed him, but rather she feared being alone during this time. Fearful of the unknown nature and pain of birth, fearful of not being able to get to the hospital, fear about not being able to waddle her way to the kitchen to find something to eat that would benefit the health of her unborn child.

Her labor started while she was searching for vanilla yogurt with apricots in the frozen food section of the Safeway in Elk Cliff. She had driven herself in Tom's clunky truck since he had called in sick that morning having not made it home until 3:00 am due to mixing his drinks with fried zucchini chasers. Waking up to his retching, made her equally nauseous and feigning some concern over his self-induced illness, she told him she was going to get him some Pepto Bismol and headed into the next town, hoping the empty level on the gas gauge was not accurate.

Pretty sure the incredible cramping was labor, she put the yogurt back into the freezer pushed the cart to the check-out stand, asked if the clerk would mind if she could keep it there while she went to the hospital. There was nothing in the cart that would melt.

The clerk, who has a significant field of zits on both her cheeks, giving the appearance of high-rouged cheekbones though in truth her face was round and not concave, immediately looked to her belly. She hesitated too long in Jennifer's short-tempered opinion. "I'm not asking you to deliver it, I'm asking you where the hospital is, I guess." Had she asked that question? Jennifer's voice must have risen more than she realized, she couldn't really hear anything but the roar in her ears from the now synchronized pain. A middle-aged man with black hair and grey sideburns joined the dumbstruck clerk. He nodded at Jennifer and asked something, she couldn't say what, and then escorted her out the door toward a Jeep Cherokee in the front spot of the store. Jennifer followed, breathing in short spurts like she had seen on television. Why they did this she didn't understand, because it wasn't helping in the least. The man said something again this time in an assuring tone, what again she wasn't sure but maybe something about three children of his own. As they were pulling away, Jennifer tapped the window toward Tom's truck as if she were waving to the unoccupied front seat, but just then her water broke and the flood of mushy water trailed down her legs. The man said something about "God's grace," and for the first time Jennifer thought maybe it wasn't a good idea for her to have gotten in this car with this man with three children.

The hospital was luckily a straight shot across two intersections from the store. She must have passed it on her way into town and not noticed. She should notice these things. That led to a lecture inside her head that she needed to be aware of her surroundings more and then that led into maybe she needed to leave the baby in the hospital and leave Arizona. She didn't think once that she should call Tom to let him know that his baby was being born. Of all the thoughts that swirled in her mind screaming with pain, this was not one of them.

When Nathan Neal came any thoughts of leaving him there to be adopted by more fit parents, left her. Here was the person who would love her, who would depend on her, who would give her reason to get up each day. Tom did come to the hospital a few hours after she had delivered. Jennifer must have given his name and phone number to someone, though she didn't remember doing so. His alcohol puffed face and breath came too close to her and her baby and she was close to batting it away. She didn't care who saw. He grumbled about having to retrieve the truck and some Christian guy yammering about his responsibilities as a father that he didn't appreciate. Jennifer was sore and exhausted from the delivery and wondered when that would pass or would this pain always be with her? She had no one to ask. Just then she heard the side-burned man's voice again, directing the nurse to give her more of something to kill the pain. Tom's voice quieted and Jennifer watched as he followed with his blurred gaze the side-burned man enter the room as if fearful he had heard his comment about the Christian guy. Jennifer was humored, though she didn't benefit from the usual endorphin effects of humor because of the pain, still she heard herself giggle. The monster-man had been silenced by the lanky Christian-man with the Jeep Cherokee, three children and bi-colored hair.

As if meeting her for the first time, the man approached her and extended his hand, making sure he waited until she had shifted the baby carefully in order to take his hand.

"Frank Reynolds," he smiled at her and then Nathan.

"Hello," Jennifer said shyly thinking about what this man had experienced with her.

"Welcome to the world little guy," he said gently to her baby and asked a bit insistently, "May I?" Jennifer did not hesitate giving Frank Reynolds baby Nathan. He took him and moved the blanket away from his face to get a full view. "He's a precious one."

"Thank you." Jennifer fell into an easy conversation with the stranger who had rescued her from the Safeway and watched her amniotic fluid stain his floorboards, and the man who made the father of her child squirm. Above anything else she liked him for the latter.

Later Frank was joined by his wife, and their three kids, who came to meet Jennifer and her new baby. They had been in Elk Cliff visiting family when Frank went to the store for a few things and instead discovered a mother-soon-to-be in distress. She later found out that he was a music teacher who taught band for a public school in Phoenix. That his passion was John Coltrane and that as a man in his twenties he had traveled to New Orleans with lofty aspirations to play music on Bourbon Street, but had instead only found a job in a strip club playing to girls removing their clothes. It was around this time that he "found God" and turned to the church for musical inspiration and personal guidance. He now played for the church jazz band and was able to work his mentor Coltrane into some of the musical productions, "un-denounced" to his pastor, he confided.

His wife's name was Nelly, and Jennifer resisted asking her if she was teased as a child, like "Whoa there Nelly." She did seem like the kind of person who was teased. Nelly had stringy blond hair that she tried to curl and instead of soft tendrils it came out as long slices of wiry string holding little curl. Today it was held into place with two jeweled, red and blue, barrettes much too young a look for a mother of three. Her two daughters Kate and Geri looked like her, but the son Jim was squarely Frank without sideburns. Jennifer smiled at the family and wondered how stringy blond Nelly had romanced a man like the trumpet playing Frank Reynolds.

When Jennifer, Nathan in her arms, and Tom trailing behind the wheelchair, left the hospital, Nelly met her at the wide automatic doors. She waited on the outside side of the doors as if she was somehow not permitted to step onto the rubber mat. Jennifer smiled at her, Nelly nodded and then at the nurse who released the handles of the wheelchair to her. Jennifer looked behind her, turning carefully since Nathan was nestled in her lap. But Nelly looked ahead as if she was a hospital employee with no obligation to speak with her, just a job to do. Jennifer caught a glimpse of the rusty truck parked at too severe of an angle next to the chain link fence that separated the hospital from a row of small industrial shops. Nelly leaned down as Jennifer motioned toward the car, "the truck is right there behind that green car" she said into her ear. Nelly nodded and Jennifer tried to remember if she had heard her speak before in the hospital or maybe she was mute.

Tom lapped the wheelchair to the left and tossed the garbage bag that contained Jennifer's soiled clothes and the few items the hospital pulled together to get the young mother started, into the truck. As it clunked in the bed, Jennifer wondered if any of the giveaways were breakable and whether she would voice a complaint to Tom. Before she could decide, he opened the passenger side of the truck and to Jennifer's surprise there was a baby seat already secured in the middle of the bench seat with the seatbelts belted tight. Tucked in the baby seat itself was a plastic giraffe whose body was unnaturally shaped into a ring. Nelly took Nathan from Jennifer's arms, "Steady yourself. Take your time." she said. She was not mute but rather had a honey undertone to her voice. Jennifer held herself up with her left hand and gripped onto the side of the truck while Nelly handed her the baby and showed her how to lower her son in the car seat from such an angle. Tom was already seated and didn't care to watch the process, instead he tuned the radio where his favorite station would begin playing once the car was started. Nelly helped Jennifer into the truck. The step was high and pain shot through her thighs burning into her now empty womb. Nelly smiled a queasy smile knowing what pain Jennifer was experiencing. "It's going to hurt a bit." Her stringy hair was on the back of her head secured by a big white plastic clip and was much too large for her sad head of hair. But at that moment Jennifer focused on her kindness and bee-sweet voice.

"Thank you Nelly," Jennifer touched the woman's skinny arm as she buckled her in.

"You're welcome," she said formally and closed the door of the truck and padded it as if she was sending a prisoner-occupied police car off to the station. How apropos. She had wanted this baby so bad so that she would have someone to love and love her back and now with the baby she was truly trapped. Two goals won; one lost. Jennifer watched Nelly push the empty wheelchair off toward the hospital entrance like a shopping cart.

"Nut case," Tom commented as he started the engine and hit reverse too abruptly. The music blared and surprisingly Tom didn't say anything when Jennifer reached over and turned down the volume.

"What do you mean? Jennifer felt the need to defend the kind woman.

"Crazy thing gave you a bunch of old stuff, it's in the back."

"Did she give us this?" Jennifer touched the baby seat and picked up the giraffe showing it to Nathan's unfocused eyes.

"I guess," Tom answered carelessly turning a corner to enter the street toward Abbott.

Months later Jennifer often thought about Frank and Nelly, how they we doing in Phoenix, what their life was like, had school started for Frank? Was Nelly still dressing the two girls alike? But most of all Jennifer wondered if Nelly had feared for her as much as Jennifer had feared for herself. What had it been like for Nelly to give birth three times and have the help of what appeared to be a loving husband?

Patrick took his hands off of Jennifer's hips when he saw the tears flowing fast from her puffed eyes. She now looked squarely at him. He seemed to be a sweet man. Was he as sweet as Frank? Would he tell her she looked beautiful even though she was now red with embarrassment and black and blue from the blows? Would he recognize a person in need and take care for them? Jennifer chirped a breath, not realizing she had made any noise at all. She couldn't understand why he was smiling.

"You sound like a squeaky toy."

"What?" Jennifer questioned and then heard herself make the sound again. "Oh," she couldn't help but grin.

"My dad used to call me squeaky. But I always worried that it was actually a respiratory disorder. I was a worrier."

"It's cute." Patrick said affectionately.

Jennifer took the time to look at him again, slowly, not that she hadn't before but before she had not risked him knowing she may really be interested, but then she stopped herself. How could she be interested?

"Don't think that."

"Think what?" she asked defensively yet too innocently; offhand.

"I can read faces really well, helps me in court." He grinned, "and in poker."

Jennifer allowed herself to giggle. "I bet. I guess I'm not good at reading faces." She said self-critically.

"Yes, you are." Patrick took her hands, which had fallen to her lap limply. "Now you are. From here on you are."

Jennifer's eyes began to fill again and this time she didn't care if they cleared, she didn't want to see clearly. She lifted her back, moved forward and found Patrick's lips. They were soft and warm. She drew a breath and he followed her into her teary passion.

CHAPTER THIRTY-THREE

Love Again

Millie's toes cramped in her slide mules and she remembered she had not eaten a banana today. She hated those things, but her doctor told her it was that or pills and at seventy Millie prided herself in not taking any prescription medication of any kind at all. But every once in awhile her joints cramped and the pain was crippling since it mainly affected her feet. Looking down she admired them - she still had beautiful feet.

Millie couldn't keep still though she knew it was driving Grover crazy. She moved into the kitchen hoping he would not know her movement there, but it's a small kitchen.

"Just go look for them," he half-pleaded, half-ordered her from the living room. Though she now had endorsement to go this didn't seem to help. Millie was a determined woman and yet still she couldn't move beyond her nervous pacing. Maybe Jennifer was coming to her senses and maybe Patrick was helping her to do so. Maybe.

Grover rose from his Lazy Boy and moved himself into the bedroom with a wave to Millie from the border of the kitchen. His eyes were heavy under his glasses, he would be asleep in minutes. She waved but it was harsh to his night greeting resenting his ability to fall asleep under these circumstances. Millie grabbed a banana walking toward the living room and opened the previously closed drapes to view her quiet neighborhood. So different than her previous life. She saw one light on across the street, but other than that the rest of the neighbors would be asleep, as would most of the town. She set the banana down, it tasted chalky, it was too green.

Millie opened the front door. Perched on the front stoop she tried to see farther down the street toward the town and the trailer parks. Was Jennifer there with Tom? Was Nathan with them? She had checked on the baby earlier and Noonie had been reluctant to give him up. He would stay with her as long as necessary. Trying to hear any oncoming cars she instead heard Grover's snoring rising from the bedroom. Even in the worry and irritation she smiled.

She had not recognized his worth when she had met him in the Tango Room on Maryland Avenue. He had become a regular with the rest of the "Liar's Club." They challenged each other over jalapeño eating contests and who had the best stories of their misguided directions in youth. Ollie had once made a miss-turn and ended up in Dallas instead of Tulsa not realizing until he got there. Barnes had loved a nun in his twenties and was the cause of her excommunication. Ed had never been to Reno though he lived in Vegas his whole life and barely recalled it was the capitol. Not a misstep of his youth, but maybe of today's youth, Grover despised the challenge-resolving game rock-paper-scissors and refused to understand it. As would be expected that was what the Club used to decide close results. Regardless, Grover typically won the jalapeno contests claiming he had the advantage because he was born in Mexico. Millie became the official stem counter, often looking the other way when Grover pulled just the stems out of the jar and placed them on the table as his opponents were suffering trying to anesthetize their mouths with ice water.

Millie was sixty-three and had long since moved off the strip to the dark velvet-papered bars downtown working as a waitress/bartender. She actually liked this crowd better and though she was still on her feet most of her working hours she was not required to wear the lavish costumes and neck-breaking headdresses. The Tango Room was the best place she had landed. It was owned by Peggy and her husband of twenty something years and touted the best collection of Jim Beam Elvis bottles in all of Nevada, beating out the Paradise Lounge over on Paradise Road by three Elvis'. It was at the Tango that Millie moved around to behind the bar when she tired and was able to turn over the trays to the younger fifty-year-old ex-showgirl waitresses that still enjoyed the looks they got when they dropped change and had to retrieve it.

Whenever Peggy's husband Ed came into the bar, almost every Tuesday like clockwork, he met up with Grover who stationed himself next to the cocktail garnish trays to pop himself a few olives when Millie "wasn't looking." When Ed and Grover got together it was not the usual banter of the Liar's Club but more gentle conversation between two elderly men fond of each other and their pasts. Millie used to love to listen to the discussions and always worked the bar when they were in together. The subject varied from politics, Grover was a "mean liberal" to baseball, gardening and lastly ex-wives. Both Grover and Ed's first wives had fallen to cancer. When they couldn't agree on who would win the pennant or whether Miracle Grow was a poison or a potion, they could agree that life had robbed them of two beautiful women. Millie found this interesting knowing that Grover had been long divorced from his wife before she had been diagnosed in her fifties, but Ed had been in his twentieth year of marriage when his wife died. Ed never made the distinction and Grover never recognized one, he had always loved Adele no matter whether they were married or not.

Ten years after Grover had moved to Vegas, Charlotte, now an adult mother in her thirties had called her father and told him a simple mole on Adele's back was cancerous and the cancer had metastasized, which Grover found out meant that it had taken over her body. Grover had not seen Adele in over ten years, the couple having divorced when Charlotte was about twenty-one. When he saw her a few months following the call, he saw her as he had before though she was nowhere near who she had been. Her hair was no longer red, but dull white with a shadow of light brown at the tips. Her voice was raspy from what Grover was not sure. She was not as thin as Grover would have thought she'd be, her narrow waist still jutted out at her ample hips. Hips he had always cherished. When he had entered her small cottage on Poli Street in Ventura she was sitting in the front room, which faced the ocean a few miles away and below her gaze. Her face was bright and she didn't try to hide her deterioration, her vanity long passed. It had been good to see him.

"Adele." He had whispered not showing the fear and shock she had expected from him. Anyone would have expected shock but he thankfully he "failed" to deliver.

"Alexander" she whispered back. Adele called him by his self-named middle name one he had taken from the great pitcher when he was playing ball. They sat and talked from hours, Adele stopping to take water from Charlotte who appeared at her side every ten minutes or so. When Charlotte had to leave and attend to her own family who at that time included two small children, Grover took over the duty of feeding Adele, making sure the bits were small enough to not require too much chewing, cleaning her and filling her with needed liquids. Adele died two months after Grover had arrived in Ventura and by the time she closed her eyes for the last time, he had fallen deeply in love again with his ex-wife who had not been a part of his life for a long, long time. Before she left the world her delicate hands held his long boney ones and comforted him as she felt herself drift to the other side. She was so beautiful in death.

After the services, Grover stayed in town for a few more months, helping Charlotte with things that she had not been able to attend to because of Adele's illness and the need for her care. But he was also there to spend time with his grandchildren, as this was one of the directives Adele had given him when she was outlining for Grover his priorities when she passed. He had never been a doter and now he was taking that role from Adele without any resentment of her instruction. She had also told him to love again. She knew in those final days that he had fallen for her hard and wanted him to understand it could all happen again just as it had surprisingly happened to him when he thought their love was over.

Whenever the conversation turned to Adele during those bar talks, Millie made sure she was in hearing distance restocking mixers and garnishes, many times unnecessarily. At first she had felt guilty eavesdropping so intentionally. But then that gave way to a need; a need to hear the story to fill in the gaps of the pieces she was able to catch from time to time. The need to know this lanky-armed old man better.

Tightening the siphons of the kegs for the draft beers, Millie heard a catch of breath coming from Grover. The intake of air to calm his sorrow made her gasp also. As she eased up from below the counter, gripping the bar's edge with both hands her eyes focused on him, Grover was taking a fresh cocktail napkin from Millie's stack and blowing his nose. Ed patted him on the back sympathetically, "I know Grover, I know" he confided. Millie was certain that he did.

In a gravelly voice, Grover offered, "I waited too long." He shook his head as if to underline the point. His face held his own disdain. Millie froze. She felt caught in her interference and the longing to console. As if feeling this pull, Grover ventured a glance at the painted bird with the red hair piled high on the top of her head. Millie's brow furrowed to focus but her eyes remained wide and Grover could see that it was not due to an attempt to see something in the distance but rather to cup and contain her tears. Her mouth quivered, and slowly moved up to a meek attempted smile. The expression was too suppressed for Millie. She was too flashy a gal to hold an expression of sorrow. Reciprocating, Grover's heart met hers and he smiled broader than he thought he could.

Ed leaned back on his stool a bit uncomfortable with the direction the silent conversation was going. He finished the last of his beer and commented to the back of Grover's head and a pat on his shoulder, "Better get going. Peggy's about to throw me out." Grover turned and patted the man's hand in return.

"Can I get you something Grover?" Millie asked and then realizing it was far too "bar speak" laughed at herself. "Sorry" she told him, for the speak or the story she wasn't sure.

Grover had been telling Ed about Adele's strength after Grover had thrown out his arm and could play baseball no longer. "She told me I was capable of anything, that I was a great baseball player but that I was a greater man." At first Grover had accused her of not understanding what all this would mean, not only was his career over, but he had nothing to fall back on. He had not gone to school, had not learned anything since a hanging fastball, and did not know how they were going to manage. His voice had been harsh. But she had continued to praise him, explaining that they would figure it out, that baseball was not the only thing he could do. A week later over much consideration and despair, Grover took on as a carpenter apprentice position with a local contractor who he had known in high school. Without shame he had told him, that his arm may not be strong enough to throw a baseball at ninety miles an hour but he could swing a hammer. Hitting the nail heads with a force unmatched, he understood that he had given up baseball forever.

When he had been injured, his coach had not accompanied him to the clinic to be checked out, he was not important enough to warrant his time. Instead the bullpen catcher, Abel McChesney sat in the waiting room with him chatting nervously until the nurse came to get him. Abel had been a bullpen catcher his whole career, he had seen pitchers move up and down and he knew a career-ending injury, and knew Grover was headed there. Grover had pitched every batting practice, giving the boys what they could expect to get in the game. In the last few months his arm was on ice more than it wasn't and the burn he felt in his elbow down to his forearm now kept him awake at night. Abel tried to make Grover slow down, but Grover was grasping at a chance to make it to the roster and he could not let that go. The day he felt his arm extend too far toward home plate, he knew too. Abel had been behind the plate grabbing the strike and he knew also. He threw off his mask as soon as the ball hit his mitt. The other team members gathered around Grover as he withered in pain, but Abel silently told him this is what he had warned him of. He was as angry as a disappointed father. But like a father he accompanied him to the clinic for the final say.

After the diagnosis he had to pay his own way back home from Idaho. It was not until the second day on the bus that he had called Adele. She had been out shopping and was telling Grover about Charlotte getting lost in a rack of bras, when she heard the strain in his voice. "I'm coming home."

Grover had told Ed that he didn't understand her strength. It had always been there, but twice in their lives he had seen her hold up when he couldn't; when he lost his dream of baseball and when she was losing her life.

Millie's hands where close to Grover's when she had pulled herself up to the bar counter. After the failed attempt at small talk, she had reached for his hands and cupped them in hers. "Sounds like a your wife was a remarkable woman."

"She was." Grover responded.

Millie searched her own mind trying to find the words that should appropriately come next. But there were none.

Grover watched this woman who had nothing in common with Adele, except a bottled attempt to capture her natural red hair. Adele never wore more that a watch and simple earrings, where Millie Flowers wrists were weighted down with bangles and her fingers protruding with dinner rings.

"I'd like to hear more about her." Millie finally offered.

Grover smiled. "I appreciate your interest, but there are other things we can talk about too."

"OK" Millie grabbed a bar towel to have something to do with her hands. She had never been this nervous around men.

"Would you like to have breakfast after your shift?" Grover ventured. Once the question was out, he feared that maybe he had misread her eyes.

"Sure." Millie answered gently.

It was then that Grover and Millie discovered that even at their age, after so many heartbreaks and careers and years that they represented, they had the ability to allow another person into their lives and to love again.

CHAPTER THIRTY-FOUR

In Control

G rover snorted loudly in his sleep, but didn't stir. Millie grabbed her keys on the key-holder near the door shaped like a San Francisco row of townhomes. A year ago, Millie had nailed it to the wall near the front door telling Grover it was a decorative addition from his home state, rather than her attempt to help him not forget where the keys were. He was becoming more absent-minded.

She carefully adjusted the driver's seat down to her height and slowly backed the car out. Her physical motions seemed outwardly in control though in her chest, her heart raced. What could she be walking into? Grover taunted her teasingly about her need to get involved in every dispute. But this was different, Jennifer was still a child, with a child and like Millie of earlier years she did not make good decisions with men. Was Patrick a good decision? She wasn't quite sure that Patrick was a good decision.

Pine Street had one light on and it was Elder Ross' porch light, which was always on no matter the time of day. The old Mormon never wanted anyone to miss his house numbers if they were driving by especially if they were missionaries looking to visit with a friendly church brother.

When she turned on to Elm she noticed that the corner lot had been cleaned up since the last time she had gone this way. She suspected the "Clean-Up Abbott Committee" had had it with the landowner's insistence that it was their land and they could do with it what they wished. Esther Begay was the chairperson of the committee and sooner or later she would get her way.

As Millie drove her heart surprisingly calmed. Breathing deeply she agreed that her intervention was in fact needed and that agreement soothed her. When she pulled in to Navajo Court she was not at all disturbed by the fact that along with the keys, she had grabbed a knife from the kitchen drawer.

CHAPTER THIRTY-FIVE

Two-Body

Solitude

Patrick smoothed Jennifer's hair against her head. It was soft and had a slight wave to it. He had noticed the wave in Nathan's hair and hoped that it would not be trained down by a hair cut. Jennifer had been asleep for a good hour, Patrick's strokes where not intended to wake her but to help her continue her peaceful sleep. She had cried with her whole body, something Patrick had not seen so close up. It was a combination of hate, fear, embarrassment and anger. Patrick had held her and kissed her and then held her while she slept from exhaustion. The dog in the adjacent yard had long ago stopped barking, possibly considering the car and the occupants to be new residents of his street or just too much to be bothered with. They had pulled over to talk after the visit to Josh's and had found this street with few spread-out houses and large yards with open space. The sun has set hours ago and with no porch lights on he didn't really know where they were other than somewhere in Abbott. Where they on a tree street?

In his two-body solitude, Patrick considered his recent choices. He had made the right one jumping off the train, maybe he had made the right one by taking the trip because it brought him here. He considered the girl under his shoulder comfortable under the crook of his arm. She was a sweet girl who had not made proper choices so far. His mother had always been frank about girls with these types of tendencies. "They will continue to make the same wrong decisions. The only difference being whether you will be involved with them." It was her own self she was talking about, he was sure. Patrick didn't understand how his mother had ever chosen his father. It seemed to be so obvious who his father was, even to a young boy. Had it been obvious to Jennifer? Patrick had questioned Millie on this but had ended up talking more about his own mother.

Millie has asked him, "Had it been a surprise?"

Patrick had hesitated, "Yes." And that's what startled him the most.

CHAPTER THIRTY-SIX

Visitor Parking

The trailer had one light on, the one over the kitchen sink. A fluorescent tube over the orange and gold ruffled curtains Millie had located at a "Dollar Days" sale at Walgreens. Millie parked in the visitor parking three spaces near the office, which were never occupied and eyed the trailer as well as she could in the dark. The kitchen light illuminated the number 19 on the trailer, but Tom had not intended to draw her to him with such obviousness. She did not see Jennifer's car or any indication that Patrick was around. She turned the ignition a notch to listen to the radio while she waited. Perry Como, "Mi Casa Su Casa" played a little too joyously. She did love him. Such a handsome man. But handsome men were trouble and men with money where even more trouble. Maybe that early notion had prevented her from taking her chance meeting with Howard Hughes seriously. What a thing to be thinking of now.

She had met him after a casino show when she was performing at The Last Frontier. One of his men had returned the next day requesting her to attend a party hosted by Mr. Hughes that evening. Millie had spryly retorted, "If Mr. Hughes would like me to attend then he can come ask me." Millie was surprised when Howard Hughes himself appeared at the dressing room door, timidly asking her if she would "honor" him in joining him in his suite for the party. Millie recalled wondering how this under-confident man had been such a successful businessman, if she had been so timid she would have never made the dance line. Here he stood, literally hat-in-hand pleading. She agreed to attend hearing the gasps of the other girls who not surprisingly listened on intently catching glimpses of Howard in their half wall mirrors or staring straight on. But in all truth it had ended up being a very boring evening. Maybe one of the worst dates she had ever been on. Howard was even shyer in social settings and Millie found herself dancing with other men the whole evening - those who gave her much more attention than Howard. She had tried, but when she would look over at him in attempts to engage him he would not, or maybe could not connect eyes with her. This was all of course decades before his demise due to obsessions and mental illness. That night she had concluded rightly that he was a sad man.

When Howard appeared at the stage door and asked to see her again, Millie quietly, but respectfully as she could declined. Grover loved to use this entry from Millie's dating history saying, "She passed up Howard Hughes for Grover Alexander Pendrell." Whenever he recited this fact his cheeks reddened at the high ends even in his eighties. He had blushing pride that she had made the right choice and it was him even though there were decades between he and Howard. Millie was not easily swayed by looks nor wealth. Grover was proud to be proof.

The next set played Benny Goodman melodies followed by Frank Sinatra and still there was no sign of Jennifer. The brass melody quickened Millie's heart again and she held her hand to her chest, counting the beats; either to pass the time or worry about an impending heart attack. Early morning that's when they come, right?

Patrick moved cautiously, not common for his age. His examination of things was deliberate, taking it all in and analyzing, maybe it was the law student in him, but maybe not, maybe it was learned a lot longer ago; farther from the last class he attended. She had noticed that he watched people's interactions carefully. He was surely gentle in nature, but his reaction to Jennifer's beating was more than a rise to the shock.

The station changed to a more mellow set of Bing Crosby, but Millie's heart continued to pick up pace. Someone who had seen a beating would not let it happen again. She clicked off the radio and opened the door, not caring if the closing door made too much noise. She looked at her watch, it was four am, 10 hours had passed since she had seen Jennifer and Patrick. She was sure the battery of the car would be dead if she sat listening to the radio any longer, and Grover would not be pleased, he had never understood her need to surround herself with music.

Millie pounded at the door of the trailer, but heard no sounds from the inside. Surely Jennifer would hear her if she was there, or would she? Millie knocked again, but not allowing any time for an answer this time turned the knob of the unlocked door. The room was dark except for the kitchen light, but she had woken someone.

"Bitch?" came a drunken sleeping voice from the bedroom.

"Yeah." Millie answered fueled by the insult meant for Jennifer.

"Who in the hell?" the voice questioned and then Tom appeared staggering down the hall toward the living room.

"Where is she?" Millie demanded.

"How the hell would I know old lady." Tom staggered to the kitchen where the light shed an unflattering spotlight.

Considering where he was, he asked "And what the hell are you doing in my trailer?"

"What did you do with her?" Millie continued her interrogation.

"I didn't do nothin'." He took a few steps toward her but Millie did not flinch, only thought of how his school system had failed him – nothin'. Tom Wheeler was a caricature of failure and the reason diagramming of sentences should still be a continued practice in public schools.

"Oh the hell you didn't, did she just give herself a black eye and swollen face?"

"None of your business bitch."

"The hell it isn't," Millie was madder than she ever remembered being.

Tom pushed off from the counter that separated them as if to appear casual, but she could tell his anger was building.

"Oh you here to beat me up? Or is the washed up baseball star on his way to do the job? You two need to get a life, there are better things to do with your time than play guard for a slut."

Millie gripped her bag and patted it, assuring herself that she had left the knife within easy access.

CHAPTER THIRTY-SEVEN

Cheerios

Jennifer awoke with a jolt and terror. Patrick had also dosed off but had woken up about ten minutes before and met her fear with a soothing smile.

"I fell a sleep," Jennifer said stating the obvious pushing off of Patrick.

"Yes, and you needed it." Patrick brushed her cheek but instead of taking it as a comforting gesture, it reminded her of her beating. She jumped and in one motion turned on the ignition.

Patrick touched her knee, "calm down Jennifer."

"Nathan," she said as she turned left at the stop sign.

"He's with Noonie." Patrick reminded her.

"She was to watch him while I made deliveries, not all night." She looked at the clock on the battered dashboard that surprisingly was clicking along with the correct time. 5:37.

Patrick sat quietly next to her as she drove recklessly down the short blocks of Abbott.

Grover stirred and with one last snore succeeded in waking himself up. The sun was starting to rise and he saw the slivers of light coming through the drawn drapes. What he did not see was Millie. Pulling his body over the side of the bed he then brought himself up with effort. The agility of his baseball days had left him long ago.

"Millie?" Grover called after his lengthy morning visit to the bathroom. There was no response. He entered the kitchen and was met with an empty coffeemaker. Even if Millie had left early for a shopping trip or other errands, she left a pot of coffee on. A marriage of kindness.

Grover looked for the car keys. He searched the kitchen counters, which were still scrubbed clean from last night. Not a pot drying in the rack.

In the living room he patted down his TV tray, no metal ring bulking below yesterday's paper. His hand left a sweaty imprint on the sports page. He wiped his forehead, he had not realized he had been sweating. Had he had too much sugar last night? He had indulged in two servings of brownies and vanilla ice milk, but he had done that plenty of times. He craned his head up, avoiding dizziness and that's when he saw the wooden key holder next to the door, it was empty, except for the extra house key Millie had had made during their last trip to Carver's Hardware store. He could argue again what good it does to have a spare key IN the house, but instead sat down, cold with the revelation that Millie had gone after them.

With the clarity and energy of fear, he bolted up grabbing the extra house key and took the twenty steps to Drew Bakkila's house.

Patrick did not want to go back to Millie's. He wanted to go home with her to make sure Tom was not there, and to make sure he would never return. Instead after they picked up Nathan from Noonie he complained of being hungry and all but invited himself to her trailer. Jennifer was in such a cloud of relief that Nathan was once again with her, that she shrugged and headed south toward the dusty row of trailers that made up Navajo Trailer Court. Nathan was cooing and giggly and Jennifer giggled with him rubbing his pudgy feet as he stuffed Cheerios into his mouth. Only her swollen eye and slightly crooked mouth would provide any indication of the recent abuse she had suffered. Only her exhaustion and timidity revealed the damage to herself, yet her son would not see them. Not until he was old enough to understand what the rise in a voice would signal, what the thud on the floor would mean.

CHAPTER THIRTY-EIGHT

Howl

P atrick had been eight when he first realized that his father's voice took on a deep-throated rapid-speak when his verbal insults turned into physical violence. He and his sisters had been so used to the routine of it, he never thought through the signs of escalation until that one-day. He was alone with his parents, his sister Amy, sixteen, was working at the local 31 Flavors, his closest sister Henrie, ten, was over at her best friend's house. Patrick having recently been excluded from a building argument by his parents was alone in his room, trying to find something to take up his lapping boredom. He had never been one of those kids who could occupy his time without some direction.

His father was telling his mother that she could stay if she wanted to. Stay where? Patrick wondered, but there wasn't any time to understand the composition of the conversation. Patrick heard the quickening of his father's voice and then the hit. A leather sandal hitting a concrete sidewalk. But they were all inside and it was not summer. Then his mother must have fallen into the nightstand because Patrick heard the gold-globed lamp hit the floor and what sounded like the rod-iron encasement hit wood and then the globe broke. The high pitch of the glass ensured that the debris would cover the room. He would have to remember to put on shoes.

"Damn it." His father yelled. "Look what you did."

Patrick answered for her. "I didn't do anything." He found himself repeating over and over as he rocked back and forth holding his knees to his chest burrowing hatred. But it would not stay there.

Patrick's mother also landed a response, but Patrick couldn't hear what it was. His father screamed longer and louder and his mother howled longer and louder in fear and pain. The combination of sounds startled him, but why? His father had yelled so many times before and his mother had cried, but never had he heard her howl. The noise was too surrendering. This was the woman who protected him and his sisters, not only from their father but, from the world. She added a blanket to his bed and made him drink pink stuff when he threw up that even over objection did make him feel better. She cornered Mrs. Robertson, his PE teacher one day, and told her in a stern, not-to-be-questioned voice not to pick on her son. Mrs. Robertson was a brute of a woman who stood a full two heads above his mother. Patrick was sure no one, or no parent, had ever talked to her in that manner. Now she was howling.

When Patrick got to the door, his mother was sitting on the edge of the bed with a washcloth on her forehead, being held in place by a shaking right arm, the other arm lay limp to her side, but already showed the bruised imprints of fingers holding too tightly. She had no shoes on her feet. His father stood too close to her his shoes crunching glass. Though she could apparently only see him through one eye, told her to "look at me." They didn't see Patrick for a good minute. Patrick watched the continued tirade of words he couldn't comprehend, not because of their complexity but because he watched the slap to his mother's exposed face, not the words, before he made a run. Jumping on his father's back he began hitting him with all the force he could. It wasn't much, his father peeled him off easily throwing him to the ground with a simple pull and throw as if he was a lizard who had foolishly attached himself to a sleeve.

Seeing Patrick in the room and crumpled on the floor, his mother lifted herself off the bed, standing, the howl became a scream and with her left arm she pushed his father aside with enough force to cause him to grab the dresser to steady himself. She scooped Patrick up and held the shaking boy to her bosom, the washcloth having traveled with her and now lay between them smelling of sweat and blood. Patrick's father took a step toward them, either to actually steady or hit her again, but he did not get far.

"Don't come near us." Patrick's mother announced. He moved again and she held her ground with still a few feet between them, walked out of the room carrying Patrick. She was talking to Mrs. Robertson and it didn't matter that he towered over her.

When Patrick was seventeen it was he who carried his mother out of her room. She had been beaten to the point of not responding, coiled around her knees. Patrick threw his father into the glass closet doors, which shattered around him. Louder than the glass globed lamps. Patrick made sure that was the last time his mother was alone with his father or ever to endure his brutality. Two days later in a small apartment they had quickly rented near his high school, the permanent restraining order had been finalized and the divorce followed a long eight months later.

Jennifer was grabbing Nathan's extended toe with her right hand when she made the left turn into the trailer park and it was Patrick who saw Millie first.

"Oh Jesus!" he shouted.

Jennifer quickly brought her attention around. Millie Flowers sat on the top step of the two-step concrete block entry into the trailer. In her hand was a long-ridged kitchen knife. A carving knife.

Patrick jumped out the car before Jennifer had slammed the brakes to stop.

"Millie, are you OK?" Millie looked up slowly and looked at him blankly. The failure of response of words launched Patrick into the house. No one in the living room/kitchen, no one in the bathroom, both bedrooms where empty. Patrick found himself checking the floor for bloodstains, but did not find any. He went back outside next to Millie. Jennifer was now at her side hugging her and with Millie no longer frozen cried audible gulps; Nathan echoing them still in the car, restrained by his car seat his fists punching the air. Millie mumbled, but none of the words were discernable. Patrick started to rattle off questions rapidly, but in response Jennifer's open palmed hand stopped him.

Patrick heard a screech of tires and saw an elderly man knuckling a steering wheel park too close to Jennifer's car. He didn't recognize the car, but it was a much later model than Jennifer's and well maintained as if it had lived it's twenty years in the safety of a garage.

"Millie!" Grover pushed himself out. He hit his head on the car's doorway but did not seem to flinch or even slow. He was not an overly tall man but his force to make contact with the metal.

"What happened? Are you OK?" he galloped over with his long arms swinging.

Millie's distorted face surfaced from Jennifer's shoulder.

"I'm fine." Her normally lip-sticked mouth, crinkled. Taking in a breath, "I almost killed him."

Jennifer pulled away so she could see her, and matter-of-factly asked, "Did you? Millie?" she waited.

"No," Millie answered. Jennifer hugged her again but then stood and relinquished her to Grover who had a difficult time sitting down on the shallow steps but got there as quickly as he could.

Patrick had not moved from the doorway, yet his breath deepened with the flow of racing blood. His eyes narrowed, but not from fighting back tears though they were there stinging. He clenched and unclenched his fists. A distant feeling caught his chest and tightened it, as constricting as his fists. He wanted to flee from this strange old couple on broken concrete steps, this beautiful troubled girl with the baby wailing in the car, yet stood hovering over Millie's back. He wanted to flee.

Patrick moved toward the car unbuckled Nathan, and held the crying toddler to his chest. The boy cried louder with the pounding of Patrick's heart. That same pounding had also made Patrick cry harder when his mother had held him that day in the bedroom. Jennifer took her son from him, talking as gently as she could to calm him. When he was safely in her arms Patrick turned to get into the car. The keys were in the ignition. He could drive away without their having time to react. He could get to him. Without understanding how she had moved off the porch and reached his side, Millie grabbed his arm. He turned to her startled by her touch.

"Don't" she demanded of him. Patrick shook his head and sat back in the front seat of the car. Millie's head jutted into his face, it was red from crying and but grew even redder with the next words. "Please don't," she pleaded and pulled her head back. Patrick was surprised to see the knife still in her hand and for a moment he was afraid. "I did this for you," she confessed, turning to stand upright and leaned against the car with her back away from him.

"For me?" Patrick realized his voice sounded too angry, but he was and he couldn't quell it. "How could this be for me?" He rose from the seat and got out of the car.

"You would have killed him." This time the words did not follow with tears. She wanted him to know, she knew.

Now Patrick needed support, he sat back down in the driver's seat but Millie didn't move to prevent his flight. He could decide to drive away.

Jennifer stood with Grover about three feet away. They needed to keep a distance, but not too much. Grover hunched over still feeling the pain of sitting on the steps and the exhaustion of fear. Jennifer took a seat and coddled Nathan who now sucked hungrily at her middle and index fingers. His little face blotchy; he would be asleep soon.

"How?" Patrick asked her, then wanting to take-up his own defense, "I wouldn't of Millie."

Millie answered him silently, then with words. "You carry it with you. I saw it when you spoke of your mom."

"Where is he?" Patrick asked.

"Nowhere. Not here." She answered. "He won't be back Patrick."

"Did you kill him?" Patrick asked without judgment. He had heard her answer before and was still not sure.

"No, but I scared the hell out of the both of us. My mama always said act crazy if someone attacks you."

The blood flooded his head again, "He attacked you?"

"No, me and this kitchen cutlery wouldn't let him." She laughed at herself, realizing she had put on an effective performance as a deranged old woman. One her mama would be proud of.

CHAPTER THIRTY-NINE

Hot Meals

Manuel put his produce carefully into small crates he had made from discarded desert-dried wood found in various places in and around town. His biggest find to date was behind Ted's Mexican Grill on the Anapamu Street side where once a creek had flowed and fed a lucky grove of trees. Amazing what people throw out as scrap. He separated the individual vegetables and fruits with cheesecloth and strips of cardboard to prevent their crushing each other in route. Rusty pulled up at exactly five o'clock and though irritated at the care and time Manny took to load the boxes, waited for him to secure them in the car and then join him in the delivery.

He had asked Rusty to allow his produce to be included once a week. He grew too much for just he and Rosie and still had much to giveaway even when he forced it on Millie and Grover. Though Grover was rather proud of his little harvests he accepted the produce. Rusty had made Manny go through some approval process with the "Meals on Wheels" people, which he thought was ridiculous but he did it anyway. He was providing fresh vegetables and fruits. This was one of the only times he "pulled rank" and explained to the "authorities" the produce varieties were actually his inventions. He held plant variety patents on them from his many days as a plant breeder. Of course Manny had to explain what a plant breeder was, but he had to do that most of his life.

People were genuinely happy receiving the fresh produce with their dinners. It would last longer than the hot sealed meals and gave them something to look forward to weekly. He had told them that without getting too technical on spoilage rates. He never wanted to out-science people.

When the duo turned into Navajo Court, Manny saw little Nathan running in the small yard about 3 spaces down at number 19. He was a rambunctious child who had walked early and now a year old or so ran wherever he could. As they pulled in slowly, thank goodness Rusty was a careful enough driver, Patrick ran after the toddler and with one arm swooped him up and with the other waved bringing Nathan's attention to the car. Nathan squirmed and then seeing Manny yelped, struggling to get down. Manuel opened the door as quickly as he could and was hugged at the knees by the small boy, "Mu" he exclaimed. It was close enough for Manuel for him.

"Well Mijo, what are you doing?"

Nathan muttered something multi-syllabled, pulled away and was off.

"Hey guys," Patrick greeted, still keeping an eye on the boy as Nathan walked to Rusty's side and did a hug-run into the old man. Even Rusty smiled with the attack encounter. Maybe the white-haired man was not so Rusty.

Patrick lifted a box from the back seat, but only Manny's box, a "Meal" was not distributed here, ...anymore.

"What do we have this week?"

"Arugula, spinach, broccoli and peaches," Manny touted proudly.

Patrick smiled. "Might have to tell me what to do with the arugula Manny."

"That little one needs iron, the greener the better," Manny was again knee-hugged by Nathan and this time he swooped him up and cradled him. "Don't you ever tell me you don't like vegetables."

Knowing only that it was a question, Nathan responded, "No." His new defining word.

"Don't take it personally." Patrick advised.

Jennifer stood at the entrance of the trailer. She no longer looked small and meek, or broken. She followed the pin-balling of her son as she took the time to greet each of the old men fondly.

"Busy route today?"

"Oh the usual suspects," Rusty muttered, "Manny thinks they are always this happy, but really only once a week are they at all interested in what I bring." He looked a little put off. Manny grinned.

"Well we'd better be off, don't want Manny's veggies to wither," and Rusty was in the car.

Manny waited, hesitated and then walked toward Jennifer. Hell to Rusty and his delivery timetables.

"Mija, see you next week." He gently kissed Jennifer on the cheek. Manny may be a quiet man but he was affectionate. Jennifer hugged him deeply in return. He turned and shook Patrick's hand, the one not holding Nathan like a bulky football with legs and arms extended.

"Good man," he assessed. Patrick gave him a quizzical look but nodded to be conciliatory.

CHAPTER FORTY

Postage Stamps

S he'd heard of these places, but this wasn't what she had heard of. Abbott was bleak; small and sun-bleached. All desert surrounded by all desert. She thought they'd end up somewhere green after Vegas, but this is where Grover wanted to "spend their years." Millie saw no obvious appeal. Grover pulled the Scout on to a street one block off of Main Street. The neighborhood looked like a kid had drawn it with a ruler. The road in was perpendicular to the feeder streets from right to left. A child or a misplaced resident must have also named them, all trees, Pine, Oak, Elm, Maple. Trees in a desert.

Grover whistled as he turned the wheel to the right on Pine Street. "Postage stamp" that's what they called these type of houses constructed after World War II. Two small bedrooms, a kitchen (usually the biggest room) and a small bathroom. Everything a veteran would need and his family could possibly tolerate post-war. These looked more like boxed trailers with wood siding. Each of the houses on the block had the same small cement pad in front that may serve as a porch and some squared off columns holding an awning. Two windows in front and a garage to the right or the left, alternating down the street.

"Well they all look alike," Millie wanted to say more but didn't want to quell Grover's obvious enthusiasm. He was whistle-happy and that should make her happy.

"I'm sure you will fix ours' up to be different," Grover smiled and padded Millie's leg. She was sure she would.

Grover pulled on to a short driveway and turned off the engine.

CHAPTER FORTY-ONE

Dusty Windows

The old sedan and the old men pulled out of the trailer court. Patrick waved, though the dust clouded the back window. This was a hot, arid town, with dusty windows, and in the summer only a few short hours that could be tolerated outside. Patrick may not belong here. He was brash to their desert kindness. But he had youth and had the stubborn ability to become successful in any way he chose. He would not be a lawyer. He would not ask his former classmates how the rest of the journey had gone. He would not make it to California. He would never see his father again.

Jennifer came to his side and waved at the dusty trail of the car that now rounded the last trailer in Navajo Court. Rusty beeped the horn in staccato, which made both of them jump. Manny's short tanned arm extended out the window in a pudgy salute.

ACKNOWLEDGEMENTS

Thank you to my gentle readers - Janet Baker, Barb Lagerquist, Silvana Kelly, Jeri Jones, Pat Burks, Karen and Kristy Prechtel-Thomson. You caught what I never would have, but also gave me sweet encouragement. Also to Gail Kearns who took the first swing at editing.

But thank you most to my family - my husband Kip and kids Marisela and Ivan who put up with my writer's moodiness and self doubt. Through it all it was their love and belief that encouraged me to get this done.

ABOUT THE AUTHOR

Leah Evert-Burks has worked in various legal capacities most of her professional life but has been writing stories since childhood. She previously concentrated on screenplays until a happenstance meeting with novelist Mark Harris while waiting in line at the post office. It was Mr.

Harris who convinced her that this story was in fact a novel.

She lives in Santa Barbara, California and Durango, Colorado with her husband who even though once fell asleep during the reading of one of her screenplays, has supported her as a writer even when she wasn't.